S0-ELA-134

All Sleek and Skimming

stories

Edited by Lisa Heggum

Orca Book Publishers

National Library of Canada Cataloguing in Publication Data

All sleek and skimming: stories / edited by Lisa Heggum.

Includes bibliographical references.
ISBN 1-55143-447-4

1. Short stories, Canadian (English) 2. Canadian fiction (English)--21st century.
I. Heggum, Lisa, 1969-

PS8321.A54 2006 jC813'.010806 C2006-900062-X

Summary: A collection of compelling short fiction for older teen readers.

First published in the United States 2006
Library of Congress Control Number: 2005939037

Orca Book Publishers gratefully acknowledges the support for its publishing programs provided by the following agencies: the Government of Canada through the Book Publishing Industry Development Program (BPIDP), the Canada Council for the Arts, and the British Columbia Arts Council.

Cover graphics and design: Lynn O'Rourke

Orca Book Publishers
Box 5626, Stn. B
Victoria, BC Canada
V8R 6S4

Orca Book Publishers
PO Box 468
Custer, WA USA
98240-0468

Printed and bound in Canada

10 09 08 07 06 • 5 4 3 2 1

For Mark

Going to the library is my favorite thing in school.
The only thing that would be better is if there was
a class where you sat around listening to records.
—Ian McGillis, *A Tourist's Guide to Glengarry*

She told me Tash had stopped believing in God. No,
I whispered. Yes, said my mom. I couldn't fathom it.
I didn't get it. That fucking library card, man.
—Miriam Toews, *A Complicated Kindness*

Contents

Acknowledgments xi

Introduction xiii

True Confessions—*Martha Brooks* 1

The Defining Moments of My Life—*Anne Fleming* 19

The Deluge—*Arthur Slade* 35

Paul in the Metro—*Michel Rabagliati* 41

Mermaid in a Jar—*Sheila Heti* 55

Real Life Slow Motion Show—*Carrie Mac* 57

The Cat Came Back—*Ivan E. Coyote* 65

The Jeweler—*Derek McCormack* 69

Recorder Lesson—*Brian Doyle* 71

The Unfortunate—*Lee Henderson* 77

Making the Dragon—*Susannah M. Smith* 105

Dawn—*Tim Wynne-Jones* 111

Fish-Sitting—*Gil Adamson* 127

This Is the Story of My Family—*Stuart Ross* 137

The Legacy—*James Heneghan* 139

Rock Paper Scissors—*Susan Kernohan* 147

The Art of Embalming—*Diana Aspin* 157

Camping at Wal-Mart—*Ania Szado* 169

Giant Strawberry Funland—*Joe Ollmann* 175

Piglet—*Janet McNaughton* 195

Alchemy—*Madeleine Thien* 201

Slice—*Gary Barwin* 213

About the Authors 217

Story Sources 223

Acknowledgments

This anthology has been a long time in the making and wouldn't have happened without the help and support of some special people. Thanks to the talented contributors, whose stories inspired me and whose enthusiasm for the project pushed me forward. Thanks to the amazing people at Orca, especially Bob Tyrrell, who made it immediately apparent the book had found a good home; Andrew Wooldridge, whose understanding, guidance and remarkable patience wowed me repeatedly; Lynn O'Rourke, who put such thought and care into the book's design; and Maureen Colgan, who helped spread the word. Thanks to Laura Reed and Blair Ratsoy for believing in this book from the start, and to the Pickering Public Library Teen Advisory Group members, especially Pamela Korgemagi, for their early feedback. Thanks to Hadley Dyer for her young adult publishing expertise and for noticing the lack of sock puppets in my desk drawer, and to Alana Wilcox for explaining the anthology ropes. Thanks to my friends at the Toronto Public Library, especially Dawna Rowlson, for too many things to mention; Brenda Livingston, for lending me *Close to Spider Man;* Susan Kernohan, for turning me on to *Simple Recipes;* and the tireless Maria A. Shchuka Youth Advisory Group members, for their reading, responses and recommendations. Thanks to the Ontario, Canadian and American library associations for the opportunities and all that I have learned through them. Thanks to Anne Fournier for translating. And thanks to my family and loved ones, especially my mother, Dorothy Heggum, for introducing me to books and the public library; Mary DeCaria, Cherie Robertson and Wendy Leavoy (then Heggum) for helping me through my teen years; and my husband, Mark Truscott, whose love, support and poetry make everything better, including me.

Introduction

What teenager in his or her right mind is going to pay attention to books shelved, reviewed or considered for awards alongside children's books? This is something I've asked myself and others repeatedly while working as a teen services librarian.

I've had countless conversations with teens who, as a result of teen literature's association with books for younger readers, think young adult books are too simple or out of touch, or both. They often skip them entirely and turn to adult books, thinking they're more challenging. But these readers tend to have trouble locating literary works that deal with issues directly relevant to their lives.

This anthology combines young adult fiction and adult fiction with teen appeal. It gathers stories of interest to older teen readers, a neglected group. It recontextualizes young adult literature by associating it with adult literature rather than children's, and I hope it changes the way books for teens are published.

If you're a teen and you pick up this book, I hope you'll delve into these stories of adolescence and that they'll make a difference in your life. They're funny, nasty, playful, heartbreaking, angry, honest, authentic and surreal. They're about family, friends, obstacles, searching, love, loss, music, sex, discovery and growing up. Their characters observe, explore, explain, confuse, disturb, create, experiment, connect, transform, rebel, excite, endure and inspire.

Once you finish reading these stories, make sure you check out the books they come from and other books by their authors. Talk to your public or school librarian to discover more great books to read. If you don't have a librarian specializing in teen services in your school or public library, then write a letter of complaint to the school or library board.

One last thing: if you happen to find this book in a children's section somewhere, please ask the staff to move it to the teen section, where it belongs.

Thanks, and enjoy!
Lisa Heggum

True Confessions
Martha Brooks

Confession of Pride
Noreen—Age 12

Gladys, Noreen's nineteen-year-old stepsister, on her wedding day, trembling fingers applying lipstick—Cherry Berry Red—rubbing it off with a tissue, applying it again, catches a glimpse as Noreen moves like a shadow past the mirror.

"Don't hang around behind me like that," Gladys says. "You are making me crazy."

"Shut up." Noreen flops down on the edge of the big double bed they've shared for seven years.

She examines the cheap shiny shoes her mother bought her for this shitty wedding. At Payless. They have straps across the tops. They are shoes for babies.

"Look," says Gladys, "I'm moving out, but I'm not moving away. Gerry and me are going to be twenty minutes from here. By bus. You can visit us whenever you want."

"Sure," she sulks. "The happy couple. You and what's-his-face."

"I'm serious," says Gladys.

"Whatever." She quickly wipes away a tear that is escaping down her face. Then she gets off the bed, stands behind Gladys for a fraction of a second and says, "You look like hell."

Confession of Lust
Noreen—Age 14

Her stepfather, Stupidhead Bob, stands in her way in the kitchen door entrance, arm high up on the jamb, grinning at her, his belly hanging over his belt.

"So you think you're going out, do you?"

"That's right," she says.

"Going with that boyfriend, are you? The one with the tattoos?"

"That's right." She's hungry, but there's no way she's going to push past him into the kitchen. She hates the way he looks at her. Not that he's ever done anything. Nothing like that, anyway. He *looks*—that is his crime. She'd like to be that ancient Greek creature, Medusa—the one with snakes for hair—who could turn people into stone with a single look. She shoots him a look of her own, one that is poisonous and stony, so he won't dare look at her that way. But when she walks down the hall, she can feel his damned eyes on her body anyway—the whole time. She stumbles around trying to get on her shoes.

"What's your hurry? You goin' out dressed like that?"

"That's right," she says.

"You look like a hooker."

"Thanks." Go blind, you bastard.

"You'll be thanking me, all right, when your skinny little boyfriend helps himself to what you got advertised. And don't you whine, missy, and tell me he's not like that. All the males of the species are like that. They just need the opportunity."

"Everybody isn't like you, you know."

"Just don't go and get yourself knocked up," he says. "Like your mother."

"Asshole loser," she says under her breath, and tears out the door before he can say anything else. Anything being the fact that her mother, pregnant at seventeen ("by some guy, he was just some guy, Noreen, I was young and stupid") and on welfare by eighteen, was finally "rescued" seven years later by Bob—a story he loves to tell—like that's supposed to make her grateful or something.

Brad is waiting for her outside the convenience store where he has just gotten off work. He pulls her around the corner and opens his jacket and wraps her up inside it until she can feel his heat and his heart thumping against hers, and his slow kisses that make her knees go weak.

Later they will go to his house, because his parents are never at home, and she won't care if what they do sometimes feels good and sometimes doesn't. She will drown in his smell and sweat and saliva and the weight of him and how much he says he loves her and how much he says he needs her. She won't care about anything else. Anything at all.

Confession of Sloth
Noreen—Age 15

Her mother, Grace, also known behind her back as Amazing, folds her arms across her nubby purple sweater and demands, "What's this?"

"This what?"

"Message on the machine. Here, listen for yourself." With a long pale square-tipped fingernail, Amazing presses the playback button, then stands back, drink in hand (cheap vodka disguised with orange juice is the recent favorite), squinting through smoke from a low-tar, low-nicotine cigarette.

It's Jolly Roger, the principal at her school. She hadn't counted on him actually leaving a message on the answering machine.

She shrugs. "So what?"

"You've missed ten days this month. *Ten days!* And this is the first I've heard of it."

"So throw me in jail."

Next thing, Amazing weaves over to the phone again and squints at the dial. "I'm calling up your stepsister," she says, like this is somehow a big threat.

Noreen rolls her eyes, drops into a chair, examines her own nails, which need to be redone. Maybe this time she'll paint them each a different color just to piss everyone off.

"Yeah, Gladys," Amazing says by way of a hello. Then yak, yak, yak, about how hard she works, how hard *Bob* works, how they can't turn their backs and "the kid" is always up to something. "I don't know what the hell she cares about." Her mouth is mushed to the phone. She looks over her shoulder, frowns at Noreen. "Okay. Yeah. Well, since you're such an expert I'll hand you over."

"Why aren't you at school?" Gladys says to Noreen.

"I dunno."

"Well, what do you do all day—while they're out?"

"I dunno. Sleep. Watch TV."

"Noreen, you have got to stop all this, you know. This goofing off. This dumb acting out."

"Why?"

"Because. It isn't healthy."

"I don't care." Turning away so Amazing can't hear, she whispers brokenly, "Why should I?"

Gladys sighs, and after a long pause, says, "Baby girl, what are we going to do with you?"

Confession of Anger
Noreen—Age 16

When they were kids it was always Gladys who was there in the dark whenever things were bad. Always Gladys who would move closer in their bed, sometimes holding her as the storms of their parents' relationship were going full blast outside their bedroom door. Always Gladys whispering, "I love you to the stars and back again. That's how much I love you. Don't forget, okay? Right up to the stars," all the while hugging her so tightly that she almost stopped breathing. It was always Gladys beside her if ever that door swung open. Then there her stepfather would be, outlined by the dim hall light, standing like a scary monster, just waiting for one more peep out of them, almost hoping for it, it seemed, so there could be hell to pay. And the first out-of-body experience she ever had happened during one of those times.

She was seven years old and she couldn't shut up. Something just possessed her. She was convulsed in nonstop giggles beside Gladys. Suddenly he was in the room. And then across it. He gave her this look. There was a sickening sharp pain in her arm as he lifted her in the air. Another part of her, she would later recollect, watched it all happen—looked down and watched Gladys cry and yell at him. After a million years he dropped her. She fell back on the bed. Silence.

"Little shit," he whispered finally, and left the room.

Her arm felt as if it were still up on the ceiling. Later, though, it began to hurt like it was being jabbed from the inside by sharp little poky things all trying to get out. She cried until Gladys left the room and came back with Amazing, who examined her and swore at Stupidhead—calling him a crazy bastard even though he wasn't there to hear her.

Gladys made her a sling out of green cloth. She wore it like a badge of honor for weeks, much longer than she needed to, and damned his eyes every time he looked at her. Even back then she was damning him to hell.

He didn't touch her after that. He picked on Gladys instead, until she escaped and married Gerry and moved out.

Whenever she remembers how Stupidhead picked on Gladys, never giving her a moment's peace, always calling her a fat cow and a whore, and how she, Noreen, never once stuck up for her, she puts her pillow over her face in deep twisting shame and helpless anger.

Amazing and Stupidhead had a trashy-mouthed small dog named Ginger that they got a month after Noreen went to live with Gladys. It was taught to beg by barking, so the thing never shut up—especially on Sundays when she was forced to go and visit them.

Gerry would put his thick freckled arm around her. "Have a great time, kid," he'd say with a big dumb smile. His eyes would go all watery. He couldn't stand Stupidhead.

"Stupidhead is *your* father," Noreen pleaded one time with Gladys. "Why don't you and Gerry come too?"

"Because I don't like Stupidhead any more than you do. And I don't have to." Gladys looked at Gerry. He looked back, still smiling. Crazy about her like she was some kind of angel. Like he thought that he was good and she was good and together they were good beyond mere mortals. It was all so sweet that it could seriously give you diabetes.

"But they don't even like me," Noreen said accusingly, hoping that that would work and she wouldn't have to go.

"Listen, we have a deal, you and me." Gladys would now pull out her weird mental contortions about family loyalty. "They have to see you once a week, or you can't live with me and Gerry. It's only fair, Noreen. They are your parents, after all. When you turn seventeen you can do whatever you want about them. Okay? That's the rule. *Seventeen,*" Gladys stressed. "So go on now. And please try to be pleasant, okay?"

"Even alcoholics deserve respect," Gerry added piously.

He had moved closer to Gladys, his arm now around her. As if they were already thinking about how, as soon as she was gone, they would breathe deep sighs and have a nice time together, finally free of this crazy person.

Sometimes she hates them both, and this feeling sits like a glowing hard lump of coal under her rib cage, right next to her jealous heart. She could show anybody the exact burning spot if they cared to ask. This is the worst anger of all. It's so bad sometimes, she thinks her heart will stop beating, and if it does, it'll serve her right.

Confession of Covetousness
Noreen—Age 17

Wesley Cuthand. She has no clear memory of how he looked when they first met. She'd been stuck between Saskatoon and Winnipeg. Walking along the highway. Fed up with the last guy she'd hitched a ride with—an asshole who'd given her the creeps, she remembers that much. (When he'd stopped his car just before Brandon and got out to take a leak in the ditch, she'd jumped out and run across a field. "Hey! Come back here, you whore!" he'd shouted. She gave him the finger and kept on running.) Ten minutes after she got up her nerve to walk along the highway again, this truck slid up beside her. She was still jumpy as hell from that last ride.

On the other hand, Wesley has no such problems remembering details about how *she* looked on their first meeting. She had a backpack on her back and the skinniest little ass he'd ever seen. "The sun was almost down, except for a piece of the sky that was still on fire. That's how I remember it. Oh, yeah, and the fields—and the hills off to the south—they were kind of blue and shadowy." That's exactly the way he says it—about the land and the shadows and how the sky was on fire, et cetera, et cetera. Sometimes he even starts there, goes on about her skinny little ass, and then, "I stopped the truck. You got in. Your eyes all big and pretty in your face."

"You said it was dark, Wesley. How could you see them?"

"I *did!* I saw them."

"Okay, go on."

He puts his hand over his heart. "I thought my breath would never come back." And gives a low chuckle.

"Go *on.*"

"I'm not going to *hurry*, Noreen. *Relax,* this is a good story."

"*Tell* it."

Next comes the part where he offered her a stick of gum to calm her. She took it from him, eased it up to her mouth, never once taking her scared eyes from him. The first words either of them spoke (the truck still wasn't moving) came from Wesley, who said, laughing, "You look like a jackrabbit."

Apparently, she almost jumped out of her skin before asking, "Why?" After which she stared straight ahead.

The best part about hearing this story is feeling safe—lying on Wesley's bed, the sheets all tangled up and sour smelling from not being washed in a while, his arm around her, her head against his chest while she listens to his voice rumble on through while he talks.

He recounts what he said next. "Why do you look like a jackrabbit?"

"Yeah. You think I look funny?"

"No. You're the most beautiful woman I've ever seen in my life." And he tells this part very seriously. Sometimes, odd as it seems, there are even tears in his eyes.

That's Wesley. He values the truth. The fact that he hardly ever gets it never stops him from expecting it.

So back at the truck, near Brandon, she said, "You are a weirdo," and yanked on the door handle.

"I'll drive you anywhere you want," said Wesley, and of course he meant it.

"Anywhere?"

"Absolutely anywhere."

"All right," said Noreen. "Drive me to Winnipeg."

"I was only going as far as Brandon," said Wesley. "And I'm almost out of gas."

"Then piss off," said Noreen, and again she started to get out of the truck.

"I'll drive you. I'll get more gas. What are you doing out here?"

"Walking," said Noreen. "And that's all you need to know."

They spent two days and three nights in a cheap motel on the outskirts of Winnipeg, with the moon outside their window at night, and at twilight the blue land that rolled flat out to the horizon. They stayed until Wesley's paycheck ran out and she suggested that he take her on home to where she lived with her brother-in-law, Gerry, and her stepsister, Gladys.

"You mean you live here? In Winnipeg?"

"Of course." She stood in the motel bathroom applying mascara, which, besides painting her fingernails unusual colors, is the only makeup she ever wears.

"But I thought you were coming from Saskatoon."

"I hitched *to* Saskatoon," she explained, examining her teeth, rubbing a finger across them. "I hitched there with my boyfriend. It didn't work out. So I came back without him. That's where I was coming from. When you found me."

In his favorite story of their love, Wesley claims he knew right then and there that he was up to his neck beyond the point of no return. She was the most delicate beautiful thing he'd ever seen, he says. He was in love with her flax-colored eyes, her long silky hair, her small hands and feet, the way she'd curl up beside him like a kitten, the way she rode him at night till the stars seemed to shower out of the cosmos and fall all around them.

Gladys met them at the door as Noreen walked in with Wesley, and right away she started in. "Where the hell have you been? I've had the cops out looking for you and everything. We thought you were dead in a ditch somewhere."

"I went with Tyler. To Saskatoon," said Noreen. "Nice to see you too."

"I'm *responsible* for you. You didn't even say you were going. Noreen, you've been gone for ten entire days! You're seventeen years old and you just keep screwing up. You're always screwing up. I can't stand it."

"I was going to quit my job anyway."

"You might have warned them. You'll never get a good reference now. I'm ready to give up on you."

"A reference for *what?* Working at a crappy burger place?"

Wesley shuffled around on the little green mat inside Gladys's door. He looked down at his feet, then at Noreen, then at Gladys.

"And who is this?" demanded Gladys.

"Wesley Cuthand," said Noreen, pushing past her. "He's my boyfriend."

"I thought Tyler was your boyfriend!" Gladys was practically shrieking.

"He's probably still in Saskatoon. He's a loser," Noreen called over her shoulder. She wasn't about to confess that by the time they'd hitched there, Tyler had run out of patience and kindness. In a hole called Bianca's Burritos and Burgers, he'd excused himself politely—that was Tyler all the way—stood up, his straight brown hair falling all over his big-boned, wind-raw face, and gone off to find the washroom. He didn't come back. After about twenty-five minutes their waitress, who had eyes as big and dark as the craters of the moon, leaned over the table and said, "I think you should know something. Your boyfriend's gone, hon. All I know is he paid for your meal just before he went out the door."

Noreen tromped into her bedroom, found a big black garbage bag under a mound of dead clothes and started stuffing things into it—whatever she thought she might need or miss, although she couldn't have cared less about most of it, quite frankly. She just figured it was the thing to do. She left her room with the bag over her shoulder.

"I'm moving out," she announced to Gladys.

"*What?*"

"I'm moving in with him."

Wesley smiled shyly at Gladys. "I'll take good care of her," he said.

"Where to? Noreen, don't you start rolling your eyes at me. Tell me where you are going to be at."

"Okay. Brandon."

"*Brandon?* Why Brandon?"

"Because. It's where he lives."

"So." Gladys folded her arms to calm herself and gather inner strength. It's what she always did, gather inner strength, Sweet Jesus (Gladys's expression), before she tried reason again.

If ever Noreen tried to think back to when things between Gladys and her got derailed, she found that she couldn't locate any actual moment. It had just been a gradual thing, until one day she realized that Gladys had stopped behaving like a real sister. Here she was, twenty-four years old, with permanent scowly lines between her eyebrows. She was getting to be a sour old woman before her time.

"Noreen," Gladys said finally, "when Gerry and me agreed to take you in, the deal was that you had to finish high school. *That* was the deal. And now just how are you planning to make a living?"

"Beats me," Noreen shot back.

She left without even saying goodbye, threw her bag into Wesley's truck, got in.

"Aren't you going to give her my phone number?" Wesley wasn't starting the truck, just sitting there in the driveway.

"Wesley," said Noreen, "I am a free woman. Now let's get the hell out of here."

But as they drove away she looked back, hoping to see Gladys at the window, or maybe Gladys standing out on her front steps waving, trying to get just one more glimpse of her baby stepsister, of the person she had once claimed to love to the stars and back again.

In Wesley's small apartment in Brandon, she stays at home all the time. Wesley goes to work at Dan's Construction. She starts her day with TV. She rolls over in bed and there's Wesley, his long black Cree hair tied back, jeans, T-shirt, boots, ready to leave for work.

"Which channel?" he asks, standing by the TV.

"Five," she says, or "two," or "sixteen." She doesn't care. It's six o'clock in the morning. Yet he wants to know, and stays until she tells him.

Then he comes to her side of the bed, makes her sit up and put on a sweatshirt, and gives her a hug and kisses the top of her head like she's a little kid. "Eat something," he says, and then leaves and doesn't get back for sometimes twelve or thirteen hours.

For the first couple of weeks, she feels that maybe he expects something from her besides sex. One day, when he comes home and asks her how her day went—and she has managed by that point to pull on a pair of jeans—she replies casually, "Oh, I was out looking for work."

He looks at her for a minute. Then he comes and sits down beside her on the couch. He doesn't put his arm around her like he usually does. In fact he looks really mad.

"What's wrong?" she says.

He doesn't answer. He gets up, goes into the bathroom, takes a shower. After that he's in the kitchen, where dishes have been piling up for about three days. He washes the dishes, puts them all away. Then he cooks hamburgers and pulls out some slaw and a bottle of cola from the fridge and brings them into the living room, where she is watching the same channel he turned the TV to before he left in the morning for work.

He sits silently and eats his burger, his dark eyes flicking back and forth between his plate and the TV. She starts to feel scared. She takes a couple of bites of her burger and can't eat any more. She wonders if she should say something. Then she starts to get pissed off. "What the hell is wrong with you?" she says. "I tell you I've been out looking for work and you go all weird on me."

He puts his hamburger very deliberately onto his plate. Brushes crumbs lightly from his hands. Thinks for a minute. Then he turns and says in a cold voice, "I don't care whether you look for work or not. That's up to you. What I don't like is when people lie to me."

"Lie to you? I don't know what you're talking about."

"Stop acting like a little kid, Noreen," he says, and goes back to eating his burger.

She tucks her legs tightly under her body and says to him, "Well, Wesley, I don't appreciate being treated like one."

"I don't treat you like a kid," he says, chewing away, staring hard at the TV.

"Yes, you do. You always do."

"When?" He's still staring at the TV. "Tell me when I do that."

"Every morning. You make me sit up like I'm some stupid invalid or something. And you make me tell you what channel. And then you make me put on a sweatshirt." She realizes even as she says this that she *is* sounding like a kid. But she goes on. "Maybe I don't want to get up, Wesley. And maybe I don't care about the stupid TV. Or my goddamn sweatshirt."

"Okay," he says. "I won't bother you anymore."

After that he leaves her alone. Every morning he doesn't wake her up—even though she's only pretending to still be asleep. He quietly rolls away until the mattress is light again with only her weight. He pulls on his jeans, makes coffee, pours himself a mug and goes with it to the open window. He stands there with his bare brown back, making her feel jealous of the sun that he is saying good morning to. After he leaves she turns on the TV, pulls on one of his shirts, hugs it around her body and then hates herself for missing him so much. Eventually she falls back asleep. When she wakes up again it's usually the middle of the day.

Things go along like that for a long time, her staying in bed most of the day, Wesley working right through into the evening. For a while she is too tired to care. She thinks she wants to go out and do something, then realizes she's been thinking the same thought for about an hour and hasn't moved from the spot where she is sitting or lying. In her spirit, she feels half dead. And lately too, she's been feeling bloated and fluish.

"Something is very wrong with you," Wesley says to her one day. "Are you sick?"

She's just come from the shower and is sitting on the sofa with the towel in her hand and her hair dripping in long strings down her back. She doesn't answer him.

He takes the towel and wipes off her back. Then he uses it to dry her hair. He takes a long time. He loves her hair. "Maybe you should go and see a doctor," he says after a while.

"I'm not sick. I don't need to go to a doctor."

"Then let's go for a drive."

"Where?"

"Anywhere."

"Why?"

"Noreen," he says, placing the towel around her shoulders, "you need cheering up. You need something, that's for sure. You don't even want to leave this apartment anymore. And you've been acting more and more like a—depressed person. It's scaring me."

"What? Now you're telling me I'm crazy?"

His shoulders sag. He takes a deep breath, avoiding her gaze. "About a year ago I was in pretty bad shape. I ended up doing something real cowardly. And that—the thing I did—got all messed up in my head. I finally had to go see somebody about it. Even then it didn't help much." He leans forward, clasping his hands. Waits for her to say something.

"I can't believe you think I'm crazy! I am *fine,* Wesley! There is *nothing* wrong with me. Nothing. Nothing. Nothing. Can't you get it through your head? *I just want to be left alone."*

But she really doesn't want to be left alone. That's the last thing she wants. She is just saying it to be miserable. One night, side by side on their backs in bed, she folds her arms tightly across her chest. She stares at the ceiling. His head slowly turns.

"Are you counting the stars?"

"What?"

"How many stars are up there?"

"Don't talk to me about stars."

"Take away the ceiling and there's millions, trillions of stars," he says, ignoring her comment. "Out on the prairies on a clear night, you can see every one of them. As long as you can find the stars, Noreen, or even imagine them, you can convince yourself that you don't feel lonely."

A little breeze riffles through their open window. She lets her arms drop to her sides. She can smell his hair, his skin. Wesley always smells real good. She scoots over to him and throws herself across his chest. She holds onto him with all her strength. There is an empty feeling coming from him that scares her. It's like he's gone away somewhere and will never come back. She keeps holding on until, at last, his arms come around her. Then she falls into a restless dream-filled sleep.

She dreams of cars. Of standing along a highway as they all pass by. Every one of these cars contains a family. As they disappear down the long straight stretch of blacktop, she looks into their back windows and catches glimpses of children's faces and the odd bit of color that stands out—like the red sleeve of a sweater or the dark profile of a silky-eared dog. Sometimes white papers with brightly crayoned lines flutter out of the open windows and swoop freely across the landscape, catching against a fence or tangling up with bushes.

In this dream the fathers drive the cars, are kind and patient with their children and never raise a hand to them. And they all wear cowboy hats. She keeps waiting for one of these hats to blow away too, but none of them ever do. Instead they vanish with the cars and the smiling dads.

The next morning Noreen wakes up and Wesley has already gone. She can't remember where she is for a moment and just lies there smelling the morning smells coming in through the window. The air is fresh. It's late June and the sun is shining. She turns her head to look out the window and the first thing she sees is the sky. It's so blue she feels as if she is floating up to meet it, becoming part of it. It is the bluest sky she has ever seen. She lies there for a while, gradually remembering that she has a body, that she's in a bed, that the bed is in Wesley's apartment.

When she gets up she's so full of energy she doesn't know what to do with it all. She finds an orange in the fridge, eats it. After that she makes coffee and, pretending she is Wesley, stands by the window, slowly sipping from his favorite mug.

She's dressed in jeans with nothing on top. She loves the way the morning breeze dances freely across her little pointy breasts. Somebody walks by on the sidewalk, a woman and her dog. For some reason the woman looks up. She does a double take and Noreen gives her a short manly wave, then goes back to examining the sky and drinking coffee, lifting it to her lips, putting her elbow way up to the side, just like Wesley.

She spends her whole day being him, and it feels great. She tucks one of his T-shirts into her jeans. She even pulls her hair back like him. Then she moves energetically around the apartment, cleaning it. She scrubs down the bathroom, takes out the garbage, washes all of their things, remakes the bed with fresh sheets. After that she still has energy. So she cleans the fridge, scrubs the stove inside and out, washes the floor. Next she starts on their tiny living room, which is also their bedroom, and dusts and tidies and sweeps.

By then the day has all but disappeared and she is hungry. There is nothing much to eat in the refrigerator. She considers making dinner, but there isn't anything very interesting in the cupboards either, so she goes on a search for money. She remembers that Wesley keeps spare change in a coffee tin on top of the kitchen cupboards. She stands on the counter, finds the tin and brings it down. She takes off the plastic lid. There's change inside, all right, but also a lot of other money, mostly twenties. When she counts it all up, almost eight hundred dollars.

She takes one of the twenties and replaces the rest. Then she goes to Safeway, three blocks down at the end of the street. She buys a barbecued chicken, some potato salad and another kind of salad with corn in it because Wesley likes corn, two tins of iced tea, a small container of chocolate fudge ice cream and a can of peaches. She struts back home. She's wearing an old pair of his boots, tied up tight so they'll stay on her feet. They make her feel tall.

At somebody's chain-link fence, a whole bunch of daisies have poked through the holes to freedom on the other side; she saw them on her way to the store. She sets down her bags of groceries to admire them and picks some. She blows on them for luck. Then she picks up the groceries and walks back to the apartment.

When Wesley gets home from work, he sees the daisies on the coffee table. That's the first thing. Then he starts to notice the other things, how tidy stuff is, how clean. He goes into the bathroom and comes out again with a great big smile on his face.

"Are you hungry?" Noreen asks him shyly.

He responds with a chuckle that is pure Wesley and says, "What—you're a cook too?"

She walks proudly past him and takes their plates out of the fridge. She sliced everything up ahead of time, with a peach half for each cut in the shape of a star. She hopes he'll notice this little detail. He does. He eats his peach half first and smiles at her. She forks her dinner around on her plate. The combined smell of chicken and potato salad suddenly makes her feel ill. She picks away at her peach and waits for him to ask where she got the money to buy the groceries. Of course, maybe he just thinks she still has some money left of her own. Besides, she only took twenty dollars.

Next morning she wakes up nauseated. She goes into the kitchen, discovers a box of saltines at the back of Wesley's cupboard, eats a dozen or so crackers and immediately feels better. After that she stands up on the counter again, taking another twenty dollars out of the tin. She goes out in Wesley's boots and walks a little farther than the day before. She finds a Wal-Mart and once inside locates the sewing supplies. She looks through material—rows and rows of flat bolts. Nothing looks or feels exactly right. The salesgirl asks twice if she can help. No, says Noreen, I'm just looking—but she's beginning to feel discouraged. Then the salesgirl, whose name is Sylvia—it says so right on her tag—directs her to a round bin that contains tail ends of material, remnants on sale.

"Go crazy," Sylvia says, smiling, leaving Noreen to her own devices.

She begins by delicately pawing through the fabric. Nothing. Then she starts hauling them out onto the long sales table, scattering the bright colors and textures everywhere. Three-quarters of the way through the bin, she finds what she is looking for, a big roll of gauzy dark blue with dime-sized white blotches splashed randomly. She unravels a length, then stands back. When she half closes her eyes, she realizes happily that you could almost think it was the nighttime prairie sky. She pays Sylvia for the material, some needles and thread and a cheap but workable pair of scissors with purple handles, and goes back to Wesley's.

At first she tries spreading the material out on the living-room floor, but that proves difficult because there isn't enough empty floor space. Then she remembers that it should be longer than the bed, so she measures it along the length and down over the end of the mattress. There is enough cloth to cut into two lengths, which she does, sitting on the floor. She sews them together up the middle and hems the ends. After the last stitch, snipping the navy blue thread with her teeth, she stands and flips out the cloth. The early afternoon breeze from the window puffs it up in the middle. Magically, the whole thing floats down on the bed, looking, she thinks—if you have a pretty good imagination—almost like a starry prairie sky.

One of the many TV shows she's watched over the past almost two and a half months since she's been living with Wesley showed a person covering a canopy frame over a bed. What she really wants is to put the sky over his head. She thinks of him at night, staring up, thinking his poetic thoughts. There is, however, no such frame on his bed. So she goes downstairs to the caretaker to ask if she has a ladder and a staple gun. The caretaker, Melissa, who is about fifty years old and always chews gum, has a ladder Noreen can borrow, but no staple gun.

Noreen takes the ladder, dragging it up five flights of stairs to the apartment. She sets it up by the bed, then goes into the kitchen and pulls down the can of money from the top of the cupboards. She takes out a twenty for the staple gun, rethinks this and takes one more twenty—just in case it's an expensive item. She also has this idea that if she bought a couple of artist's brushes and a few pots of silver and gold paint, she could make points around some of those white spots and then they'd really look like stars. So she helps herself to another twenty.

At the end of the day, when she finally comes down from the ladder and looks up at the billowy blue material, all sparkly and celestial, she can't believe she has made this—made it just for Wesley. She lies down on the middle of the bed and looks up. Surely it's the nicest thing she's ever done for anybody. It certainly is the prettiest. She tucks her hands inside the waistband of her jeans. She's feeling bloated again and kind of ill. She undoes the button. Then the fly. Places her hands gently on her abdomen.

A dull memory, insistent as heat, creeps over her. She thinks back over the past couple of months. Tries to remember when she had her last period. Thinks about that time the condom broke when she and Wesley were going at it. And there were a couple of other times when they didn't bother with protection at all.

Her mouth goes dry. Her whole being begins to shake with a terrible, sickening recognition.

Later, she doesn't hear Wesley come home. She doesn't hear his truck pull into the graveled side lot under their apartment window, or the tiniest dying rattle the engine always makes just as he turns the key and pulls it from the ignition. She doesn't hear him come into the apartment or close the door or set his boots down in the hall. She doesn't hear him move across the carpet, or the familiar soft *clunk* his key chain makes when he places it on the coffee table.

She doesn't hear him standing there, breathing—looking at the expensive staple gun, the paints and the paint brushes, and her lying under the canopy of stars—or him going through the plastic bags to locate the sales slips, pull them out and read them. She doesn't hear him as he stands thinking about all this, putting it together in his mind; or when he goes into the kitchen, pulls down the coffee can, pops the lid, takes out his money and begins to count it.

What actually wakes her up is one, single explosive word: *"Shit!"*

Then he is standing over the bed, towering over it, over her. Just like a bad little monkey, she sits up and scoots over to the other side so he can't hit her, or grab her, or do whatever it is he's going to do to her.

"I'm missing a hundred dollars here, Noreen! Why the hell didn't you just ask?!"

"I'm sorry. I'm sorry. I'm sorry," she says, putting her hands over her ears.

He looks up at the stars now sparkling dully from his ceiling and says again, *"Shit."* Then he turns abruptly, strides to the door, pulls on his boots.

"Please don't go."

"I need to get out of here. I need to think."

"Wesley, please please please don't go. I'll do whatever you want."

"And just what would that be," he says coldly. "Get a grip, Noreen."

He slams out of the apartment. His boots make a terrible angry sound down the hallway, down and down the five flights of creaky wooden stairs, out of the building, onto the sidewalk. After that everything is quiet. She sits at the edge of the bed, thinking.

She thinks about her stepfather and how there was once a time when he was nice—before he married Amazing. "Just wait," Gladys had told her, the day after he gave her a Barbie doll she really wanted. "He's just doing that to impress everybody. You don't know him like I do. He's a crazy bastard." Gladys was right. He gradually changed into Stupidhead and didn't budge from there on.

She doesn't feel a single thing, she realizes now, shaking her head, and that's good. After all, she knew this was coming. Sooner or later Wesley would have grown tired of her and things would have changed. Taking his money without asking has just helped to speed things along. It's almost a relief this has happened. Now she can leave.

The purple-handled scissors she bought earlier are still lying on the floor. She picks them up and takes them into the bathroom. In front of the mirror, she solemnly regards the silky long blond hair that Wesley always loves to stroke. She lifts one section away from her head, moves the cool metal blades in until they are a few inches from her scalp, then snips. Instantly a long snake of pale gold slithers into the sink. She does this with another section and then another, until soon Wesley's sink is filled with her hair.

Then she takes the few belongings she arrived with, plus the money remaining in the coffee tin, coldly picks up his keys, locks him out of his own apartment, goes out and gets into his truck and drives away.

The Defining Moments of My Life
A Chronology in Two Parts
Anne Fleming

Part One: The Defining Moments of My Life as Envisioned by My Mother when Pregnant with Me

-1-

I am, like David Copperfield and most other people real and imagined, born. This event occasions my mother enough pain and struggle to be worthy of the word "labor," but not so much that she begins to believe my entry into the world will be her exit.

During these difficult but ultimately meaningful five or six hours—eight at the outside—her husband frets with worry in the waiting room, absently ripping the petals off the flowers he bought in the first giddy half hour, and whose stems he snapped soon thereafter from too much anxious clenching.

He is not disappointed in the least to learn his first child is a girl.

-2-

I am an attractive baby, even as a newborn, with enormous eyes and long lashes. All the nurses love me on first sight. I breastfeed easily and happily.

-3-

Eight weeks later, my christening takes place in St. Clement's Anglican Church. I wear the slightly yellow but still gorgeous lace gown that my mother's grandmother tatted by hand for her first child's christening and that has seen eight christenings since. My father holds me proudly by the baptismal font. After handing me to the priest, he coughs in a weak attempt to mask his deep emotion and rubs his strangely watery eye with his knuckles.

My mother takes his hand. She too, bites back tears. Afterwards they have a fabulous luncheon at which no one gets drunk and everyone coos appreciatively at me and my mother.

We are pretty as a picture. She does not leak breast milk onto her best dress, the blue silk. I smile.

-4-

I am an easy baby, gurgling happily in my crib. Each stage described in the baby books I enter into promptly and exactly. At X days, my eyes focus past ten inches and I display an interest in the mobile above my crib. At Y months, I roll over. At Z, I begin to crawl.

All this while, my mother is utterly absorbed in me, and so, when he hurries home each night from his job with the great future, is my father.

-5-

At two, I chatter away animatedly and am almost completely toilet trained. My father gets a promotion. When they learn the happy news that my mother is again pregnant, they put a down payment on a house in Moore Park. We are nicely ensconced there by the time my mother gives birth, even less painfully than to me, to my little brother, on whom we all dote, me included, in my clumsy toddling way.

-6-

I have a happy childhood, which consists of:

a) An easy adjustment to school after making shy and clinging to my mother's skirts when she delivered me on the first day;
b) A cute and unshakeable conviction at age six that I will marry Timmy Mills, the adorable blue-eyed first-born of my mother's best friend, Peg;
c) Well-attended birthday parties, creative Halloween costumes sewn by my mother, fun family Christmases at which no one passes out or kicks the dog, and many other seasonal festivities;
d) Skating lessons, swimming lessons, piano lessons, ballet, tap, and lessons at anything else I happen to be good at;
e) Sunday school; and perhaps
f) One sorrow: the death, in old age, of my grandfather. My grandmother lives till she is at least ninety, or whenever my mother can conceive of losing her.

-7-

I get my period. Of course my mother has lovingly explained my entrance into womanhood before the sacred event. I embrace my womanhood with bashful pleasure, feeling closer than ever to the woman who brought me into the world. I turn to her with the difficult questions in my life, like how to let a boy know you like him without going too far, and how to get blood stains out of underwear.

-8-

a) I continue to be attractive, as my brother also turns out to be. We are popular and have lots of friends. Mother makes us a nutritious lunch each day.
b) I go on my first date.
c) I have my first boyfriend.

-9-

I get the lead in the high school play, preferably *West Side Story*.

-10-

~~I have my first abortion.~~

Sorry. -10-

I am valedictorian and give a moving speech, thanking my parents for their support.

-11-

I go to university on a scholarship I don't need.

-12, 13, 14-

I have a brilliant career as well as a brilliant marriage, and several children as adorable as I was.

And so on.

Part Two: The Defining Moments of My Life as Seen by Me

-1-

I am not, if you go by Shakespeare's way of thinking, born. I am untimely ripped from my mother's womb via C-section. (I always did think that was a bit of a plot cheat—one may be untimely ripped, but one is still of woman born.) Before the decision to open my mother up, labor is a monstrously painful and long process, and I hear about it often, every time I am deemed an ungrateful child.

-2-

I am a startlingly ugly baby, with a big swath of coarse black hair down the middle of my head and onto my low brow, and a bumpy red rash over my entire face. The effect is not unlike that of a black-haired pig we see some years later at the Royal Winter Fair scratching its flaky skin against the door of the stall.

The hair falls out, the rash goes away, and I am still none too pretty. I cry almost constantly. It drives my mother to distraction and causes my father to yell at my mother to shut me up, he needs his sleep, whereupon he storms out of the house in a rage swearing he'll sleep in his office, which he may or may not do. This is what he does when my brother, though not biologically related, takes after me in the vocal cord department.

-3-

One of my earliest memories—I will call it my first—is of a geranium on the kitchen table. Just that. The geranium—red and green on the pale gray table, lit up by a small patch of sunlight—and the sound of traffic outside. Apparently I pulled all the petals off this geranium, in fact off any flowers I came in contact with, but I don't remember that. I remember it whole, in the sunlight.

-4-

My other early memory is of playing with the nap of the beige carpet under the ironing board as my mother works above me. The iron hisses across spritzed shirts. The air smells of seared starch. And then there are spots on the carpet under the place where my mother is no longer standing. Putting my finger in the biggest spot, inches across, I lick it to make sure it is what I think it is. Yes. I am a wound-sucker; I know that metallic taste and I love it. It's the taste of me, my cut finger or knee or lip. The same taste coming from someone else makes me feel funny.

-5-

My adopted brother arrives. He has black hair and brown skin and hollers all the time. I can't believe I ever hollered that much or that loudly, though I am told repeatedly it is true.

-6-

I have a childhood in which:

a) I hate my clothes. My mother makes them or gets them passed down from her sister's daughters. I lobby for hand-me-downs from my boy cousins, to no avail. The clothes are cute skirt-and-top outfits or cute patterned pant-and-top outfits.

   One weekend at my cousins' I steal Jeff's red-and-yellow striped shirt. I'd take his blue corduroys too, but I'm afraid my greed would reveal me. I start carrying the shirt with me in a plastic bag and change wherever I can, in friends' garages or in the bushes in the park.

   Seeing myself in a mirror at school, I realize the shirt doesn't do much to change the overall effect. I am still wearing a brown skirt with gingham appliqué mushrooms.

   I continue to wear the shirt anyway until a close call with my mother wanting to know what's in the bag forces me to stow it in my hiding spot in the park. The next day I discover it half-burnt, sodden and unrecoverable. I cry.

b) Timmy Mills calls me and my brother ugly. This follows on my mother telling me gleefully and regularly—every time we see an infant, in fact, cute or ugly—that I was an ugly baby.

   She has told me I look cute in various outfits. More accurately, she has said that outfits look cute on me. "It's a pretty little outfit, isn't it?" she will say. "You look sweet in it." She has not said that I am pretty. Not that I want to be. Handsome suits me better. But for the first time I notice my mother makes a distinction between me and my clothes. She herself is pretty, as my father is handsome. I have heard my mother say to her friends, joking, "We get by on our looks." I look like my father, and the effect is not pretty.

My brother is only five, and too little for me to have thought much about his looks. Sometimes, when people ask, I say our father is a Cree Indian and that we spend summers on the trapline. You don't look Indian, they say, and sometimes I say, *You better sleep lightly 'cause you never know when an Indian is sneaking up on you, and you never know what we'll do either, because we're dangerous.*

"Yeah," my brother will say.

c) I realize words can have unexpected consequences.

My brother Danny, though almost four years younger, is a good companion. He is game for almost anything. He can keep up, he never whines or complains or tells on me and my friends when we smoke in the park and light fires, burning mitts and hats lost under the snow in winter, or other articles of clothing that we find. (I am on the lookout for boys' shirts, but mostly we find underwear and socks and wonder how their owners came to leave such things behind.)

But he has nightmares, my brother. Our father says he is too old to sleep with his parents, so when he wakes up in terror he comes to me, the person who put the seed of fear in him in the first place.

He dreams his real father has come to kill him in his bed.

I get my period when I am ten. Not expecting this for a couple of years at least, Mom has not yet given me her Soon You Will Be a Woman speech, but I know what's going on. I don't think I'm bleeding to death with some mysterious disease. I know what menstruation is. I have read my friend Elaine's copy of *Are You There God? It's Me, Margaret.*

There's an unofficial club of girls who have read this book. They whisper and giggle and make like they have a superior knowledge of the world. A friend of my mother who has a daughter a couple of years older than me says she doesn't care what the school board thinks, this book is a true representation of girlhood and should be on the curriculum. She has started a petition.

I do not like the book. If it is a true representation of girlhood, then I am not a true girl. All of Margaret's friends look forward to getting their periods and are happy when it arrives. There is talk of small amounts of rusty-brown blood in the underwear.

The blood in my underwear has never been rusty brown, not even on the very first day. It is brilliant red. There is lots of it. I am always getting up in the middle of the night to find I've bled through my nightie onto the sheets again and have to scrub them out with cold water. I learn to sleep a light, uncomfortable sleep on my side.

I stain things: car seats, couches, swings. At school I work on ways to casually lean over so I can check between my legs for blood. I perfect a light probing gesture down the back of my pants to check for wetness as I get up, but several times I notice people notice.

My mother is not a big help. After giving me her modified, My God, You're a Woman Too Early talk, she provides me with a box of pads and the instruction never to use hot water on a blood stain. She seems to blame my inability to manage my period on my general inadequacy at being female rather than on a startlingly heavy flow. Not that she says anything; it's just these looks she gives. She claims to have a heavy flow herself, so I assume that she must be right, that there is some innate girl thing, some tidiness and cleanliness gene that I simply don't have.

It's not until I'm fourteen that I figure out that I can stick a second pad to the back of my underwear at night to catch the flow. Finally I can lie on my back and get a few nights' rest, but it's no help during the day.

I determine to use tampons. I open a box of Kotex snuck from my mother's bathroom. They look like white bullets on sticks. I crouch over the toilet and try to insert one. It feels like a white bullet on a stick. I push. I swear. Push. Wince. Pull it out. Dump. Flush. Pull another tampon from the package. Reread the instructions, noting the approximate angle of insertion. Try the foot-on-the-bathtub method. Adopt a speedier plunge. Am pleased with the success of this. Put my foot down. Try to walk around the bathroom.

I finish the whole box and hope Mom is not having her period. The next day I go to the drugstore and buy a box each of Kotex, O.B. and Tampax. It costs my entire allowance. I manage to insert a Tampax.

It lasts three-quarters of an hour.

-8-

The same friend of my mother who championed *Are You There God? It's Me, Margaret* gives my mother *The Diary of Anais Nin* for her fortieth birthday. She has inscribed it "Here's to spotted G's." I read it after my mother is finished. It is not as racy as I expect, but there are bits I read over and over. With my door closed and my hand between my legs.

-9-

At seventeen, I win a part in *West Side Story*. I am the tomboy, always trying to get into the gang and always getting ridiculed and kicked around instead. My character's name, interestingly, is "Anybody's."

My mother is appalled. She knows I could not possibly be Maria, but she thought maybe a chorus girl, maybe even Bernardo's girlfriend, or Riff's. Anybody but Anybody's.

The girl who plays Maria, who I've always thought was a flirty snot, turns out to be okay. Her name is Sara, and while she waits for her scenes she drinks coffee and does the *New York Times* crossword puzzle, which I've never heard of before. The first time I meet her she asks me for an eight-letter word for crazy. "Um," I say. She is a year older than me. She's sitting with Colin Vogl, who I know from track. He does javelin. He is Officer Krupke in the show. I keep saying "Um," because I can see she is in the process of writing me off and I don't want to be written off. I can't think of a single word for crazy except mad, which of course is five letters short.

"Cracked," says Colin.

"That's only seven," she says after a pause.

"Demented," I say, my mind suddenly unleashed. "Deranged, insane, nuts, cuckoo, off your rocker, loopy, lunatic, unhinged, bats."

"Unhinged," she says. "Thank you."

We begin to give each other vocabulary tests we get out of *Reader's Digest*. We score well. When we don't do the crossword, we smoke drugs in the parking lot, me, Sara and Colin, who supplies the weed. Getting high is not the point of this exercise, at least not for me, because I don't, not at first. The point is Sara and Colin and me. Maria, Officer Krupke and Anybody's. Or, as we soon become to each other, Santa Maria (being a Christian icon cracks Sara up because she's Jewish—the irony is not lost on us that so was the original Mary), just plain Krupke and Buddy. Me.

-10! 10! Let's Sing a Song About 10-

I get high for the first time. Sara and Krupke and I lie in the middle of the football field after smoking up behind the dumpsters, and for the first time I really feel it. The clouds are stupendous. "I love you guys," we all say. Other times we say it like fakey-fakey actor types, "Oh, I just love all of you guys," blowing kisses, but this time we say it like we mean it. We sit up and put our backs together, leaning in a circle. Sara holds my hand. "I feel pretty," Krupke hums. Sara and I take his hands. We get up and skip around in a mockery of an interpretive dance circle, singing the song. I realize that Krupke is gay.

-11-

Timmy Mills is paralyzed after plowing his mother's car into a telephone pole on the big hill on Mount Pleasant south of St. Clair.

-12-

My brother gets busted for shoplifting a water pistol at the variety store. I used to steal Dubble Bubble from there by bending down and putting them in my socks. The one time I got caught, the guy put me in the bathroom for five minutes, saying he was going to call my parents, but then let me go after I blubbered like an idiot and swore I'd never steal again. On my brother he calls the cops.

My father picks my brother up by the shoulders and shakes him. Danny scrunches up his eyes and kicks as hard as he can. He gets Dad in the hip and the thigh and when he almost hits the groin, Dad slams him into the wall and lets go. Danny howls.

My father has previously thrown plates full of food, dented the fridge with his fist, torn the door off its hinges, and smashed my mother's antique dining-room chair, but he has never hit my mother or me. Or my brother. "Don't you ever hit him again," my mother says and then tells him to get out. I am amazed that he does. He comes back sometime while we are asleep because he's there the next morning. When he apologizes to us at breakfast, we don't look at him.

-13-

I cut my hair for the performance of the play, though the home ec teacher doing costumes has said, "Just tuck it up under a cap, dear. No need to go too far."

My parents freak. "You look like a boy," my mother says.

"I'm supposed to look like a boy," I say.

"You're supposed to look like a girl trying to look like a boy."

"A facsimile," my father agrees, "not the thing itself."

"What can you do?" I say, shrugging. "What's cut is cut."

"Are you being flip with me?"

"I'm just saying what is."

My father paces a few steps away and adopts a considering tone. "She's just saying what is. She's just—saying—what—is. Does she actually know what is?" He paces back, looking at the floor, finger to his chin. "Does she? No, I don't think so. Should I tell her? Is she old enough to know what is? Or should I tell her if she takes this play too seriously, she won't be taking it at all? That her career in drama is hanging by a thread?"

He looks me up and down to see if I am quivering or not, to see if he's got me. He has. He says, "Get out of my sight. You look obscene."

"Talk about a career in drama," Sara says of my father when I tell her about this the next day.

My brother comes and sits on my bed while I cry and plays with his Rubik's Cube. "I like it," he says. "I think you look good."

-13.5-

My father steps up his scrutiny of my appearance, leaving for work only after he has seen what I'm wearing each morning. Of course I am careful to look like a girl. I wear earrings and bangle bracelets and high-waisted pleated pants. I even wear blouses, though it pains me emotionally and the shoulders are too tight.

He does not come to the play itself, which is fine with me. My mother comes with my brother and Peg Mills, who hasn't gone out much since Tim's accident. Mom is teary-eyed afterwards—it is, after all, her favorite musical and the one she starred in when she was in high school. She hugs me. She hugs Sara. "You were great," she says. "You were all just terrific. Oh, does it take me back, though!" She hums a bar from "I Feel Pretty" and takes a couple of waltz steps. "Oh!" she says, wiping tears from her eyes.

After the opening night pop-and-chips party in the drama room, a bunch of us go to the Morrissey on Yonge Street, a bar famous for not asking for ID. The strategy is to mix up the younger-looking people with the older-looking ones. I wait nervously in line with Sara, who has fake ID, and Krupke, who's looked old enough to drink since he was fourteen. Except that I start debating the relative merits of successive Doctor Who's (I'm a Tom Baker fan, myself) with Winston Yeung, and Sara, who played her part like a star, is now being mobbed like a star, so by the time they get to the door I have fallen far behind them. The bouncer lets them in. He lets Winston in. He lets everyone in. Except me and the boy who plays Baby John. Baby Bob, we call him.

"Nice try, boys," he says, laughing. "Come back when your beard starts to grow."

Sara and Krupke don't see what's happening. Baby Bob and I turn away without looking at one another, sensing that each other's eyes are too full to bear being seen. We put our hands in our pockets and head up the street toward the subway. I walk slowly, hoping that Sara and Krupke will come after me.

"He thought you were a guy, eh?" says Baby Bob. I shrug. "That's so weird. You don't look like a guy to me." Oh no, I think.

Baby Bob drapes his arm across my shoulders. I twist away from him so it falls off and pick up my pace. I immediately sense that I've hurt him more than if I'd just said "Don't, Bob" Other girls, the ones with the girl genes, would have known that ahead of time. Thankfully we take different routes at the subway station.

On the way home I take my childhood shortcut through school grounds and backyards, darting like Anybody's from shadow to shadow.

-13.67-

There is a long line-up for the bathroom at the closing night party, and Sara comes in with me. "It won't make the wait any shorter," I say. I close my eyes while peeing, and the room spins a bit. It has just hit me that evening that I only have another month of Sara and Krupke—three at the most—before they go away to university. Next year they won't be here. Next year they will forget about me, their little high school friend.

No, no, they have said between tokes. Never, they have said.

Sara idly flashes the light on and off in the bathroom, then leaves it off. Streetlight comes in through the frosted glass. She pees, saying, "Help me up" when she's done, though she doesn't need it.

She hangs onto my arms. She looks into my eyes. My stomach is full of happy bumblebees tumbling all over one another. She kisses me. This is exactly what I've wanted since the first day I met her, though knowing it is news to me. I kiss her back.

People start pounding on the door. "Let's get out of here," Sara says, pulling up her underwear.

Though tempted, we don't ditch Krupke. He is now as maudlin as I was earlier, only about the jock who takes him for "rides" after school but won't otherwise talk to him. We climb the fence into the cemetery and spend the rest of the night communing with the dead and dodging security. A couple of times Krupke turns to find us holding hands, whereupon we take his as well.

-13.99-

My mother is in the kitchen waiting for me when I get home. I expect an earful. More than an earful. I get it, but a different kind than the one I was expecting. It turns out I am not the only one who did not come home last night.

"Good!" says my brother when he hears the news. "I hope he never comes home."

-14-

My father returns the next afternoon and sleeps for two days before checking himself into rehab at Homewood.

-15-

Sara and I skip school and go to Toronto Island. We stop for crusty rolls and shaved salami from Poko's Deli. In the line-up we stand close enough that our clothes touch. It is unbelievable. The bees inside me zoom around in wild abandon. We stop again for kiwis and a bag of Oreos at Dominion. In this line-up, I read *The National Enquirer* over her shoulder. Her hair is against my cheek, the front of my left shoulder is against her back. I have never been so aware of a few square inches of skin. If you gave me a pen today, I could draw you an exact outline.

Because it's the middle of the day, we are able to find an unpopulated section of beach near Hanlon's Point. We eat our lunch. We talk. Sara, who is never shy about anything as far as I can tell, is suddenly shy. We lie in the sun with our sides touching. She turns over on her stomach and puts her arm across me. I stroke her hand. I lift it to my mouth and kiss it. I kiss each knuckle, each nail, the pad of each finger, the palm. I want to kiss the whole rest of her, but I don't know where to start; I don't know how this is done. Luckily, she does.

She has her hand up my shirt when movement down the beach makes us hurl ourselves apart. A Doberman trots up to us, a friendly one who licks our hands. We laugh at ourselves. Just a dog. We sit up, waiting for its owner. Our hands touch where we support ourselves on the sand.

The owner appears. "Gorgeous day, eh?" he says and looks out over the water. "Sure would be nice to be sailing." I make the mistake of agreeing.

He tells us he used to have a sailboat but had to sell it when he got divorced. Sara runs her hand over mine. He tells us what kind of boat it was and what kind he wants for his next boat. Sara's fingers make the hairs on the back of my hand stand up. He tells us he got the dog 'cause he was lonely. Her fingers run over my wrist, up my forearm. Cinnamon is the dog's name. Cinnamon Girl, from the Neil Young song.

"Go away, go away, go away," Sara starts chanting without moving her lips.

"Well," he nods to Cinnamon, "my girl's waiting on me. You have a nice day now."

"You too."

"Ha," says Sara when they're out of sight. She rolls on top of me. Her weight is splendid. Her tongue is as liquidy-thick and inevitable as molten lava and almost as hot. Her hands are acrobats. This is it, I think. This is it.

$-15^{\infty}-$

I have my first non-self-induced orgasm, there on the beach at Hanlon's Point, sometime around 2:30 on a perfect day in June.

$-15^{\infty+1}-$

We get to know Toronto's parks by night, all the wonderful dark out-of-the-way pockets where two bodies will fit together.

$(n\text{-}2)$

Sara goes to Trent. We write a lot of letters. "My bodacious beautiful Buddy Budski," Sara writes. "When are you coming to visit?"

> I did it. I TOLD my roommate about us. I was very nervous but pretty sure she'd be cool about it, and she was. Her parents—the ones who called her Rainbow, natch—have lots of gay and lesbian friends, in fact, her two godmothers are lovers. Whoa. I told her about your godmother, the Anglican nun who sends you crucifix jewelry every birthday. What's her name again? Anyway, slight contrast. So I'm liking her a lot—Rain, that is, not Aunt God—and she says it's no problem, she'd be happy to find a place to crash whenever you come to visit. "YOU-MUST-COME, YOU-MUST-COME" (said like the Daleks on *Doctor Who*, "EX-TERM-EE-NATE, EX-TERM-EE-NATE"). I'm sorry you are so bored and lonely. Of course, if you came here and visited me, you wouldn't be, n'est-ce pas? Mais non. Pas solitaire. Tout ensemble encore. So come, okay? Next weekend? Oh, except I forgot, you have some family do then, don't you. So the one after. I have to go to my appallingly simplistic Canadian Geography course now with the patronizing prof. I think I should drop it. Except it's a prerequisite for things I do want to take. Argh.
>
> Love you more than Barney loves Fred. No, I mean Lucy loves

Love you more than Barney loves Fred. No, I mean Lucy loves Ethel. I mean just a heck of a lot. Your Santa Maria ("Oy, these blue robes, they weigh a girl down!").
P.S. A "nullipara" is: A. an empty subset in Venn mathematics; B. a meaningless comment; C. a woman who has never borne a child; or D. a ciliated micro-organism.

I am not able to go to Trent until the end of October. Halloween. This is because my father wants weekends to be "family time" now, so he can think he's making reparations for the damage he's done and is turning us into a loving and supportive family who will help each other (i.e., him) through this difficult time and all other difficult times to come.

I would like for Sara and myself to spend our first weekend together since the summer closeted in her room, reading, talking, doing crossword puzzles, kissing, touching. Sex would be nice too, but it's Sara's touch I've been missing more than anything. Just her hand running through my hair or across my back.

But there's this Halloween party she and Rainbow don't want to miss, it's going to be great, they're going as Starsky and Hutch. As lovers. "I mean, the subtext was always there, wasn't it?" Rainbow says.

Sure, but what am I supposed to go as? The car? The bad guy?

"You could be the girlfriend we're not interested in," Rain says. When I don't laugh she says, "Kidding. It's so nice to meet you finally. I feel like I know you."

Rainbow came with Sara to meet me at the bus station and has not left us alone since. I don't know yet whether I like her or not. If I hadn't met her through Sara, I almost certainly would. Whether she likes me, I can't really tell.

All fall I have been writing to Sara about how worried I am about my brother because he doesn't want to do anything anymore, how he hardly talks at all, even to me. He eats. He sleeps. He listens to music in his room.

I've been writing to Sara about my father and how in some ways he's worse now, if only because he's around more. He comes home after work and hovers over us, watching everything we do. He tells us how we're not doing it right, whatever it is, math, chopping the beans, cleaning the bathroom. He tells my brother he can give him extra help in school since my brother seems to need it, which of course he doesn't and only confirms what my brother suspects, that my father thinks he is stupid because he's an Indian.

I have written about how hard all this is on my mother and how she seems to take it out on me.

Sara should know I'm not in the mood for a party with a bunch of yahoos I don't know drinking their faces off.

"Can't we go as Pete, Linc and Julie?" I ask. Rainbow has blonde hair not unlike Peggy Lipton's.

"Where would we get an Afro wig in the next two hours?" Rain says.

I lie back on Sara's bed. I think I might cry. Halloween is like New Year's Eve. You have to either get right into it or ignore it, and I have never been able to do either.

"Let me look in my Tickle Trunk," Rain says. Maybe I do like her. She stands on a chair and rummages through the top shelf in her cupboard. "Cowboy hat. You could be Stan the Man from Alberta." She tosses the hat down. "Pig nose. You want to be Miss Piggy? A little mascara, flouncy dress?"

Sara laughs.

"Okay, maybe not. Little old lady? World War I flying ace? Colonel Klink?"

The party is at another residence in a big hall. We go latish, after drinking beer in our room with Marcus, another costumeless friend of Sara and Rain. Marcus wears the cowboy hat. "Marcus. Cowboy. They're just two words I never thought I'd hear in the same sentence," he says. He practices introducing himself on the way over. "Hi, I'm Marcus. I'm a cowboy. Yup, Cowboy Marcus, that's my name."

He asks me how I'm going to introduce myself. "I'm not," I say, turning up my jacket collar. "I'm too cool to introduce myself."

Sara has dressed me as James Dean, starting with a tensor bandage wrapped around my chest so my breasts don't show, then an undershirt to hide the bandage, and then a white T-shirt. Jeans. A red bandana. A bomber jacket. She has gelled back my hair and got me to bite my lips to redden them. I look in the mirror. I like what I see. It's not James Dean, but I like it. It's Bud.

Starsky and Hutch are all over each other all night. Predictably, I guess. That's what they said they were going to do. I doubt it occurs to anyone but me that they aren't just two straight girls having some fun at the expense of fags and a seventies TV show. I think even they think they are just playing. They get a good reaction.

And then a drunk boy dressed as Hitler says, "Starsky? Starsky? Vat kind uff a name iss Starsky?" and I think that Sara is going to rip his face off or at least knee him in the balls. I start forward, but Rain has already got him spun around and is remarkably smoothly, as if she'd done this before, handcuffing him with the toy cuffs she bought. (She tells me later she and her sister spent countless afternoons practicing this. They didn't have a TV, so they acted out their favorite shows instead.) Sara rips the paper swastika off Hitler-boy's sleeve.

"Hey, hey, hey," he says. "It was only a joke."

"You're an asshole, Matt," a big guy dressed as Julius Caesar says.

"Yeah, yeah, okay, I'm an asshole," he says. "Sorry."

"Go home, Matt."

"Okay, okay," he says and wanders off, still handcuffed.

I put my hand on Sara's back and ask her if she wants to go. "No, I don't want to go, I'm not going to let some sophomoric prick ruin my night."

But then she cries. I hold her, glad it's me and not Rain, thinking it's significant it's me and not Rain, that I still have the right to be the one to hold her when she cries.

Back in the room Rain gets out her guitar and we sing songs; we sing "Will the Circle Be Unbroken?" in three-part harmony, and it feels like it used to feel with Sara and Krupke, like we all love each other and it will always stay that way. We pull the beds together and sleep with Sara in the middle.

(n-1)

On the bus on the way home I look out the window at all the bare trees in the wind out there on November 1. I see a big-framed skinny dog trotting down the shoulder like he had a purpose. I think I'd like to be a dog going somewhere in the rain. I remember the lonely guy on the beach, calling his dog Cinnamon Girl, how pathetic I thought it was—I could be happy the rest of my life with a Cinnamon Girl—how Sara and I made fun of him afterwards. How I kinda liked him.

The Deluge
Arthur Slade

I committed a fatal error at the Tacky Party.

The festive event was three blocks away at Sandra Woodrick's. I arrived, squeezed between several Jock Tribe members congesting the doorway, and helped myself to a pink lemonade–based punch. I sniffed gingerly. Conclusion: alcohol free. I sipped nonchalantly, bobbing my head to the music. When in Namibia, do as the Namibians do, my father often said. Teens in colored shirts danced wildly through the living room, others sat on couches or the floor shouting to be heard.

I stood near the bathroom, jammed between a bookshelf and a life-size statue of Rodin's *The Thinker*. Hung behind him was a framed picture of card-playing canines dressed up like gangsters. I smiled. Anthropomorphism at its best. Mr. and Mrs. Woodrick must have a fabulous sense of humor, judging by the juxtaposition of those two articles. Or no sense of taste.

My smile faded as Michael and Nicole strode into the room. This was my fatal error. I broke a basic law of survival: always have an escape route. I ducked, but they veered in my direction like two lions stalking a lone antelope. Until this point no one had conversed with me.

They approached, clad in matching garb: lime green shorts and bright yellow T-shirts emblazoned with a red sun and a bird bearing a laurel branch. They absolutely *had* to talk to me: God's orders.

You see, they were from the Born Again Tribe. They viewed me as a misguided mammal and hoped to save my "soul" from hell.

"Percy," Michael said, "it's great to see you."

I straightened my back. "It is?"

"Of course." His light blue eyes were ethereal. His face flawless—smooth white skin and a glistening smile. His teeth had been artificially straightened by a dentist.

"Are you having fun?" Nicole asked. She too had perfect teeth. Two large friendly eyes. She tucked a brown curl of hair behind her ear.

"I experience a modicum of enjoyment."

"Modicum!" Michael echoed. "I like that. You have a real gift with words. It's a blessing."

"Thank you." I was flustered. I hadn't expected them to attend this function. Believed it would be against their beliefs. But here they stood clutching Canada Dry cans, looking ... like they belonged.

"Fun party!" Michael watched the cavorting students. Did he see them as souls; some smudged with the darkness of sin, others shining bright as a thousand candles? "Drink?" He offered a can dangling from a plastic six-pack holder.

"No, thank you." I raised my glass.

He moved five centimeters closer. "I still have questions."

My heart sank. "Not another Wilberforce," I whispered.

"Wilberforce?" Nicole asked.

"Bishop Wilberforce of Oxford," I huffed, annoyed that they didn't know their theological history.

"Darwin's arch enemy. He gave *The Origin* a bad review. Asked whether man was descended from monkeys on the paternal or maternal side. He knew nothing about science. He died when he fell off his horse and hit his head on a stone."

"Oh," Nicole offered. "Really."

Michael's smile hadn't retreated. "That's interesting. But what I'm curious about is the fossils. I know you think we're crazy."

"No," I said emphatically, "religious beliefs are not an insanity. All societies consider it normal to believe in supernatural beings and forces."

"So you don't think we're crazy?" Nicole said.

"I just made that point."

"Good to hear." Michael lightly squeezed my shoulder. His hand was warm. I stared until he removed it. "Anyway, about the fossils. You know how they date them and stuff. I asked our study leader why the scientists got it mixed up."

"Mixed up?" I asked. "Oh, that's right, you believe the world is only ten thousand years old."

"You don't have to yell, Percy," Michael said softly, "the music's not that loud. And the earth is six thousand years old. Adam was created in 3975 B.C."

Nicole edged nearer. "And don't forget that lots of scientists aren't sure carbon dating even works. Or that evolution is true. It's just a theory."

Michael used his opposable thumb to open the last can of ginger ale. It fizzed so he brought it to his mouth. "Anyway, it's the fossils we want to talk about. They're real."

"They are?" I asked.

"Yes." Nicole was now face to face with me. They were a spiritual-philosophical tag team. "But you've been fooled by ... well, you know—*him.*" She pointed at the floor. "Evolution. Devilution. Soul pollution." It was a tribal chant. "*He* made you think they're millions of years old. He does tell the truth, but circles it with lies. There *were* dinosaurs."

"There were?" I sensed a breakthrough. "In the Bible?"

Michael fielded this question. "On the ark. Two of each species is what God told Noah. And when the ark finally was caught on Mount Ararat the dinosaurs stepped out into the new world. Rain had swept everything away. There were new diseases. All of the dinosaurs got sick, died, fell into the ocean and were compressed by the weight of the water, hardening their bones instantly into fossils. Do you see?"

"I understand," I answered, though the idea the ark could hold enough animals to repopulate the world was ludicrous. A population cannot sustain itself with only two of its species. The gene pool would be too small. I wouldn't even bother mentioning that water pressure can't harden living flesh into stone.

Thankfully, I glimpsed Elissa across the room. She had chosen a flashy pink shirt and a giant gardening hat that could have doubled as an umbrella. She looked my way. I waved. She removed her hat and held it like a shield against her bosom, dodging overexcited dancers.

"You know," I began, "the age of the universe can be measured using the speed of light. Astronomists have devised a formula that proves light from distant stars began traveling toward Earth billions of years ago."

Put that in your philosophical pipe and smoke it, I thought.

"The speed of light has not been measured properly," Nicole spoke carefully, as though to a child. "Everyone knows that."

I slumped.

Michael drained his ginger ale. "You should meet our study leader. He'd like to talk to you. Bible study isn't formal, you know. Not like other churches."

Agitation built in my nerves. A simple command to get out. *Out.* Elissa was halfway across the room, surrounded by a chain of revelers doing the locomotion.

"You know, you're okay, Percy," Nicole said, briefly touching my shoulder. "You're really okay."

I furrowed my brow. Okay? I was okay? My tear ducts welled up.

"Did I say something wrong?" she asked.

I shook my head. Elissa joined us at last, nodded at Michael and Nicole. They smiled back.

"I … I left my stuff in your car," I said to Elissa.

"What stuff?"

"Those … uh … field notes I took today. I must retrieve them. Now."

"Yes," she said, recognizing the crisis. "You should."

I walked past Michael and Nicole, pulling Elissa behind. We wriggled through the sweaty, yuk-a-flux-soaked congestion. Outside, I sucked in fresh air. Two teens lay gazing skyward. A tribe of skateboarders, heads shaved, some wearing toques, rolled again and again over a jump on the sidewalk, like mice endlessly repeating an experiment.

"What was that about?" Elissa asked.

"They—Michael and Nicole—they have all the answers. They're just so … happy."

"Yeah, freaky, eh? Sorry I didn't rescue you sooner. But you should have returned my call."

"Oh. I didn't get it." I breathed deeper. "Really, I didn't."

"You're lucky I came. I stopped by your house and your mom had no idea where you were. Why didn't you call me?"

"I—I just couldn't …"

"Don't … don't get worked up." She grabbed my hand, squeezed it softly between both of hers like she'd caught a butterfly. "You take everything so seriously."

I had to take things serious. How else would I get my work done? "Elissa, I … " My thoughts were too random to express. "I'm sorry. I—I hurt. You. Your feelings, I mean. I didn't intend. To."

"Percy, it's … I think I understand. This'll all blow over soon. We'll spend the summer catching rays and drinking daiquiris. We'll survive grad week. Where there's a will there's a way."

It was one of Will's favorite sayings. A joke. I gently pulled back my hand. "I could have stopped him from jumping," I said. "Should have."

"What?" A pause. "Will, you mean?"

"He told me. About Marcia. He asked whether I thought he had a chance to be with her. I—I was too literal: I said it was unlikely. She wasn't from our tribe."

"You couldn't have done anything, Percy. Sometimes things just happen."

"Things never just happen," I said. "There's always a reason. I wish I'd lied."

"That wouldn't have changed a thing. It was more than just Marcia. He was—he just kept so much to himself. Who knows what he was thinking half the time."

"Did he tell you about his crush on her?" I asked.

"Yes. I almost fell over backward to hear him talk about his own feelings. And not make a joke."

"What did you say, when he told you?"

"I—I don't really remember. Something like it was good to fall in love. Something like that."

She'd been encouraging. Loving, not logical. "He was lucky to have you as a friend."

"He was lucky to have both of us," she corrected. "And we were lucky to know him."

I opened my mouth to say something else.

Elissa put a finger to my lips. "Shh," she whispered. "You're getting that dazed look. It always happens when you think too much." Her skin tasted salty. She pulled her finger away, put it to her lips. "Shh. Just forget about everything for now."

I nodded. She grabbed my hand and led me onto the street. "Enough tribal interactions for tonight," she said. "One can only pretend to be tacky for so long."

We wandered silently for several blocks. She didn't release my hand. I tried not to think about what this contact might mean. I just enjoyed the warmth. We walked onto Broadway, the neon lights advertising bars and restaurants. It was too bright. We cut across the street and headed into the darker lanes.

"I like your hat, by the way," Elissa said, finally. "It's cool."

Pride swelled up, but then Dad's hat felt loose, like a small wind might lift it from my head. Without thinking, I pulled my hand from hers and held the hat down. Only after several steps did I realize my mistake.

Stupid. Stupid me.

Though we walked for another twenty minutes, I never found the guts to reclaim her hand.

At midnight, Elissa and I hugged in front of my house. For a long time. Then I went inside, my legs all wobbly.

Mom was meditating in the living room, surrounded by candles and a haze of pine incense. *Ommmmmm* emanated from somewhere deep inside her throat. Her lips didn't move. She could *Ommm* for hours, contacting various internal organs, willing them to function in perfect harmony with the rest of her body and the universe.

I padded past her. Stopped. Changed my course and sat down.

She opened her eyes. Smiled. "You're home," she said. "Nice outfit."

I slipped off the hat. "I was at a party. A tacky dress-up party."

"Was it fun?"

I shrugged. "It was... well... entertaining."

"Good."

A long silence followed. She continued to smile.

"Mom. Tell me again. What happens when we die?" I asked.

"We ascend to the next stage of existence. Shed our flesh. Become pure spiritual energy. We have so much more to do. To become."

"What if I don't believe that? What happens to me?"

"Your doubts are natural. All will unfold as it should."

I nodded. "That's good to know," I said.

I retired to my room. Everyone had an answer. But I had none. I sighed. My lot, apparently, was to be an analyzer.

I went to my desk and recorded the day's events. Finally—arm tired, mind emptied—I collapsed on my bed and dreamed of jungles, tsetse flies and Elissa's warm hand.

Paul in the Metro

MICHEL RABAGLIATI

MONTREAL, AUGUST 1973. BY THE END OF SUMMER VACATION, ALAIN AND I WERE BORED OUT OF OUR MINDS. SO WE RODE THE SUBWAY, JUST FOR THE HELL OF IT.

ONE OF OUR FAVORITE DESTINATIONS WAS THE DOWNTOWN EATON'S STORE.

FIRST, WE WENT TO THE BASEMENT TO WATCH THE AUTOMATIC DOUGHNUT-MAKING-MACHINE AND BUY TWO FRESH, HOT DOUGHNUTS.

TRANSLATED BY HELGE DASCHER HAND-LETTERED BY DIRK REHM

"Q-TIP" WAS ONE OF THE HOUSE DETECTIVES. WE CALLED HIM THAT BECAUSE OF HIS HAIRCUT. HE KNEW OUR FACES, SO WE HAD TO AVOID HIM.

GROUND FLOOR
RAY-DE-SHOW-SAY

GOOD DAY.
BONNE JIOUR.

I WAS CRAZY ABOUT THE ELEVATOR GIRLS, WITH THEIR ENGLISH ACCENTS, THEIR UNIFORMS AND THOSE PRETTY WHITE GLOVES.

WE'D GO UP TO THE 9TH FLOOR TO CHECK OUT THE RESTAURANT.

WE LIKED THE RETRO MOVIE-STYLE DÉCOR. AND IT WAS ALWAYS EMPTY.

WE LET OURSELVES BE SEATED IN THE DINING ROOM AND ORDERED A SMALL SNACK, JUST TO BE THERE.

IT WAS LIKE BEING ON BOARD OF OF AN OCEAN LINER. I FOUND OUT MUCH LATER THAT THE RESTAURANT IS CONSIDERED TO BE THE FINEST EXAMPLE OF PUBLIC ART DECO ARCHITECTURE IN MONTREAL.

THEN WE WOULD GO SPRAWL ON THE LaZ-BOYS ON THE 8TH FLOOR.

ONE FLOOR DOWN, WE OGLED THE GIRLS ON THE BRA BOXES IN THE LINGERIE DEPARTMENT.

BUT THE SPORTS DEPARTMENT ON THE 4TH FLOOR WAS OUR FAVORITE SPOT.

IT WAS USUALLY EMPTY. WE COULD PLAY THERE FOR HOURS.

GOTCHA!
WHAM

THE GAME'S UP, GUYS. SCRAM! YOU'VE GOT NO BUSINESS BEING HERE.
YES SIR ...

MAKE SURE THEY GET OUT OF THE STORE.
RIGHT.
SAD PUPPY FACES.

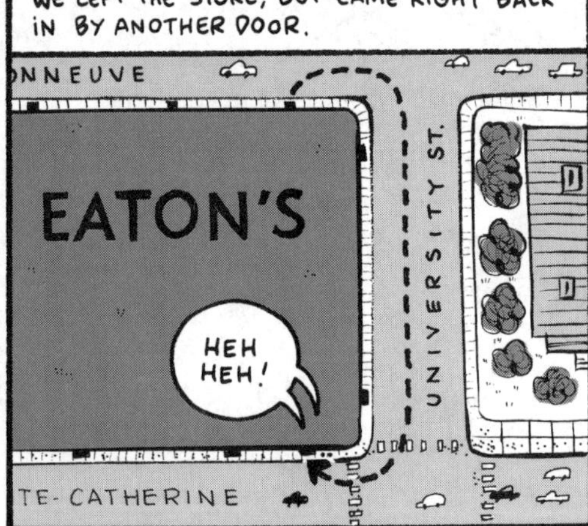
WE LEFT THE STORE, BUT CAME RIGHT BACK IN BY ANOTHER DOOR.
ONNEUVE
EATON'S
UNIVERSITY ST.
HEH HEH!
TE-CATHERINE

THAT'S WHEN THE FUN STARTED, BECAUSE NOW WE HAD TO STAY ABSOLUTELY INVISIBLE.
SSSHHH!
ON SALE
ON SALE
10% OFF

WE BECAME A GERMAN SPY COMMANDO.
WUNDERBAR! THE COAST IS CLEAR.
29 99$
19 99$
GUT.

TO GET EVEN WITH Q-TIP, WE CARRIED OUT WHAT WE CALLED "INDUSTRIAL SABOTAGE" (PRONOUNCED WITH A NAZI ACCENT).
SCHNELL, SCHNELL!
Couleurs de DIOR

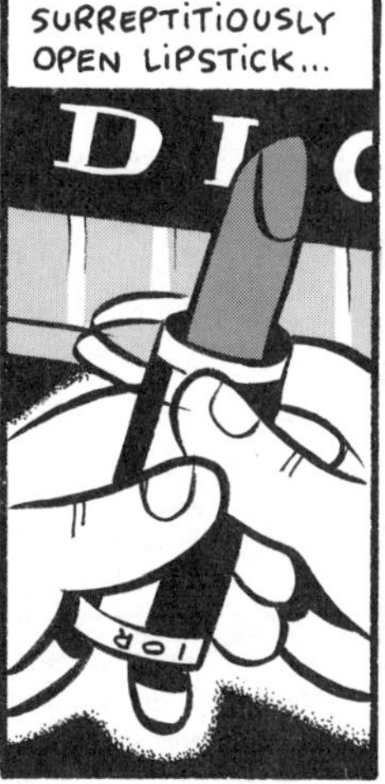
SURREPTITIOUSLY OPEN LIPSTICK...

...CRUSH IT INTO DISPLAY CASE.
SPLOTCH

UNCAP BARGAIN-SIZED SHAMPOO-BOTTLES, TURN THEM OVER ON THE SHELF...
VOILA!
PLUNK

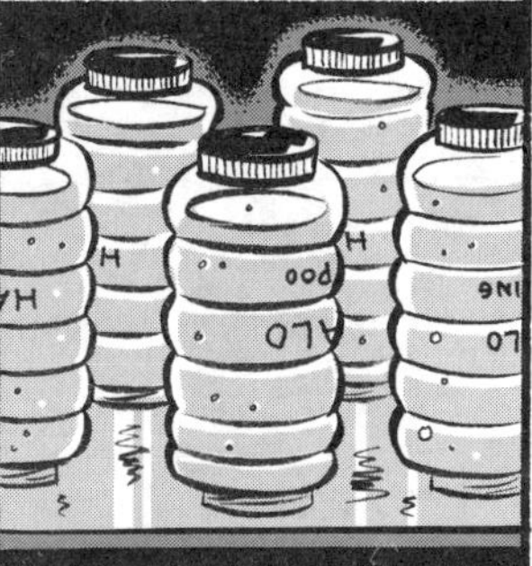
...PLACE LID ON TOP.
HARMLESS, UNTIL SOMEONE LIFTS A BOTTLE.

EMPTY PERFUME BOTTLES INTO SHOES, ETC.
GLOOP

ONCE WE DID SOMETHING REALLY BAD.
OH LOOK! PNEUMATIC MESSAGE TUBES...
YEAH!

HEH HEH...
PFF HOHO...
PSSSSSS

AUF WIEDER-SEHEN!
FSSHHHH
CLICK
SEND
HA HA!
5

ANOTHER DAY IN THE SUBWAY, WITH TIME TO KILL, WE DECIDED TO VISIT EVERY SINGLE STATION ON THE MAP.

THE POINT OF THE GAME WAS TO COLLECT TRANSFERS FROM ALL THE STATIONS. IT WAS STUPID, BUT IT WAS SOMETHING TO DO.

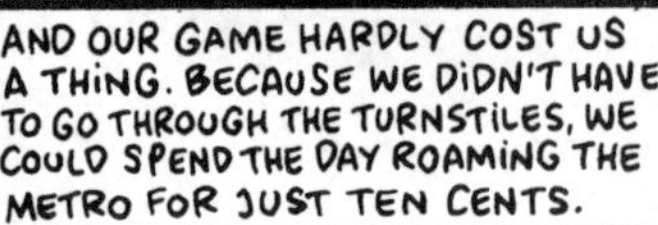

THE BEAUDRY STATION HAS A MOVING SIDEWALK THE LENGTH OF A WHOLE BLOCK.

WE SPENT AGES WALKING AND RUNNING IN THE WRONG DIRECTION.

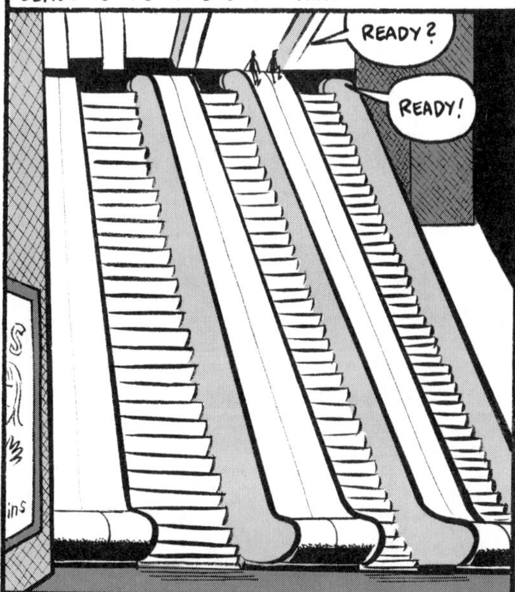
AT BERRI-DE-MONTIGNY, A LONG, STEEP ESCALATOR LEADS TO THE LONGUEUIL TRAIN.
READY?
READY!

AT THE TIME, THERE WERE NO BOLTS ON THE CASING AND WE COULD SLIDE ALL THE WAY DOWN.
YEEEEEE HAWWW!

Berri-de-Montigny
Île-Sainte-Hélène
3
Longueuil
N
COOL! WE'VE GOT THEM ALL!

WITH THE TRANSFERS FROM THE YELLOW LINE (BERRI-LONGUEUIL), OUR COLLECTION WAS COMPLETE.
WANT TO GO TO EXPO?
OK.
on est 6 millions
faut se parler.

ÎLE-SAINTE-HÉLÈNE
TERRE DES HOMMES
MAN AND HIS WORLD

BY 1973, MOST OF THE EXPO 67 PAVILIONS HAD BEEN TORN DOWN AND THE EXPO EXPRESS TRAIN THAT HAD CONNECTED THE EXPO AND LA RONDE ISLANDS TO CITÉ DU HAVRE WAS NO LONGER IN SERVICE. ONLY A FEW BUILDINGS REMAINED AND ADMISSION WAS FREE. THE SITE WAS A GHOST TOWN. EXPO DIDN'T INTEREST ANYONE ANYMORE, ESPECIALLY NOW THAT OLYMPIC FEVER HAD GRIPPED MONTREAL, WHICH WAS PREPARING TO HOST THE 1976 SUMMER GAMES IN THE EAST END OF TOWN.

HARD TO BELIEVE THAT JUST SIX YEARS EARLIER, FIFTY-FIVE MILLION VISITORS HAD CONVERGED HERE TO SING AND DANCE TO GROOVY POP TUNES CELEBRATING THE DAWN OF A NEW AGE OF PEACE AND LOVE.

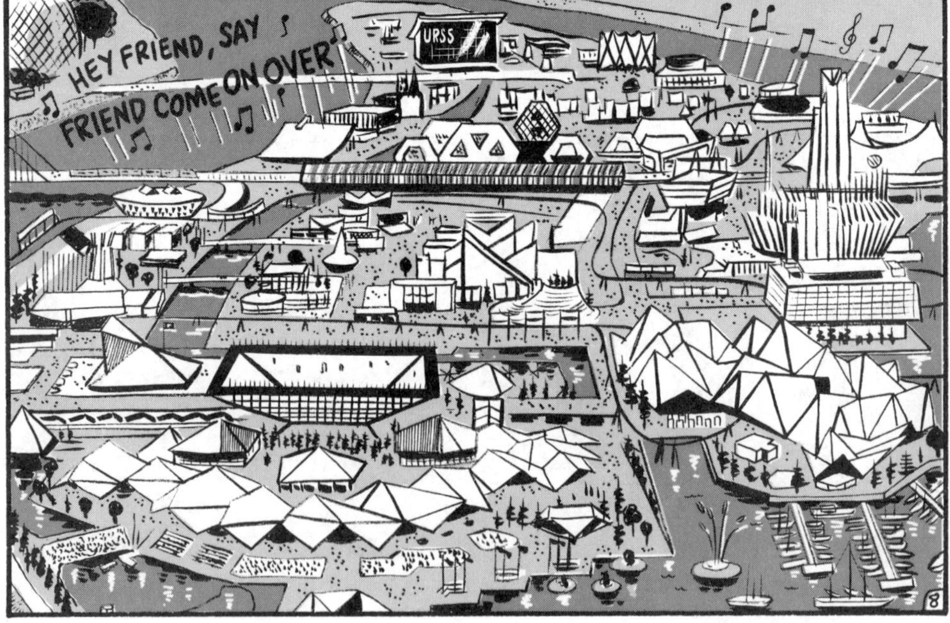

I DON'T REMEMBER MUCH ABOUT EXPO 67. I WAS TOO YOUNG, JUST SIX YEARS OLD.
67
GUIDE

WHAT I DO REMEMBER IS THE AMERICAN PAVILION AND THE MINIRAIL THAT DROVE THROUGH IT.
expo67

AND I REMEMBER THAT THE GROUNDS SMELLED OF STRANGE FOODS, THE CROWDS WERE ENDLESS, I COULD NEVER SEE ANYTHING...
Pentax

... AND I THREW UP IN A GARBAGE CAN. THAT'S ABOUT IT.

EVEN IF EXPO WAS VIRTUALLY EMPTY IN '73, I LIKED IT MUCH BETTER THAN IN '67. IT HAD KEPT A GOOD PART OF ITS OLD MAGIC.

ONE OF THE THEME PAVILIONS WAS STILL OPEN. THEY HAD RENAMED IT "STRANGE, STRANGE WORLD."
VILLON DE
SOLITE
9

FLYING SAUCERS, UFOS AND THE PRESENCE OF EXTRATERRESTRIALS.

TEXAS 1949

OREGON 1951

I'M SURE THEY EXIST, BUT THE GOVERNMENT DOESN'T WANT US TO KNOW.

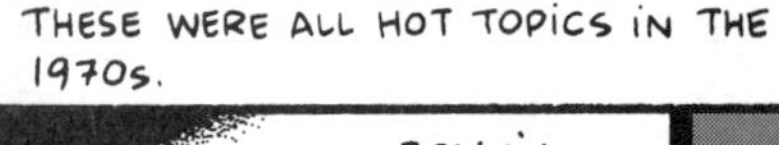

THE DRAWINGS FASCINATED ME. ESPECIALLY THOSE BY ROBERT LA PALME.

I THOUGHT HIS CARTOONS HAD AN INCREDIBLE VERVE. AND TO THIS DAY, I STILL THINK OF HIM AS ONE OF THE BEST.

THERE WERE ALSO ORIGINAL PAGES OF EUROPEAN AND CANADIAN COMIC STRIPS THAT I KNEW.

THE EXHIBIT MADE A HUGE IMPRESSION ON ME. LOOKING AT THE ORIGINALS, DRAWN IN INK ON PAPER, I REALIZED THEY HAD BEEN MADE BY REAL PEOPLE.

IT MADE ME WANT TO GIVE CARTOONING A TRY AT HOME.

I STARTED BY COPYING CHARACTERS OUT OF ASTERIX.

LATER, AFTER DISCOVERING SPIROU AND GASTON, I INVENTED TWO CHARACTERS LIKE THEM, SHAMELESSLY IMITATING FRANQUIN'S STYLE.
Tourlou
GASPAR
MIRADO HB

BUT WHEN THE TIME CAME TO DO A REAL COMIC BOOK, WITH A STORY AND EVERYTHING, I GAVE UP.
Apollo 1
AW, FORGET IT! IT'S WAY TOO MUCH WORK...

BACK AT EXPO, OUR DAYS ALWAYS ENDED WITH A LONG RIDE ON THE MINIRAIL. WE WERE THE ONLY PASSENGERS ON BOARD.
Montréal
Montréal
15

WHEW! WHAT A DAY! I'M WIPED OUT!
ME TOO...
MONTREAL

HEY! LOOK! A FLYING SAUCER!
YEAH YEAH. FORGET IT...
MONTRE
12

BUT IT WOULD BE FUNNY TO SEE MARTIANS IN THE SKY OVER EXPO, IN A FLYING SAUCER...

YEAH! THEY'D STOP OVER THE AMERICAN PAVILION...

CAUSE THEY'D THINK IT'S SOMETHING FROM THEIR PLANET, AND THEY WOULD PICK IT UP AND TAKE IT AWAY!

HEE HEE!
HAHA!

DJJJJJJJJJJJJJJJ
CLUNK

HEY! WHAT'S GOING ON?? WE'RE NOT MOVING!
I... I DON'T KNOW ...
MON

WHAT TIME IS IT, ALAIN?

UH... I DON'T HAVE MY WATCH, BUT I THINK THAT

AHHHHHH!
CLICK
CLICK
CLICK
CLICK
CLICK
CLICK
13

IT TURNED OUT THAT AT NIGHT, THE MINIRAIL MOVED IN SMALL BURSTS OF 35 FEET, WITH 5 TO 6 MINUTE WAITS IN BETWEEN.

DJJJJJ

IT TOOK US HOURS TO GET TO THE PLATFORM. BY THEN, THE BUSES AND SUBWAYS HAD STOPPED RUNNING.

CLUNK.

WE WALKED OVER THE JACQUES CARTIER BRIDGE AND ALL THE WAY HOME TO ROSEMONT. WE GOT IN VERY LATE AND WERE SEVERELY PUNISHED.

DJJJJJ...

Mermaid in a Jar
Sheila Heti

I have a mermaid in a jar that Quilty bought me at a garage sale for twenty-five cents. The mermaid's all"I hate you I hate you I hate you," but she's in a jar, and unless I loosen the top she's not coming out to kill me.

I keep the little jar on my windowsill, right behind my bed, right near my head so if I look up in the middle of the night, up and back, I can see her swimming in the murky little pool of her own shit and vomit, and I can smile.

"Hello, mermaid! How are you this fine evening?" I can say, and sometimes do. "How very sad it is that you're so beautiful, and you're so young, and you're so fucking trapped you'll never get out of that bottle, ha ha!"

Once I went on a class trip and brought my mermaid along, just for the hell of it. We were going to Niagara Falls and I was thinking, "Right, well, maybe I'll hold her over the rail, give her a little scare, put her in her place." Or about letting her loose down the falls and out of my life. But once we got there I forgot her in my little brown lunch bag with my hot cheese sandwich, under my seat in the little yellow school bus. But she got jolted on the ride there and jolted on the ride back and that was enough for me.

Once I had a party and invited all my friends, seven little girls to play and sleep over, and having called every number flashing in our heads, and having already called the pizzas twice and seanced out of our minds, I just thought, "Oh, why don't I bring my mermaid out to show? They could make their faces at it, they could have their fun, and we'd be able to toss it back and forth like a real little football." But then Emma fell asleep, and then so did Wendy and Carla and the rest, and the mermaid just stayed locked in the closet where I'd put her that afternoon.

Once when I thought she needed a bit of discipline I rolled her measly bottle down Killer Hill in the ravine. Another time I threw her deep into my best friend's pool.

Now she's getting old it seems. I even saw a gray hair on Friday, and wrinkles are spreading all across her skin, and as much as I liked her before, I like her even less now. I was thinking sort of what to do with her, but I think I'll just keep her there a little while longer. At least until I'm happy again.

Real Life Slow Motion Show
Carrie Mac

On his way back from fishing—he didn't catch any fish—my father shoots a deer, but it's off-season, so the only people he can brag at is us.

"Right out the window, Junie!" He's come home to get us so we can help him lift it into the truck. "I'm driving along and there she is and there's nobody around for miles and my gun just waiting and pow! Got her on the first shot. A beauty. A real beauty."

My brother, Tyler, stares at the gun on the seat.

"Change your shirt, Tyler." My mother steers him back inside. "Find something you won't mind getting mucky."

Tyler does not want to go. Dad says he won't be any help; he's so scrawny and weepy.

"But he's coming anyway," Dad says when Mom suggests leaving him behind. "Do him good to see some real life."

Tyler's eyes brim with tears. He comes back in his WrestleMania shirt with the scary-looking guy scowling on it. He hates that shirt and would've thrown it out except Dad's favorite brother brought it all the way from Las Vegas. Dad's so excited about the deer that he takes no notice of Tyler's choice of shirt.

"That's right," Dad says. "Cry all you want, life and death is all over the place and you got to get used to it."

The deer is up a logging road in the middle of a clear-cut. We can't drive the truck right to her, so me and Dad and Mom roll her onto a tarp and drag the tarp over the brush to the truck.

"Her eyes are open," Tyler says. He throws up again.

"That's right, you look her in the eye. That's death right there for you," Dad says. "Some kids never see death, and that just isn't right. Now, son, what you can do is lift her head while your mother and Bea and I get the legs."

Mom wipes Tyler's mouth with a handkerchief. "Maybe he shouldn't, Ken."

"This one here's going to grow into a man. Now, what kind of man do you want to be, Tyler?"

Tyler squats. He lifts the deer's head into his lap.

"There's the man." Dad grabs hold of the deer's back legs. "Just caught a glimpse, there. Tyler, the man."

Dad backs the truck into the smaller garage behind the gas pumps and hangs the deer in there so no one can see it. He skins her and cuts her up and Mom wraps the meat and I pack it in the freezer. Dad makes Tyler sit on the workbench and watch. As I hose down the floor, Tyler falls asleep, his head on an empty jerry can. Mom carries him inside and puts him to bed. There's not a spot of blood on his shirt.

A couple of days later, Mrs. Anderson pulls her car into the gas station. Her baby is asleep on the backseat, just a little baby in a diaper. I get my dad and go back to the paper. The obituaries are my favorite. I like trying to guess how the person died by the charities listed at the end or by their age or if there's words like *taken from us suddenly* or *after a long battle with*, that sort of thing. If Mrs. Anderson's baby died, sailed clear through the windshield for example, what would the obituary say? When her husband died in the spring it said *loving father* and *devoted husband*. He was forty-eight. I guessed heart attack. I was right.

"Mr. Lancaster," she says when Dad starts the pump. "I got a few words for you."

Dad watches the numbers on the pump. Mrs. Anderson leans out the window.

"There are bastard pups from your effen' dog all over this town," she says. "Everyone knows it's your dog. The least you can do is get him fixed."

"Twelve dollars even." Dad peers into the car. "You should have that kid in some kind of seat."

"Well, you got words for me and I got words for you then." Mrs. Anderson gives Dad the money. "If you don't deal with your dog, Horst will, and he's known for taking them up the mountain and shooting them in the head rather than have the town pay to keep them in the pound." Mrs. Anderson stuffs her wallet into her purse. "In this case, I'm not sure I disagree with him taking things into his own hands."

"Is that right?"

"Yes sir, that's right. My Maggie found four of them pups drowned in the pond by the dump. She's having nightmares. She's only *ten*."

"And did you have a car seat for her? The one that made it to ten?"

"I can honestly tell you that I do not like your attitude, Mr. Lancaster, and as someone so new to town, you might give that a good hard think."

"I appreciate your concern, Mrs. Anderson. I do." Dad puts his fingers to his cap. "And, of course, my apologies to your Maggie."

"Well." She starts the car. "You just see you do something about it, Mr. Lancaster."

"Will do. Bye now," Dad says as she drives off. He rips the paper out of my hands and smacks my head with it. "You hear that, miss oh please, please, please can I have a dog?"

"Yes sir."

At dinner, Dad stares under his glasses at Tyler and me.

"If I recall correctly, I did not want anything to do with this dog," he says. "I said, the hell with it, what did I care? Get the damn dog, but keep it outta my way. I said no funny business, didn't I?"

"Yes sir." I rest my feet on Duke lying under my chair. I wiggle my toes and Duke wags his tail, thumping it against the linoleum. Dad scrapes his chair back, grips the table and peers under.

"Out!"

Duke sits up, half asleep.

"Go lie down where I can't see you, you damned dog."

My mother's hand hovers above the plate stacked with bread.

"Well? I don't need this damn dog making me any enemies in this town, do I?"

"No, Ken, you don't."

"I didn't think so."

"It's just that he doesn't know any better, Ken." Mom deals us each a slice of bread and then offers one to Duke. "Now, go to your bed."

Duke pads over to his blanket in the corner by the fridge, circles twice and settles down. "There's a good dog," she says.

As Tyler and I clear the table, Mom says, "There's money by the back door for you two to go swimming. Your towels are in the dryer."

Tyler and I walk barefoot down Sequoia to the public pool. The sidewalk is still warm from the sun minding it all day. Our towels are knotted under our chins like superhero capes. We stop when we hear the voices and splashing from the pool. Tyler and I slow way down for the last block. We call this the Real Life Slow Motion Show.

"How slow can you go?" I dig my chin into my neck to make my voice low.

"Slow, slow, slow." Tyler takes giant steps, hands out like a zombie.

Tyler can't swim. Mom signed him up for lessons but he's too scared. He hides in the change room every Tuesday afternoon. No one knows except me. Tonight he sits at the edge, kicking his feet in the water while I swim around the pool, pretending not to care that no one notices my perfect stroke, the way my fingers curve together like mermaid fins, the way I barely have to lift my head above water to breathe. I dive under and do three somersaults without coming up for air, see if they can ignore that. When I break the surface, Curtis is waiting for me.

"Hi, Bea." He tugs at his shorts. He's wearing a bathing cap with orange spots on it. No one else in the entire pool is wearing a bathing cap. "You're real good."

"Thanks, Curtis." Maggie Anderson and her frilly friends are watching now, sure. Of course, *now*.

"You want to play marbles sometime? Or hockey cards?" He wipes his nose with the back of his hand. "I got great cards."

"Don't talk to me, Curtis." I pull myself out of the pool.

"Why not, Bea?"

"Just don't, okay?" We've been living in this town for ten months and Curtis, town retard creep, is the only one who talks to me. I tell myself I can do better. I tell myself it takes time. I tell myself Maggie Anderson is a bitch and who wants her for a friend anyway, and besides, she ratted on my dog.

Curtis just stands there, shivering and staring as I walk over to Tyler. He's sitting on the farthest deck chair reading a women's magazine someone left behind.

"Let's go, Ty." I wrap my towel around my waist.

"I should go under the shower," Tyler says.

"You don't have to. Your hair would be dry by the time we got home anyway. Mom will never know."

"She can tell." Tyler stands under the outside shower for a minute, coming back covered with goose pimples. Neither of us brought anything dry to change into, so we run the four blocks home, our superhero capes limp.

There's Mom sitting on the stoop, the cherry of her cigarette glowing in the dusk shadows.

"Don't come home yet," she calls to us when we reach the gate.

"How come?" I ask. "What's going on?"

"Did you have a good swim?" She hands me a five-dollar bill. "Why don't you two go get something at the Tasty Freeze?" She winks at Tyler. "How about that, Superman?" Tyler chews on a corner of his towel and steps closer to me. Mom looks at me. "Please, honey Bea?"

There is no room for saying no. It's not just the pause, but the tone too. More an order than a plea.

"We can see if Charlotte's working," I say to Tyler. She babysits us sometimes.

"Okay," Tyler mumbles. "I guess." He takes the five dollars from me and puts it in the zip-up pocket of his swim trunks.

At the Tasty Freeze the teenagers park their cars side by side so tight that they have to climb through their windows to get in and out. They sit on the bumpers smoking hand-rolleds and drinking Coke mixed with booze in Tasty Freeze cups. The boys wear rocker shirts with the sleeves ripped off, and the girls hang off them in striped tube tops and stretchy jeans. I hold Tyler's hand as we cut through.

"Hey, look." A boy on the hood of a Camaro blows a smoke ring at us. "Little kiddies in bathing suits."

"Out after dark, beware of the big bad boner!" A fat guy grabs his crotch and howls like a coyote.

"Go on, Dwayne, you like 'em young!" Another boy makes Ozzy Osbourne eyes and pounds his fist on the car. They all start drumming on their cars. I stick my chin up a bit more. The word, I believe, is *impervious*. I-m-p-e-r-v-i-o-u-s. Spelling Bea won the spelling bee with that one; Maggie Anderson left out the *u*. Tyler stretches his arm over his head, covering both ears.

Charlotte gives us hot chocolate for free and a cup of extra whipped cream each. We sit in the staff booth with our knees under us, eating the whipped cream with our fingers.

A family sits across from us. The father is tracing a route on a road map with a yellow marker. The mother reads the funnies on the Tasty Freeze place mat to the little girl. The boy stares out the window at the teenagers and notices me looking at him in the reflection. He turns and stares back, picking up his Rubik's Cube and adjusting the squares.

I don't look away. I want to tell him I can solve any Rubix's Cube in less than seven minutes, that I got a fifty-dollar cash prize for doing that and roller-skating at the same time. That was in the last town we lived in. He looks away first.

I stare enviously at the boy's sweatshirt. The air-conditioning is on. The muscles in my arms and legs tighten against the chill.

"I'm cold too," says Tyler. From where I sit I can't see his swim trunks. He looks naked.

Charlotte lets us out through the kitchen so we don't have to go through the parking lot again. We wander home the long way, across the highway overpass. At the middle, we climb up the railing and spit at the cars, pulling our fists for the truckers to honk. The rest of the way we play the Real Life Slow Motion Show, walking on all the lawns, our feet sore from so much barefooting on cement.

"What happened?" Tyler asks when we get to our gate. "How come we had to take so long?"

"Do I look psychic to you?"

The house is dark in front. I can see into the backyard where the kitchen light spreads onto the overgrown lawn.

"What's psychic?" Tyler takes my hand and pulls it to his cheek.

"When you know things before you're supposed to," I say.

Dad is at the table reading the newspaper. There's blood on his Lancaster Family Reunion shirt. My skin feels suddenly hot. Tyler and I stand in the doorway. Tyler rubs his cheek against my hand.

"You're back." Dad keeps his eyes on the paper. We nod.

"Put these on. You're both blue." Mom hands us the snowflake sweaters Auntie Pat sent us at Christmas. I slip Tyler's over his head and pull his arms through. I'm too hot to put anything on. Tyler sets his cheek against my hand and rubs. He closes his eyes.

"Who wants to be first?" Dad nods at the basement door. It's shut, which is unusual.

"What for?" I steer Tyler into a chair, his eyes still squeezed shut.

"I tried to take care of the dog problem, but it kind of backfired. I don't think Duke is going to make it." Dad pulls his glasses off and pinches the skin between his eyes. "I'd say he's on his last legs right about now. I will say, and then I won't say it again, I am sorry, I am. I made a botch job of it and I'm sorry."

Tyler starts to cry silently, his thin body shaking and heaving. Mom puts a hand on his shoulder, but he shrugs it off, reaching for my other hand and pulling it to his other cheek.

"Big sister first, then." Dad folds the paper. He opens the basement door and ushers me ahead. "After all, the dog was your idea."

Duke is on the floor at the foot of the stairs. He's covered in blood, so is the towel he's laying on, an empty whiskey bottle and the cement for about two feet around. I kneel beside him and stare at his bloody belly. Duke's testicles sit in a tin pie plate beside the dryer. They look like a dead rodent. On the stairs behind me, Dad lights a cigarette.

"I am sorry, Beatrice. I gave him the whiskey and then figured he was as good as out and cut them off, but he's not doing so hot now. He just wouldn't stop bleeding."

I stroke Duke's silky black ears. His eyes are closed. I put my hand over his heart. The beats are slow and long in between. The blood is sticky and cold.

"I said I'm sorry. I didn't think it'd be this bad, really."

"Go away."

"Now, Bea, I only meant to fix him like they do at the vet."

"Go away." I lean in to kiss Duke's dry black nose.

"Be reasonable, Honey Bea."

"Go away!"

He backs up the stairs. When he opens the door Tyler bolts down and freezes when he sees Duke. He sits behind me and chews on a corner of his towel still pinned under his chin.

"Oh no, Bea." He rests his cheek on my bare back. "Did you psychic this?"

I want the heartbeats to stop. They get slower and slower, but do not stop. I think about breaking his neck, or smothering him with a towel, and decide I can't do either.

Mom comes down, steps over all of us and moves the laundry from the dryer to the basket. With a slippered foot she slides the bloody pie plate closer to the floor drain. It scrapes against the rough cement. Above, Dad walks from the kitchen to the family room, the floorboards creaking. I hear the television click on, then the squeak of his chair reclining.

"Oh, poor old Duke." Mom dumps a pile of bloody towels into the washing machine and then leans down to stroke his head. I'm just about to remind her that Duke is only two years old, but she cuts me off. "I'm so sorry, Bea. You know he was trying to fix things. Try to understand." She picks up the basket of clean clothes, steps over us and heads upstairs.

Duke breathes slow all night. Tyler and I stay with him, using the clean towels from the dryer to keep him warm. In the morning we lug him up the stairs and out the back while our parents are still sleeping. We lay him in the wagon with two good quilts under him and one on top. We take him to Horst's place and he calls the vet. That afternoon Horst writes Dad a ticket. There's a fine too. Dad makes us pay him back for it, so we spend the fall pushing an old baby carriage up and down the roads, collecting bottles from the ditches.

Mrs. Anderson pays the vet bill, so she takes Duke home when he's all fixed up. I wait for Maggie Anderson to pull out all the stops. I wait for the rumors to zing back to me and pierce my skin. They never do. She tells Curtis, though, and Curtis makes me kiss him twice, every day, with tongue, or he'll tell everyone what my dad did. Maggie watches us sneak behind the utility shed every day at recess. Curtis tastes like rot and gets a boner every time.

"That's a hundred kisses," Maggie tells Curtis one day. "Now you leave her alone." She takes my hand and walks me to the cool side of the playground, where her frilly friends are waiting for us on the monkey bars.

The Cat Came Back
Ivan E. Coyote

When you're Irish, and Catholic, and the oldest, you babysit a lot.

I have thirty-six cousins, so I pretty much had to book my weekends off if I had plans of my own, plans that didn't involve the baths and bedtimes of any number of little ones in pajamas, most of them with blue eyes just like mine. We all vaguely resembled each other, me and my cousins. This made it easier to get mad at them, and harder to stay that way for very long.

There was a routine, which changed only slightly, according to which aunt and/or uncle I was sitting for, which house I was in, and how many kids I had being the variables.

I would ride my bike over, or get picked up if it was winter. My uncle—no matter which one—would pull his truck up into our driveway and honk the horn, because invariably he was late. I would skid across the ice in my running shoes, because snow boots were so uncool, and climb into the cab of his pickup, which was usually a four-by-four, and almost always blue.

This was how things were done in my family.

This night it was my Uncle Rob behind the wheel. He was a car salesman, and always smelled like aftershave, and sometimes like rum and coke.

"Watcha got in the backpack?" he would say.

"Homework," I would answer, usually lying.

"It's Friday night, for crying out loud," he would reply looking at me sideways, his right arm draped over the seat between us as he backed up the truck. "You read too much."

I would shrug, he would shift into first, and we'd be off.

There would be chips, and pop, and sometimes a video. There would be bathtimes, and bedtimes, and numerous glasses of water, and eventually, finally, all my cousins would be asleep.

Leaving me blissfully alone. To do whatever I liked.

This is how I discovered *Playboy* magazines, vibrators and dirty videos, condoms, feminine douches, hemorrhoid creams and vaginal suppositories.

I have to admit that most of my earlier knowledge of the strange and smelly world of adult bodies came from snooping in the bathrooms and under the beds of my mother and father's brothers and sisters and their significant others.

Nobody had cable back then, and a girl can't keep herself occupied with CBC North all night. Boredom forced me to it, you see. My parents either had a remarkably unaccessorized sex life, or they hid things better.

Anyway, it was a Friday night that had passed like any other, and I was alone in my Uncle Rob and Aunt Cathy's bedroom. It had apparently been the scene of a rather frantic fashion crisis on his part earlier, because his clothes were strewn everywhere.

I took off my T-shirt and slipped on one of his car salesman suit jackets. It was scratchy wool on the outside, with suede sewn over the elbows. But it was lined with caramel-colored satin inside, and felt cold and kind of nice up against my nakedness.

There was a walk-in closet, a big one, with a sliding door. Everybody had them, you know the ones, covered in mirrored tiles with gold veins running through them.

My pants didn't match, so I took them off. There was a tie, tied and then abandoned on a chair back. I slipped it over my head and slid the knot to the base of my throat. I looked left and then right at myself, sucked my cheeks in, flexed my biceps. I tried on his cologne, slicked my hair back, and danced with myself in the mirror, singing "Jessie's Girl" by Rick Springfield.

I was a twelve-year-old dork, and I didn't care.

Except my legs looked too skinny protruding naked from his suit jacket, so I dug a pair of his clean underwear out from an open drawer and put them on. I grabbed a pair of dress socks too, the ones made of all man-made fabrics. I believe I had every intention of putting them on my feet when I originally removed them from the drawer, but somehow they ended up down in the front of the underwear. I was on my way to finding a pair of his dress pants when I was again distracted by the mirror.

I believe it was the Rolling Stones I was singing when he walked into the bedroom.

I froze, covering the bulge in my—I mean his—underwear, and just tried to act… natural.

"Forgot the tickets," he said, perfectly calm, reaching for an envelope on the dresser. He stuffed the tickets into his inside pocket, turned without even cracking a smile, and was gone.

I stripped in a panic, I don't know why, having already been caught quite in the act. I couldn't believe he hadn't said anything. In my family we rarely turn down an opportunity to torture and harass each other, and he had just been handed the opportunity of a lifetime. Maybe he couldn't think of anything good right away, that was it, I would be in for it later, I'd never hear the end of this one, I knew it.

But he never did say a word to me about that night, not the next day, nor the next. Not even years later, both of us drunk in his boat, talking about why we both like girls, did he even ask me about it. Maybe he didn't know what to say. What do you say to your half-naked niece when you catch her in your bedroom with a pair of your dress socks stuffed down the front of a pair of your underwear, singing "I Can't Get No, Satisfaction" and licking your gold-veined mirror-tiled closet door? Maybe the shock was too much, maybe he blanked it out.

Or maybe the black panties and fishnets I found under his and Cathy's bed weren't Cathy's, who knows?

He always was my favorite uncle.

The Jeweler

Derek McCormack

Jason skimmed dead minnows and leeches and dumped them in the stinkbait pail.

I sat at the till. A man bought do-ball hooks. A man bought Hoochy Trolls.

A girl came in. Her hair was wavy and blond.

After supper Jason and I drove to Sophie's Lake. We hauled in Dad's minnow traps.

"She's beautiful," I said. "She looks like Carole Lombard."

"Her name's Sara," he said. He baited traps with dinner rolls, tossed them back. The sun dipping across the lake. Jack pines like fish bones.

I pulled my sheet over my head, put my flashlight on my pillow. The troll was a silver chain with five blades. For landing bass. I glued a green rhinestone to each blade. Then I laid it in my tackle box and pushed my tackle box under my bed.

Jason pulled the branches off the boat, hauled it from the woods. I paddled out.

"Are her ears pierced?" I said.

He shrugged, rigged his line with sinkers and a rubber crawler that smelled like pork.

Something struck. Took half his line. Zigzagged beneath us.

"It's a keeper!" he said. He played it out. I netted. It was a pike. It flipped out, flopped all over the boat. Oozing slime.

"Ugly bastard," he said. He dropped down and pinned it between his knees. He gouged out the eyes with a jackknife. He threw it back. Speared his hook through the eyes.

❧

I pulled the weedguard off a Spinning Frog and glued a safety pin to the belly. I dipped Crippled Minnows in glue and dredged them in yellow glitter. Filed down hooks.

My flashlight died. In pitch black I rummaged through my tackle box.

Jason woke. He called from his room.

"Nothing," I said.

❧

Jason dug a reel out of the junk box. He oiled the axle and the pawl. "Sara's coming so don't ask her any dumb questions."

She rode in front with him. I got the back of the truck. Bouncing down the ministry road, weeds fanning the engine.

She helped with traps. One had a little pike in it. Jason slit it and six minnows slopped out.

She oohed and shivered. Jason laughed and went for the boat.

I pulled a box from my jeans and gave it to her. LIMP SPINNING LINE, it said.

She opened it. "That's sweet," she said. "My first lures."

"They're not lures," I said. "That's a brooch. And that's a charm bracelet. And those are earrings. I made them myself."

Jason yelled. I went down to the shore.

"Think you could guard the truck a while?" he said.

I shoved them off. I put on my sweater. I shone my flashlight at the lake. Walleye eyes glowed white. Then disappeared.

Recorder Lesson
Brian Doyle

I played the recorder.

I had a summer job at the Ottawa exhibition playing the recorder outside our church's bingo tent.

The recorder music was to attract people to the tent to take a closer look at the cute guy with the curly hair playing the recorder, whose curls and charming music would somehow seduce them into buying a bingo card or two.

Across from the church bingo tent was the beginning of the midway and the "girlie show," as it was called.

Beyond that was the Alligator Man, whose skin was so thick he invited audience volunteers to come up and try to cut through the soles of his feet with a hacksaw.

Next to that was a show with huge billboards outside with crude paintings of different kinds of torture. A head sticking out of the sand with ants eating its eyes and tongue. Inside, however, was just a wax-museum type of display—lights flashing, phony screams of horror and a curtain that cost an extra dime to go through and see a bloodied head on a platter.

Next was the fantastic boy who was "brought up by reptiles." For fifteen cents you could go in and watch a guy crawl around in the mud.

Down toward the end of the midway was the "Siamese Triplets Inside" show. The paintings outside showed three children, attached at the hips and heads, dancing with little umbrellas on a stage with a huge symphony orchestra and acrobats and monkeys and clowns. Inside, you got a dark passageway, strange music and then a little stage area lighting up a big jar. Inside the jar, floating, was a membrane or something; maybe it was a dead jellyfish, or just a couple of pieces of rubber—it was hard to tell.

Back to the girlie show at my end of the midway.

Every hour a drummer, a saxophonist and a trumpeter would come out on the deck in front of the girlie show tent, and a loud guy on a vicious microphone would give you a sample of the action you could see inside if you bought a ticket.

While the music blared and the microphone blasted, out would come half a dozen dancers in high heels and wiggly little skimpy outfits, bells on their ankles and feathers on their wrists and piled-up hairdos.

It was hard to play the recorder while this was going on. Not only would I be completely drowned out, but my imagination was so inflamed by the sight of all that wiggling, jiggling, bouncing girlie flesh that I couldn't get the recorder to do what I could normally make it do.

My boss at the bingo tent was concerned I would be corrupted by this sinful display. She was a friend of my mother's and the reason I got the job. My mother must have asked her to keep an eye on me. She must have told her I was at a very susceptible age. My mother would do that kind of thing. And it explains why my boss would leave her bingo duties and come out and protect me from the girlie show whenever it appeared on the platform.

Her way of screening me from being sucked into a sewer of sex forever was to get me to play louder on the recorder.

If you've ever played the recorder, you'll know that you can't play *louder* on the instrument. A recorder must be played with gentle breath. You can't force your breath on a recorder and make it louder.

But my boss would stand there and urge me on to compete with the music and the screeching microphone.

"Louder! Louder!" she'd shout. "Keep playing! Keep playing!"

The hymn "Abide With Me" was what I usually played during this time.

One hot afternoon I noticed that the girlie on the end of the line of jigglers had me riveted with her eyes. Once she was sure I was watching, she gave a couple of extra twirls on her breasts, fluttered the flat of her hand at me and then ground her pelvis, bumped her crotch and flashed me a big wink and a delicious smile.

"Louder. Louder!" shouted my mother's friend, as I played "Abide With Me," the hymn that asks God to stick by you even as the darkness thickens.

Next to the girlie show tent was a trailer where the dancers changed costumes between acts. They would exit the trailer down three steps and pick their way daintily over ropes and pegs until they disappeared behind the tent.

And then I could see them run back when their dance was finished, bangles and beads bouncing, bells jingling, heels clacking, breasts and bums pushing and straining the shimmering fabric of their tiny outfits.

"Keep playing," my mother's friend would hiss as she passed behind me with a handful of bingo cards.

This particular day, as the girls left the trailer to go backstage, the last one, the one who'd been giving me all the attention, shouted "Nice piccolo!" and then twitched her ass at me, a gesture that nearly knocked me off my chair.

At the end of the act, instead of following the others into the trailer, she cut across and, to my disbelief, came up to my chair.

She stood with the August sun behind her, bathed in gold, her form shimmering, her perfume washing over me in a glorious vapor.

All detail around her flowed away like a watercolor painting in the rain.

She leaned and placed her lips to my ear.

"Could you teach me to work that piccolo?" she whispered, causing a ripple of gooseflesh to run down my spine, playing it like a xylophone.

"It's not a piccolo, it's a recorder," I said, turning my head slightly until our eyes met.

"Whatever it is," she said, "you could show me … " She blew a little burst of breath into my ear.

As I drowned in her eyes, the voice of my protector stiffened me up.

"Excuse me!" she boomed. "Is there something I can do for you, young lady?"

"My name is Nan," said the lips at my ear. "My supper break is at six. Meet me behind the trailer."

"Pardon me, miss," persisted my boss. "I think you'd better clear out of here and go about your business!"

Nan gave my hand and my recorder a squeeze.

Then she clicked away in a little hurricane of perfume and feathers.

I could see that my mother's friend was about to make a speech so I put my recorder to my lips and played "Abide With Me" until she gave up and left.

It was the best I'd ever played it, trills and all. Since we were in a quiet time, I thought Nan might hear it while she stripped off her costume in the darkened trailer.

At six o'clock, while my boss was down the midway buying hamburgers, I walked across, shoving the recorder into my pocket to disguise the lump in my pants.

She was sitting on a bench behind the trailer, holding a mirror, trimming her hair. She wore a red kimono decorated with designs of musical instruments in black thread.

Around her, the cables and tarps and boxes and discarded makeup packs and usual backstage litter took on a prettiness in the early evening light.

The shouts of the children on the distant rides and the rumble of the grinding machinery reached our privacy, muffled, from another world.

The air awash in waves of the scent of candy floss, thick hemp rope, tent canvas, mustard, diesel fuel, fried onions, lipstick, sweat and cold cream was a sexual soup to me.

"Would you like to come in?" she said. "The others are away at supper."

She took my hand and led me up the three steps into the trailer.

There, in the gloom, I could make out two narrow cots, rows of costumes on hangers, a long mirror with lights over it, four stools, a small, dirty window, a little table.

"Would you help me with something?" she said, sitting on the first cot.

"I'm trimming my hair down here," she said, opening her kimono and stretching her legs straight out. "It's hard to see," she said. "Could you do some for me?"

She handed me the scissors and opened her legs wide and leaned back on her elbows and smiled a beautiful smile.

I didn't move.

My eyes were used to the light now.

I'd never seen a naked woman before.

She seemed sweetly, mildly amused.

"Is that your piccolo in your pocket?" she said. "Mmm?"

"It's a recorder," I said.

"Oh yes, recorder," she said. "May I see it?"

I removed the recorder from my pocket and handed it to her, my hands shaking.

"You're not going to be able to give me a trim shaking like that. Come here." She pouted, like a mother about to readjust her kid's clothing.

She took the scissors from me and placed them on the little table.

She undid my belt, unzipped my fly and pulled down my pants and underwear.

"Is this your first time?" she said.

"Yes," I said, my voice hardly working.

She handed back the recorder.

"Show me how you play," she said.

As I put the recorder to my lips she shifted on the cot and leaned into me and gently fed me into her mouth.

I began to play "Abide With Me."

Out the little window I could see my boss, my mother's friend, standing in front of the bingo tent, holding hamburgers, cocking her ear, listening. Was that a recorder she could hear, faint, faltering, hesitating, then fading plaintively . . . ?

That night I looked deep into my face in my bedroom mirror, searching for any kind of change that I might have undergone. I saw none.

The next day, Monday, I was shocked to see a whole new girlie show move in. A big sign went up:

ALL NEW GIRLIE SHOW!

I sat in my chair in front of the bingo tent and glumly watched the new dancers come onstage to the blaring music.

They looked old and bored.

"Where'd you get to last night?" my boss asked me. "I had your supper for you and you never showed up."

"Sorry," I said. "I forgot."

"And why aren't you playing?" she said.

"Can't find my piccolo," I said.

The new dancer on the end had skinny legs and bony knees. Her face looked like she was in some kind of pain.

"Piccolo? You mean recorder! What happened to your recorder?"

"I lost it," I said and went home.

That night and nights to follow I nightdreamed visions of Nan, in some trailer somewhere, reclining naked on cushions, her legs stretched straight out, her pubic hair glistening, practicing on my recorder the basic fingering I showed her, working toward her own rendition of "Abide With Me."

The Unfortunate
Lee Henderson

Not a monster, but not simply disfigured, the boy was born during a cold snap. His mother was in labor for three hours before she relented to the forty-five minute drive to the city hospital. I don't want those doctors looking at me with those, with those instruments, she said. They lived on an acreage with pigs, goats, a few dogs. It wasn't a farm and his father wasn't a farmer, but he sold central heating to farmers and that was close enough. They lived in the country, and on a winter day such as this a woman might prefer to try to give birth in her living room on the wall-to-wall rather than brave the freeze. Sixty kilometers of white ice between here and some idiot doctor. Her husband smoked and sat in his easy chair and watched CNN while she sweated and grimaced. Are you ready to go now? he asked her.

No, she said. Damnit.

The unborn boy's older brother was in another room looking at catalogs that had come in the mail, women's apparel.

Ah, shit. She stood up with her big belly. Go get the Pathfinder warmed up.

Now for the second time her husband became a father. The child came out headfirst as usual, with an unusual head. A nurse backed away. The doctor squinted at what he saw. He delivered the baby from her and lifted it into the light, cleared the newborn's mouth with a deft turn of the finger, told her she'd just had a, Well, let's see, okay it's a boy.

Another one? she gasped.

Her husband lovingly untangled a splatter of hair that stuck to her white forehead, A boy, he said, that's just great.

The doctor slung the baby in her arms and she saw him for the first time, his little body, fresh skin, head shaped like a football, and she said, Damnit what is this?

After keeping the boy on observation for the next few days the doctor sat the parents down and told them he had suspicions.

What suspicions? the mother said.

Well, the doctor put his hands in his lap and looked at them, it's too early to speculate.

Her husband reared up from his seat, Too early to, you mean you don't want to tell us because you, what suspicions, answer the question my wife asked.

Please, the doctor said, please. The husband flattened his shirt and sat back down.

At first he had difficulty learning to walk. His head was way too heavy. They would find him ambling sideways, dragging his head along the carpet; he'd be sitting up and suddenly his head would tip backward and he'd start crabbing forward; lying flat on the floor he'd run in circles; when he stood up his head would still be on the carpet. This kind of thing. His older brother watched him roll around, Goddamn dud brother. You're the kind of creature that gets killed in other cultures.

That's not nice, his mother said. Take that back. She returned to her knitting, a game show on the TV for background. The Panasonic there in the corner was next to the gas fireplace they had rigged up to a clap mechanism. Clap and the fire ignited. Clap again and it vanished. On the TV someone spun a big wheel and clapped and the fireplace stuttered explosively. His mother looked at her knitting, then the TV, then her youngest son, as if they were connected somehow, in a way that didn't seem to please her.

His features, his pencil-dot eyes, for example, were pinched together as if all tacked to his nose, the back of his head formed an equidistant cone to the cone of his forehead, and sad blond whiffs of hair came out of nowhere on the pink baldness of his scalp. It was common for the child to get headaches, and later, as he matured, these headaches turned into migraines and nosebleeds, earaches too. If he got a cold or the flu he might go blind for hours at a time. He begged for the phone to stop ringing when it wasn't ringing.

His father bought a horse. One morning he took his baby boy out to the fence, holding him on his shoulder. The wind was nimble and snow traveled through it in dancing flecks. The sun was white. The horse came to the fence and snurfled, Look at that brown horse, he said to his son, that's your horse, I bought it for you, happy birthday. He had just turned four. What a beautiful animal, hey kid, what a beautiful animal a horsey is. The boy leaned an arm forward to touch the horse with a finger, but his head was too heavy and he slipped off his father's shoulder and fell in the snow. He cried. The snow was cold. His father brought him back inside huddled in his trembling arms, I'm sorry, I'm so sorry, goddamnit.

They had beef stew for dinner.

Why'd you buy him that horse when he can't even ride a horse? He's only four.

I've boughten you lots of things. I can go and buy your brother something too.

But he can't ride a horse.

Just eat your dinner.

Afterward they had vanilla cake and sang Happy Birthday. The boy squealed and then started to cry. His brother gave him something stick-shaped wrapped in a newspaper and a wrinkly bit of ribbon and he tore it open and there was a Mars Bar inside.

Don't eat that all at once, his mother said. You'll get cavities.

Once they'd eaten and had put the boy to bed, while sorting the dishes into the dishwasher she said to her husband, We can't afford a horse.

Now you too? Can't I enjoy this?

I'm the one sorting through the bills.

It's too late now.

Later that evening his father went back out and rode the horse at a gallop and lost track of time and he rode and he rode and when he got home one of his ears had been frostbitten and finally a week later a small chink of dry red ear fell off. He put the piece of ear in a Sucrets tin and put the tin at the back of a drawer in his office desk. The company he sold central heating for didn't cover the cost of his gas when he had to drive halfway across the damn province in his Pathfinder to try and convince some hick couple with three TV's and three VCR's and a giant cardboard plate with six remote controls glued to it to get central heating instead of the oil heating they were used to. The man of the house never even looking him in the eyes, just going from remote to remote, flicking and switching and suddenly recording. The prairie wind outside was full of icy razors. Arriving home late that night with nothing to show for the time, goddamnit, he stood and watched the horse graze through chunks of hard snow. The horse pushed around in the snow and found yellow grass to eat. His father never rode the horse again and eventually the horse became unhealthy. They fed the horse and cared for it in all other ways, but it was never ridden. The horse became skittish and would run in tight circles and rear up; or for many days the horse would stand at one corner of the fence and look at the ground and at night it would fold up at the knees and sleep, and again like the day before, the horse would stand and stare at the ground it had just slept on. And the horse did this for what seemed like months.

The boy turned five and they brought him in at the doctor's request for more X-rays, covered him in a heavy black blanket, It's okay honeycakes, it's okay I'll be right on the other side of the door. She backed away from him and the door shut and the boy was alone, Mama, the boy said and wept.

Flicking on a switch, snapping the X-ray against the lit glass, the doctor detached a pen from his shirt and traced the icy glow of the boy's skull. He looked to the parents and took a deep breath and nodded. Is that, well, that looks like an awful lot of bone there, the father said.

The doctor nodded, At least three inches at the back, here, well, four, and again, here, at the forehead.

The mother chewed her lip, held her husband's hand firmly in her own, Is that a good thing, no, no it's a bad thing right?

No, yes, it's not a good thing, the doctor admitted.

Damnit, the mother said and stood up, I hate all you doctors, you know I fucking hate you, you're telling me he's stupid.

No, no, that's—.

Helping put on her son's mitts, toque, then wiping her eyes, out the door, and back into the van. The long rutted road below the Pathfinder, out past the last restaurant in the nearest town, the curling rink, and then nothing but dead wheat and white loaves of snow.

For dinner scalloped potatoes, ham shank heated and with gravy, fruit salad with whipped cream, string beans, Can I show you my marks? his brother said and ran and retrieved some tests from his grade three class.

Oh, you're so smart I can't believe it, you're the one I tell you, in this family, going all the way to university isn't that right, she said turning to her husband.

That's right, he said.

He's a genius isn't he? his mother said.

You can bet on it, his father said.

Pretty soon you'll be teaching me things, she said.

Can I have a girlfriend? his brother asked.

His mother frowned. Concentrate on your grades and girls will be begging for you, and stop thinking about girls, don't think about girls.

Mama, the boy said.

Hey it's suppertime here, his mother said, pipe down.

Mama.

What did I just say?

His brother said, Shut up, you dud.

Don't call your brother a dud, how many times?

The boy turned and stuck his tongue out at his older brother and then got his head pushed against his supper plate, food up his nose. The family laughed, his father crying, tears, dabbing a napkin against his eyes, Oh I'm sorry but that's, I'm sorry, that was like a clown running face-first into a pie instead of the, you know, the opposite. His father had to sit back from his meal and just breathe for a moment. Meanwhile the boy could feel another headache coming on, rippling outward from behind his eyes, across his skull, screaming behind his ears, down his neck.

He was blinded. The headache got him. His mother guided him to bed, They're just teasing you okay, okay. The boy nodded. You got to understand your brother, he's a very smart boy, and it's not, you can't blame him really, he's very smart like your father says.

Things were bad and then he was a teenager and things got worse. In high school his desk directly faced the desk of his teacher. She had an electric pencil sharpener she used on her chalk and it made a tortured noise as it ground down to a point in that little battery-powered box. The entire class sat behind him and he could hear the soft murmur of their mendacious voices, the seedy stamping and stretching of legs and arms. He could hear it but see none of it. If the teacher sat at her desk—which she always did—it was inevitable that the class had to look over his deformed head to see her, and he knew this, but there wasn't anything he could do about it.

Sitting in the desk behind his was this girl with curly hair. A note was passed forward while the teacher read passages from a book of Canadian stories. The note came over his shoulder, pinched between the fingernails of the girl with curly hair, Somebody passed this to me, it's for you. A folded note on looseleaf, he opened it and saw a drawing of a thick square-shaped boy with meaty fingers and monster arms, goofball short legs (like his own) in ill-fitting pants, and a football complete with stitching replaced the head of the boy. This was a caricature of him, he knew that, he wasn't so stupid.

He turned and looked at the girl and she was blushing. He stood and faced the class and spoke in a steady voice over his teacher's lecture, said, Fuck you, you fucking fucks.

And was sent promptly to the principal's office where they seated him with a line of delinquents to await guidance counseling. He fell into the same slouch as the other boys, the pregnant girl. The handicapped kid. He sat there, the dud, and tried to will his head to shrink. But no, it wouldn't.

Sit down, the counselor said, right there, and pointed to the only chair in the room other than the one behind his desk. How are you? he said.

What d'you mean? the boy said.

Hmm, he wrote something on a legal pad. I was looking through your, through the list of your classes, the counselor said, history, do you like that?

The boy looked past the counselor to a map of the world taped to the wall behind him, I like it okay.

The counselor nodded and smiled and nodded, What do you plan on doing this summer?

I don't know, I thought I'd get a job.

That's good that's good, so I wanted to ask you before we really get started, before I get into—, you know my son is in your history class, and also your algebra class I see, do you know him, did you know my son went to this school?

Yes.

Oh good because, before we start, I thought maybe you might know how he's doing. Yes, ha ha, sometimes a father doesn't know everything, even if he's a guidance counselor, ha ha, things a boy keeps even from his dad, I'm sure you know how that is, well.

What do you want to know?

Have a pear, the counselor said. He gave the boy a pear. Try it, go on, give it a big bite.

The fruit was rock hard. He put his teeth against it and dug them as far as they would go into the meat.

That's good pear isn't it, it's delicious, personally I love pears.

The boy nodded and broke the piece down into smaller pieces with his back teeth until he could finally swallow it. The counselor dropped back into his chair, That's good, so, I guess I want to know, and don't misunderstand me, but, I worry of course, a father, well, ha ha, is he on drugs?

Oh, the boy said and put the pear back on the counselor's desk, it's not ripe.

I'm sorry I thought it was I'm sorry is there anything else—.

No, thanks. No, he's not on drugs as far as I know.

The counselor rubbed his hands together, Good, that's nice of you to be honest with me, thank you, now. Tell me, tell me about what happened today in class.

There was a knock on the door and a secretary's head appeared and rolled her eyes at the counselor and he was up out of his chair and told the boy he'd be a moment, and the door shut and he sat in the leatherette chair and waited, let his head rest against his shoulder.

In the hallway during a break he stood in front of a change machine flattening a five-dollar bill. He took the bill and pressed it against his chest and studied the diagram on the machine and then followed the directions and put the bill to the machine's lips. The bill came spitting out. Having some trouble, she said, the girl, suddenly she was right there beside him.

Oh, he said, well I—.

It won't take wrinkled bills, here, she opened a little bag slung over her shoulder and gave him a perfectly flat five-dollar bill. Try that, go ahead. See, she said, voila, change. It came jangling down and he collected it. What was that note about that made you freak, she said, you know in class today?

A sproing of hair fell across her eye and she tugged it beneath a clip, Someone drew a picture of me with a football for a head, he said and she looked at him very seriously in the eyes.

That's sick, it's really, doesn't that hurt your feelings, because if it was me I'd be bawling, I used to, this is so embarrassing but, I had a limp? My hips were at an angle, I wore these special leather pants all the time? Oh my god, you can't tell anyone this. You won't tell anyone will you? She put a hand on his arm.

I won't say anything.

Okay, she smiled. I trust you. These leather pants were so painful. They were cut so I had to walk against the natural angle of my hips and—.

Who drew it? he asked her.

Who drew what I don't know, how do you, why would I know?

It made me mad, he told her, How am I supposed to change the way I look?

Sure, you can't, it's not your fault.

I wish I looked normal too, like I could get special leather pants for my head, people think I'm stupid because, and I'm not stupid, why'd you give that to me?

No, I don't think you're stupid, I always thought—, no, okay, you know two desks behind me and on the left?

On the left, he shut his eyes and lifted his left arm, Yeah okay I know that guy. Well that's who drew it.

He made up a plan in his head. Beat that kid up.

When the snow stopped coming down and the clouds broke away and the days got colder and the evenings even colder than that, their old horse started to look weaker. His knees kept nearly giving out, either that or they'd lock and the old horse would stand in one spot for hours, afraid of falling over. Even with the TV on they could hear him braying, Maybe it's time we put the guy out of his misery, his father said.

He took his son outside behind the old gray barn and showed him how to use a shotgun, firing old books off a chopping block, not so much for the aim—he'd have his son stand right over the book—but simply to get used to the recoil and the noise. The horse tramped about, the smell of cordite and the terrible crack of the gun puzzling him.

Ah, maybe we shouldn't do this, his father said.

Okay, he said.

Don't chicken out like that. This is an important lesson. You know everything dies?

Yeah.

Well then. Okay, his father said, I can't watch this, I'm too old myself. Good luck, and he went inside.

The boy stood there with the gun against his arm. The air was cold and the barrel of the gun was cooling fast. He loaded another two shells, walked over the creaking snow toward the stable and the horse. Climbed over the fence, the horse taking a couple steps away and then no more, tossing his head and then staring at the boy, two quiet eyes looking, watching.

He aimed the barrel, closed his eyes, and did it. The horse froze, then buckled, slumped to the ground.

The screen door clanged shut and his father came out. He walked toward the fence and almost stumbled. He said, Oh.

On flattened snow his old horse lay, head turned back, blood coursing out hot and steaming. The boy looked down at the miserable horse and said, I feel like I'm going to be sick.

His father fell on his knees, You stupid stupid boy, you think I was serious, my god this was my horse, I can't believe I let you—, why didn't you, you fool, you're so goddamn stupid.

The boy replied, You told me—.

Why didn't you ask me, you could have asked me why, haven't you got a mind of your own, to do something like this, stupid and senseless? Falling back into the snow beside the dead animal his father gasped for air and pawed at the gore and liquid of the old horse's life. This would be what the boy remembered of the day his father lost it.

He returned his father's gun to its rack in the shed and walked over to the stable and looked at all the hay, the hay the horse slept in and ate.

Could I eat my own bed? the boy wondered. No I couldn't, he answered. Too bad maybe.

He picked up a shovel and wandered out the back door and walked some distance into their acreage, stabbed the blade at the frozen ground. It took him nine hours to dig a hole six feet deep, and the next day when he got home from school, another three and a half to get it deep enough to fit the horse in. He brought a skid over and found he could get the horse on it by using its stiffened legs as leverage, tied some rope to the skid and dragged the horse across the snow to the hole he'd dug. He shoveled the dirt back over the horse and packed it down and within three days the snow had it covered so thoroughly it was impossible to remark on which plot was the horse's and which was just plain dirt.

That night he went to bed early. He lay in bed and looked at the walls in the dark. He thought about things. That old horse trembling and collapsing. He heard the TV coming from the basement all grunts and moans, then heard his brother coming up the creaking stairs, shifting foot to foot, and the bathroom door shutting. His brother now a high school senior, still without a girlfriend. The bathroom door opening, his brother come knocking on his door, What is it, what d'you want?

Do you have any soap?

Soap? No I'm sleeping, what d'you need soap for?

There's none left.

What d'you need it for?

Having a Jacuzzi.

It's midnight, and you've had, you've already had two today.

I know, *dud*, I know that.

Well what d'you need another for then, and don't call me a dud.

There was a pause before his brother said, It's none of your business what, where, and why goddamnit, and then he heard his brother walk away.

His father came and knocked on his door and he thought it was his brother,

Go away. The door opened with a splice of light and he saw his father standing in his housecoat, I'm sorry, Dad I, I thought you were—.

His father raised a hand and made a fist and punched the air, Ah-hoo, his father barked, this is the new, you see, this is the new time for you and me, the new whatsit, the new epoch, get a job, you hear me?

Yes.

Good, get a job.

All right.

All right good, get a job or, or you know. His father tightened the belt on his housecoat, turned and walked away leaving the door open. The boy heard his mother quietly say, Don't give him a hard time, he's simple right, don't be so rough.

The central heating kicked in and he could feel his lips begin to dry out before he fell asleep.

There were very few places in the school during lunch to hide. He had to spy out empty classrooms and eat in the back row. High schools were not developed with the solitary in mind, and so when a group of boys appeared at the door to look at him he wasn't surprised, What're you doing in here? the kid said, stepping through the doorway. The kid had an awful grin and a stale giggle. He was the one who'd drawn the caricature.

I'm eating my lunch, what does, what d'you think I'm doing? he said and put a final bite of bologna and macaroni sandwich in his mouth and crushed up the plastic wrap and shoved it into the paper bag.

The kid smiled, I came to say, you know, that I'm sorry about you know.

About what? the boy said, a headache so close behind his eyes he could feel the hard melody of it. Now was when he should start beating this kid up, but he was too afraid.

To say I'm sorry about that drawing, he came closer, that was you know, pretty mean of me. The unfortunate boy leaned against the desk behind him, I mean, that wasn't very nice of me, the kid said, smiling. I feel kind of bad about it, the kid said, here let me apologize. A fist came up and connected at the boy's jaw and he was turning out of his desk, the remains of his lunch going down with him, and another fist.

When it stopped there were more boys around, smiling but silent, and the kid who drew the picture was flushed and tired. You like that? the kid huffed.

The boy climbed up from the floor and sat back down in the desk, his head lolling from a headache—now he was stinging blind, What d'you think? he said.

What did you say? the kid said.

You asked me if I liked that and I said, what do you think?

The kid looked to his friends, You just can't get enough can you? What, freaks can't get enough, is that it, is that it? A sloppy tired punch just above the ear, Is that it?

After they left he stumbled out of the classroom with a bloody nose and out the front door of the school, paid the fare to ride the bus to the nearest town and sat in a Chinese Canadian restaurant watching the owner feed a stray dog overcooked rice and bits of gray hamburger, You what? his mother said when he got home, you can't do that, what're you stupid?

No, Ma, but look at me.

His father folded down the day's newspaper and slid each section back into order and then looked up at the boy and said, You can't just, see, you'll have to get a job or I'm sorry, that's right. He was still in his housecoat.

His brother was watching TV in the den and eating mini pizza-bagels. He stood up and went to the bathroom and came out again in five minutes without flushing the toilet or running any water, Well there's no way, his mother said, if you ever thought you were going to be like your brother and get to go to university, count that out, not even high school I don't know what can you do without high school, what job can he get?

His father leaned back calmly, Oh there's, I mean there's a type of job that, manual work, I think that should be your goal. And then he fell off his chair. More than once at each meal his father would lose his balance and fall off his chair and his mother would have to go and pick him up off the floor and prop him up in the chair again saying, Bend your knees damnit, bend them.

The next morning he rode his brother's bike to town and stopped in at the family restaurant where the curling teams met after games and got an interview as a dishwasher.

No, the manager said, and he walked out the glass door while an electronic alert bell went off. He got back on the bike and tried the gas station, the hotel, the store, the wallpaper warehouse. It seemed that no one had any work for him. When he got home he parked the bike in the shed and walked back to the stable and picked up the shovel and went out and started to dig a hole. When the hole was deep enough he filled it in again. He came in the back door and took off his boots and jacket and didn't answer his mother's questions.

What the hell're you doing out there, is that, is your dad paying you, no, what? He had a shower instead. And then he sat and ate dinner. Thank you for dinner, he said and went to his room.

At 6:00 AM he pulled himself out of bed and dressed and went out and started to dig another hole. At nine he came in for some raisin toast and cinnamon butter. By five in the evening the sun had already been guttered and the wind had picked up and he'd finished filling the hole in.

At the same time the next day he was out again, no snow coming down, the sky a veiny blue and a gelid white sun burning off the ice and his work was a bit easier. And by the time summer rolled along he'd dug a hole every day for the past five months—that was one hundred and fifty holes—and he'd filled in just as many.

I'm watching you out there, his father said.

It's good work, he answered.

When I was your age I worked for money. I got paid. What you're doing, I don't know. His father rubbed his nose furiously.

Well. I work and don't get paid. You get paid and don't work.

He started to go out in just an old pair of shorts, no shoes even. The dry ground was warm and soft, and then cooler and wetter as he dug deeper. The smell was rich and mellow. He began to notice the crease of the hole's chilled shadow as it drew up his body and he was comfortable with a hole's size when he could stand completely in its shadow. That was when he'd begin filling it in. There were worms now that it was summer, and dead mice, and long milky insects like he'd never seen before. He dug a hole and sealed it up. His fingernails were black, there was no use trying to clean them. He'd forgotten about his old high school, as far as he was concerned they were all dead and buried, What are you doing out there, hey, yeah, hi, what is that, a hole you're digging?

He leaned against his shovel and ran his hand across his forehead and cleared away the sweat, it's a hole.

He walked toward the car stopped on the rural road beside the split log fence and saw his guidance counselor behind the wheel of a Toyota, Why're you digging a hole, is that something, may I ask why?

The boy walked toward the car and stopped at the fence and looked at his guidance counselor, then looked at his own dirty feet, I've been digging them all year.

What, since you, since you left school?

That's right, I guess that's when I started.

His guidance counselor turned off the engine to his car and leaned farther out the window and looked at the upturned land behind the boy, the random wildflowers dribbling red here and there, the long ambient stretches of umber weed, the wavering heat exhaling and warping the low sky, Looks like you have, well, is this a job, I mean, for pay?

No, the boy answered.

It isn't, well, I guess you're just passing the time then.

I guess so.

His guidance counselor nodded.

What're you doing out here? the boy asked him.

Oh, ha ha, I came to see how you were doing, I came to see, but it doesn't look like you're interested in school anymore.

No, the boy shook his head and kicked a clump of dirt from his shovel, no way.

Hmm, well, can you take a break? I thought, it's pretty hot out, I'll buy you a beer.

He squinted his eyes at the counselor, I'm not old enough.

That's all right, I know a place.

On the stage a lonely cowboy rubbed the strings of his guitar and his bony partner played a Casio keyboard with programmable drum sounds, bass sounds and a little sick trickle of piano. There was an exit sign above a door near the men's washroom that read: IT. The whole place smelled of stain and salted nuts. The boy wondered if that was the scent of puke or just old beer. He saw a farmer sitting on a stool at the bar repeating numbers off a ledger into a cellular phone. The boy's head felt kind of loose and soft and he rested both hands on the red shag-covered table between him and his old guidance counselor. A delirious man approached them and showed them the contents of a greasy paper bag, Fish, the man said.

There was a freshwater salmon in the bag, No thanks, his guidance counselor said and the man continued on to the next table, saying, Fish.

The boy watched the foam deplete in his mug of beer, I phoned your parents when I saw you weren't at school, his counselor said.

The boy looked up, Why'd you do that?

I was, it's my job, that's what they pay me for, I was concerned, I mean, also, it wasn't just my job, I was concerned.

What'd they tell you?

The guidance counselor turned the handle of his pint toward him, raised it and drank, put the mug down, They said you found school too hard, that you didn't do well on tests.

That's true, the boy said, I didn't.

Well okay, but, hey I'm asking you, hear it from you.

Fish.

No, no, you already asked us ... hey?

What? the boy said.

The guidance counselor leaned forward, Why'd you leave school?

He raised his head and pointed his eyes to the ceiling and then rolled them down again and he was hoping the whole world would be different, but it wasn't. He said, You think I'm going to tell you that I couldn't handle school because I have a head shaped like a football, well, that's what I'm telling you.

From the stage the cowboy singer said into a microphone, This one goes out to all the women, how many of you are women?

The guidance counselor turned his head to the band and then looked back at the boy, And you think I'm going to tell you that I think that wasn't a good reason.

He came in one night covered with dirt and showered as usual and came out to watch TV for a change and there was no one in the house, he was alone. He went to his brother's room and opened the door and looked around. In his parents' room he found a photo album with pictures of him and he suddenly realized how ugly he was. He went back to his brother's room thinking about pictures and found a bunch of curled-up photos of naked women stuffed into film canisters—and an unopened box of ribbed condoms.

Your father had an accident, he's in the, they've got him in the hospital, he fell trying to sit down to dinner again, his mother was wailing as she fell in the front door.

Should I go see him? he asked while trying to help her off the carpet.

No, god, no just stay here.

Well, what's wrong?

Goddamnit I'm no doctor, honey, I'm not a doctor, I don't know. I need to be alone right now, okay honeycakes? She pulled at her hair. Give me a hug, she said.

He gave her a hug. Now go away, she said.

He started up the stairs toward his bedroom.

I love you? she called after him, almost as a question.

I love you too Ma.

Later his father came home and laughed and laughed, Ha ha ha, for what seemed like too long and then fell asleep.

He dug another hole and filled it in. The next day the same. There were lumps like blackheads everywhere, fresh earth shoveled and packed down again. The oldest winter holes had sprouted odd little green tendrils here and there, Hi.

The boy walked toward the car, What time is it?

His guidance counselor looked at his watch, Five-thirty.

He threw the shovel against the side of the fence, I said, didn't I say six?

Yeah you, six, yeah, I'm early, should I leave and come back?

No, come on. They walked into the house and he introduced his guidance counselor to his family, shaking his father's shaking hand, How do you do I'm fine, his mother said, Well I've heard your voice so many, sheesh it's nice to finally meet the man, his brother said, Yeah hi.

You needn't introduce me to your brother, the guidance counselor said, winked and followed the family into the living room where his mother had set out a bouquet of flowers she'd bought a couple years back, made of polyester.

I'm going to have a shower, the boy said.

There's no hot water, his older brother said. It ran out halfway through my Jacuzzi.

I'll have a cold shower, and he left them alone.

Dinner was spare ribs, steamed carrots, corn on the cob, boiled potatoes, lime aspic. They drank iced tea. Outside a cherry sky turned purple then black and dancing clouds of mosquitoes followed the smell of cooked meat to the screened windows and waited there, Well this is the best meal, I mean, these are the ribs to end all ribs.

His mother blushed, Normally the man of the house would make, but today, she looked to her husband whose drooping head almost touched the table, but today I was the meat chef, ha ha.

It's just delicious.

His mother said, Leave room for the dessert I cooked, well hold on. She brought a pecan pie from the oven and they sat and ate it à la mode, and then his brother disappeared, then his father, so it was just him, his mother and his guidance counselor.

Let's move into the rumpus room, his mother said and clapped the fireplace on. Bring your drinks.

I'm going to bed, the boy said.

He shook the guidance counselor's hand, I'll talk to you soon, the counselor said.

His mother smiled like a precious schoolgirl.

Before the sun came up he started another hole. He noticed construction right on the horizon, way off there in the distance. They were putting up a Petro-Canada gas station, he could see the sign.

At dinner that day his father said, I think what we think is that you should be starting to look for a place of your own.

His father was old now, prematurely gray in the hair and in the eyes, limbs thin and stiff.

The boy finished chewing and shut his eyelids for a moment, You want me to move out?

His brother put down his fork, See you can't justify it, you can't just live here not educating yourself or bringing in any money either, just, you've got to—.

His mother interrupted him, Honeycakes, each person's got to learn his own way how to live and—.

You all talked about this?

His mother started to cry.

His father said, Oh we talked about it all right.

The boy walked into the living room and pulled out the old Nintendo and untangled the entrails of black cord and hooked the thing up to the TV and sat playing Super Mario Brothers 2, thinking about what he should do next. The music was plinky and stupid and he felt nostalgic. His reflexes were a bit off, but he was surprised to know that he could still remember where all the secret bricks were, the extra lives and gold coin hideaways. He bounced on the hardback shells of big turtles. He made his own way.

Hello, she said. Hi, he said, sorry, maybe you don't remember me, I was in your history class, I sat in front of you? Oh, she said, and then, will you shut up I'm on the phone—just a second okay? Okay. I'm on the phone, shut the, shut the door, okay, yeah, I remember you, how are you? I'm fine, how are you? Good. He sat back on his bed and realized he didn't know what to say, she sounded vital and alive: he said nothing. Did you drop out or something? she said. I guess so. Wow, what's that, I mean, do you miss school? No, he said, I've been busy. What? Working, I've been working on the acreage.

That's cool, that's good to keep busy. There was a pause. Look I'm sorry to call but, it's that I need a place to live and I don't know anybody, and I had your number. Another pause, he wound his finger in the coil of the phone cord. You need a place to live, you're getting your own place? I guess so. That's cool, she said, man, that's I mean, that's *really* cool. Do you know anybody who needs a roommate or something? No, I mean, no. Okay sorry to bother you. No, don't worry about it, shut up, sorry my little sister, I better go, my parents.

After hanging up he thought about her hair, the way it dangled in front of her eyes in perfect coils. He needed to use the bathroom but his brother was having a Jacuzzi so he sat and held it and thought about her and then let her disappear again the way he'd been able to let her and everyone else from school disappear, and he fell asleep, his head to one side, large, heavy, and thick with bone.

The next morning he met her at a steakhouse where she worked as a busser. On her break they ate steaks with steamed broccoli and French fries and she looked older and he loved her for a moment, Have you been to that, to the mall in the city?

No, he said.

You've never been to the mall?

I've been to some strip malls.

Oh, it's, you'd like the real mall. They have a store that's just hats.

Maybe I should go there.

But yeah, no big deal, she said. It's pretty boring at the mall. Just like everywhere, I guess.

Is this a good place to work? he asked.

No, the manager's a prick.

I'm looking for a job, he said.

Well, my dad got me this job, maybe, do you, well.

He put his arm against the frame of the window and looked out at the gas station and the field behind it, My dad doesn't know of any jobs for me.

He picked at the last sinew of his steak, he watched a car pull into the gas station, it was the guidance counselor's car. His counselor got out and filled the tank, leaned down and someone stepped out, it was his mother, she went inside and paid. They drove across the street and parked in the parking lot of the steakhouse, Hey that's the guidance counselor, she said, holy look at that, that's not his wife 'cause she's, you know, she divorced his ass, do you see that?

Yeah, the boy watched them cross in front of the window of their booth arm in arm and go toward the door.

Maybe it's sweet to see him like that with another woman. Think she sucks his tooter? I wonder if she does?

That's actually my mother.

The steakhouse door opened and the boy kept looking out the window. They were checking for a table, he could see them out of the corner of his eye and saw them jolt at the sight of him, he kept looking out the window, the door opened, they went around behind the steakhouse and came up quickly to the guidance counselor's car and drove away.

Oh my god I'm so embarrassed. That was your mother? Well, but, did you know that? Your mother and him? I feel like such a loser.

No, he said. I better go, he said.

She took her napkin off her lap, Really, okay well, thanks for lunch, I well, I'm glad you called I mean, feel free to call anytime, I'm so *bored* this summer I can hardly—

Sure, he said, I will. But he never did.

Have to say I'm glad you called, thought maybe I wouldn't hear from you again, ha ha. I think you're going to like this guy. He's got a good sense of humor. They drove down a highway and he watched it become autumn and wondered why things went so fast even when it seemed like he was doing nothing. He sat where his mother had sat as a passenger how many times? his arm out the window.

Been busy? his guidance counselor asked.

I worked for three days washing cars but they fired me.

Why'd they fire you?

Because of my head, the mechanics didn't like looking at me.

That's ah—, he said.

The money was pretty good.

They drove a little while longer. I think you'll like this guy, he's a bit of an oddball but you know, heart of gold, listen, about—.

But they didn't talk about it, the conversation quieted, they went over a hill.

A blackened rusted barbed wire fence followed the road until they came up to a steel gate and the guidance counselor stepped out of the car and opened the gate, returned to the car and drove along two bald streaks in heavy grass. Dragonflies followed the car, How are you?

Good, how're you?

I'm fine, good to see you.

Good to see you. The man leaned down in his lawn chair and picked up a bag of tobacco and began rolling a cigarette in the lap of his sweatpants, It's sure fucking hot today, I'd say it's the fuckenest hottest day we've had this summer.

The guidance counselor looked up at the screaming sun and then back down. Under the shade of a plastic awning rigged to the front of a little house no bigger than a fist sat the man, It sure, it's hot I'd say. The boy watched the man twist the paper up, lick it, light it and smoke it.

Fucking addiction I tell you I tell you, he spat at his feet. What's wrong with your head there? the man said.

The boy stopped. The guidance counselor smiled or squinted. I've got a malformed skull, I've, well, there's too much bone.

The man waved a hand in the air, Yeah yeah I can see that, but why's it red and flaky like that?

The boy put a hand to his scalp, Oh, oh, that's a sunburn, I well, I don't grow much hair so—.

Fuck, the man said and pushed some smoke from his mouth. Well that's the crapper, and no hats I bet.

No, the boy said, no hats.

Beside the house was a chicken coop bigger than the boy had ever seen, above which a white haze hovered. The floor of the chicken coop was flush with movement, white puffs skittering and circling, feathers floating up and scooping down through the air. There was a chicken wire door to the coop and a flatbed truck parked near the door with big tractor tires covered in the splatter of offal, the guidance counselor waved a hand at the man, This is my brother by the way, I'd like you to meet my brother.

He stuck out his hand and the man put his cigarette in his mouth and passed his hand to the boy and the boy shook it.

It was a few degrees cooler in the shade. That's a lot of chickens you got there, the boy nodded his head in the direction of the coop.

Is that the fault of your school, bro'? Don't you teach kids grammar? The man rubbed his armpit.

I'm a dropout, the boy said and the three of them had a real laugh.

The guidance counselor sat down on the slat-wood deck next to his brother's chair and smiled at him, What, what why're you looking at me that way, what?

Nothing, just, no nothing, the counselor said.

Well fuck, see, this is why, are you trying to figure out what's going on inside this slush pile up here? He poked his head with his finger. Because there is no way to parse this gooey mess of a brain.

The guidance counselor laughed and wiped some ash from his pants, No, no, and I don't want to know.

D'you see they're building a Petro-Can up there? the man said.

It's going to have a restaurant attached to it, I saw.

I heard it was an Internet café, the man said with a laugh. I'm just kidding, but wouldn't that be fucking funny?

What you'd be doing is this, the man said as he unlocked the door to the chicken coop and walked in. Chickens instantly surrounded him, pecking and clucking. He picked one of the chickens up casually by the neck and gripped it by the head and with a deft turn of the wrist broke the chicken's neck. The chicken's head fell to its breast and dangled there loosely while it went into spasms. He dropped it to the ground. The chicken ran butting into other chickens, doing hectic backflips before finally falling over dead. He picked the chicken up and threw it into the back of the truck. How does that look for you? the man asked.

The boy nodded, I can do that.

All you have to do is break their necks, I'll hack their heads off.

Okay.

He walked through the door and was attacked immediately by chickens. Little pecking beaks. The noise was infuriating. Don't think about it, just grab the fucker, go on, the man said and gestured. The chickens gobbled and jabbed one another with their dirty orange faces. He reached down and found one kicking between his fingers. He brought the chicken up off the ground, not so much heavy but unwieldy, and grabbed its head and cranked it around.

No, no don't let it go it's not dead yet, it's not dead, give it another twist.

He heard a crack, or felt it in his hand, and let the thing down, watched it freak a bit and then die.

They broke open a few beers and sat under the awning, Can you work everyday? The boy said that he could.

I'll pay you a nickel for every chicken you kill.

He looked to the guidance counselor, That's good pay, don't worry.

A nickel doesn't sound like much, but think it doesn't take long to kill one chicken.

I need a place to live, do you—, the boy said, have you heard of any?

The man put down his beer and began to roll another cigarette, Well fuck, I've got, up in the barn, I renovated the attic, it has a bed and whatever, there's a toilet and a sink—I was thinking about it as a guest room but.

I'll take it, the boy said.

Ha ha, the man said, all right.

His guidance counselor smiled, See, now, see this is good; more beer in the fridge? He stood up and opened the screen door and went inside.

The man sat forward in his lawn chair and picked tobacco off the floor of his porch. Fucking heat it's the fucking crapper I hate it.

He told his mother he'd found a job and a place to live. She said, Oh that's just, goddamnit, look at your father. His father was in the living room wearing a housecoat and his head was folded over the edge of the easy chair with the TV blinking and dimming in the background as if maybe a tube had broken inside it, but no, it was just a rock video on the religious channel.

And you're going to just get up and go, what about me? said his mother.

He wondered if his father was asleep, and then said to his mother, I thought you wanted me to find a place, get a job, for my own good.

Haven't you been listening? Your father, he's sick. The doctors say.

Now he noticed that his mother was very agitated, her eyes were silky with water and her clothes were on all backward, she whispered to him, You can't leave us like this.

But you said.

I need your help, honeycakes, please. I'm not a doctor.

I should get away for awhile, he said.

You, I don't, I don't, hold on, she picked up the ringing telephone, Hello? Yes, here it's for you.

For me?

Of course for you, here, she handed him the phone, his brother in the living room took notice, breaking his concentration on his textbooks.

Get back to studying, his mother snapped, don't pay attention, I don't want you learning anything stupid from your brother.

Hello? he said into the phone. They talked, he told her to come over later if that's what she wanted, she did, she wanted to come over, Okay then, come over later. There was a beep but she ignored it. His heart tripped when she said it. There's a beep but I'm going to ignore it. Come over later, he said again. When later? When it's dark, All right when it's dark.

Here on the prairie there were more than just stars, there were layers of stars that threaded together into gauzy strips, diaphanous against the empty black face of the universe. The fabric static of the universe, he said in a way a man might say something like that to a woman. Under a wool blanket they huddled in the chill of the summer night on the back steps of his family's house. She was warm and smelled of an expensive soap, a soap she must have bought at the mall in the city; he couldn't help but imagine her life, she said, Can I come and hang out in your new place?

He said, Sure. They watched the family goat off in the distance mount a shallow body of rocks, stand erect and watch the tidepools of stars motionless but alive in the sky. What d'you think is *up* there? she put her head on his shoulder and shivered dramatically. I don't know, I see stars and planets but of course, they say there could be more. I saw this show, it was about space, she said, her eyelashes brushing against his neck, and they well, how did it go, I can't remember, but it's like the universe is still getting bigger. I'll bet it is, he said. She leaned away from him and he looked at her. Can I touch your head? she asked. Okay, he said. He wanted to close his eyes but he wanted to watch her. She lifted her hands out of the blanket and put her fingers on his temples. She smoothed the random tufts of soft hair and brushed the dry skin away, she followed the dips in the skull and the near-point at the back. Down the nape to his shoulders and then up behind his ears. She kissed him, I'm only seventeen, she said.

Well, he said, I think—in his brother's room he remembered seeing that box of condoms. They were ribbed. But he couldn't very well go in there now at two in the morning and ask to have a couple. He said, I don't, no, but if you think, I mean.

She kissed him again, on the peak of his forehead this time, My uncle runs the confectionary. She kissed him on the lips.

Sure, he said, I know the one, come on, he pulled her out of the blanket and looked down her body.

She followed him to the house, I can't come, right, he's my uncle, he'll—.

He sat her down on the couch in the living room, Sure okay, sure, just wait here, is that okay? Okay, don't make any noise or you know—.

She ran her finger over her lips and whispered, Zippered shut.

He drove without the headlamps on, his heart rattling. He parked and ran in the confectionary doors, Hi there, her uncle said. Hi, he shuffled up and down the aisles picking out candy bars, a jar of pickles, a box of condoms, a newspaper, Okay that comes to ten eighty. The uncle looked at the boy casually, dropping the condoms into a plastic bag with the other items. Thank you, he said and ran back to the van huffing and scared out of his wits.

He drove down the cobbled road toward the house and at the main gate he pulled over and decided to walk the rest of the distance so as not to wake up any of his family. He spilled the contents of the bag onto the seat of the van and put only the condoms in his jacket pocket. The air was cold and the night was dark by the half moon. The wind seemed to sing a high note, giving him the first edge of an earache. Now and again he stumbled over the freshly turned earth of some hole he'd recently made. Nervously he broke open the box and separated a link of condoms and transferred them to a pant pocket, put the rest back in the box. He crept up the stairs to the house and tenderly put the key to the lock and screwed it around and clicked open the door. Removed the key and careful not to let it touch the other keys on the chain hung them on a peg. The hall was dark and he walked through it toward the living room.

She was on the couch, below his brother, her body moving as he'd hoped it would move against his own. They had not heard him. He'd been very quiet coming in, he was sure of that now.

You can't leave, no, you can't no, you'll leave your father like this, she cried, tearing the clothes he'd packed out of his Samsonite. He put them back in his suitcase only to have her throw them out again.

We bought you these goddamn clothes, these are ours, we goddamn paid for them, dig holes all year, these, none of this is yours. She turned the suitcase over and dumped his belongings on the floor of his room.

His brother came and stood in the doorway with his hands solemnly in his pockets.

Get the fuck away from me, the boy said.

I don't know what happened, his brother said. What can I say?

Get away from your brother. She pushed him out of the room and shut the door. She started working at the Scotch tape, putting his old rock posters up.

In his parents bedroom his dad was sitting bolt upright on the Sealy with an *US* magazine in his lap open to a picture of a robot. He waved a hand to the boy and smiled, Okay well, it's been great, I mean, you'll come for dinners sometimes, right?

He said, I think I might but it's hard to say.

His father nodded, Great, and coughed. I remember when you were born, he said, and everyone thought you were going to die, with that big huge head, but I thought no way, not this kid, he's tough, and hey, look at you now what do you weigh, how much?

About two-twenty.

All muscle too I can bet by the look of you.

I guess so.

I'm proud, really, no, I think it's just great.

Okay, he said. Dad? he said.

What? his father said.

I'm sorry I shot that horse, I shouldn't have shot the horse.

His father said nothing. His father made no noise. He looked at his father, saw his eyes shut as though maybe a strong thought had passed by, but he still didn't say a word.

His mother screamed from another room, See? He's all delirious, he's sick, I can't help him I'm not a goddamn doctor, I'm not and he doesn't know that.

His father laughed through a grim rasp, She's hysterical but it'll pass. Don't worry about me, the stinky stretch is over for this one, he pointed to himself. No way, he said.

At dawn he woke naturally and he was in a new bed, much lower to the ground, a softer, less resilient bed. The attic walls were stapled with old newspapers, the plumbing pipes protruded like knuckles from the dry skin of the walls. He washed his face in the sink and opened his little beer fridge and made himself a bowl of cereal, and someone said, Can I come in? and a pair of hands hoisted themselves up the ladder and his guidance counselor followed behind them.

Hungry, I can make cereal for you?

Love some.

They sat and ate. It's warm up here.

It's a bit too warm, the boy said.

I think he'd let you make a few more windows, if that's, you could if you wanted.

It's a good idea. He poured them each another bowl.

I stopped, maybe you already knew this but, I stopped seeing your mother.

The boy put his spoon in the leftover milk, I didn't know that, no.

Yeah, I did.

Why?

Why? Oh I don't know, your mother, she's an interesting woman. But she wasn't with me because—, I know she was wanting some guidance that's all.

Some guidance.

She was, that's right, but I couldn't give it to her, she thought I could, but ha ha, I'm not very good at my job, I guess. She's having troubles dealing with your dad.

I'll say.

Look, the counselor said, my son, he's not ready for this kind of thing. He doesn't know about any of this.

I don't think I do either, the boy said.

The counselor nodded, like a child being reprimanded for a small misdeed.

How are you? the counselor asked. How are you doing?

He thought about this as he stood up and gathered his clothes and began dressing, Don't worry about me. He shrugged. I think I should start work now.

The guidance counselor wished him luck and they stepped down the ladder and into the barn and the guidance counselor said goodbye and went to his car and the boy went to the coop.

He gathered up the first chicken by its pimpled, bony legs and swung it up and clenched its neck, broke it quickly, threw it into the truck. The other chickens pecked at seeds. He raised another off the ground and killed it just as fast, That's good work, the man said, leaning against the coop. I eat lunch at noon, come on over to the house. The boy said he would and got back to work. He snorted feathers from his nose and blinked them out of his eyes. The coop was hot and there was no shade.

By his twentieth chicken he was lathered in sweat. He went up to his attic and ran a towel under tap water and wound it around his big head then went back to the coop and began killing chickens again, one by one, throwing them into the truck. At any time two or three of the chickens in the truck would still be kicking and flapping and stirring around in there atop the growing mound of dead ones. White feathers floated everywhere, the more he killed the more this seemed to raise the feathers off the ground. When he broke their necks he noticed this sometimes caused a spasm that released a puff of feathers all at once. They were sticking to his body, he was dappled with white.

By noon he'd killed two hundred, You'll have to work faster than that to make any money, the man noted. They ate tuna sandwiches and drank beer, it was good to be in from the heat because he was exhausted and dizzy. Either that or I'll have to raise it to ten cents a chicken, he laughed. He rolled the boy a cigarette after lunch and they sat on the porch and smoked and watched a dust storm in a neighboring acreage peel away a layer of dry weed.

You see they put the lights up in that Petro-Canada sign?

No, I didn't see that, the boy said.

I guess we'll have to go to that restaurant sometime soon and check out the waitresses.

Sure.

You smell like dead chickens, the man said.

I've been killing them, the boy said.

That's too fucking funny, you've been killing them, well no shit.

The boy laughed, And I'm going to go back there and kill some more.

Go to it, the man said, and the boy walked back to the coop, picked up the first chicken that came near him and broke its neck. He threw the bird into the back of the truck.

Later that afternoon they drove to the city, to the mall in fact, to sell a dozen birds to a butcher. He asked the man if they could stop a moment to take a look at the mall since he'd never been.

I'll wait in the truck.

He stepped out and walked in the front doors. The air was cold and the floors were smooth and the light was odd. He looked at a rack of baby clothes and watched a man do karate chops and then a row of children try and imitate the chop. He listened to music come from the ceiling and he thought to himself, So this is a mall, and then he felt naive. Someone bumped into him and screamed when they saw who they'd bumped into, and then burst out crying and apologized for the whole thing. A group of teenage girls huddled closer and closer together as they passed him and he decided that he didn't like malls all that much. He smelled the food court and then saw the corona of food outlets around the tables. Old men sat with their coffees, men that reminded him of his dad but were in fact much older, and he wondered when he'd next see his family, and the thought made him sad, because he really didn't ever want to see them again. And he asked someone in a pet store, Where's the store that only sells hats? Hats? the clerk said, a store that only sells hats? The clerk looked at the boy's head. There's no store that only sells hats. The boy nodded, I thought there was, I'd heard that there was a store here that only sold hats. No, there's no store like that. Is there another mall? the boy asked the clerk. No, this is the mall and there's no store that's just hats, there's a store that only sells nylons, women's stockings, but no, not hats. Okay, the boy said, thanks for your help, but the clerk had already walked away.

Making the Dragon
Susannah M. Smith

Nothing objective ever happens on the train.
Except: the wheels are joined and go fast.
Together.
Faster. Quick. Soon. Quick. Soon. Quick.
I hear them move.
Sometimes when I look I see Shadow running alongside.
She wears black rubber boots loosely on her bare feet.
She looks for puddles.
I like to see her breathe hard,
trying to keep up.

"Destination … "
The Conductor uses a long wooden pointer.
He taps it on the map at the front of the compartment.
Where the stick rests there is a small black dot.
No one looks.
They think black dots are irrelevant,
believing that what matters is the journey itself.

Across from me is the Priest.
I know him from the way his eyes roll back in his head,
and from the smile trembling around his mouth.
If I were to close my eyes for an instant and then open them quickly,
he would speak to me:

(In a whisper)

Look. See what I have…

(Takes a black case out from under his seat. Opens it.)

Look. Closer.

Lays pieces of animals on the table. Parts of rabbits and birds.
Paws. Entire limbs. A wing.

See? No blood—only swift meaning.
Pieces form the whole…

But I keep my eyes open and he remains still and quiet.
A thin line of saliva trails down from the corner of his mouth.
I watch it move.

Drake is stroking Mink's hand.
Up. Down. Quick. Slow. Quick. Slow.
In his other hand he holds a paperback.
Something tattered and opened to page six.
His eyes are looking out past the glass.
Out the window at the smeared world.
Mink holds a pen.
An empty page bites into a full lip.
Her hand strains but not hard enough to break the skin.
Quick.
Quick.
The pen moves.

Halfway, the train slows.
It almost stops and Shadow is there.
Still outside, she is closing in,
pressed up tight against the cold metal of the train.
I can smell her incense.
I can hear the low song she sings.
She bends over to dump water out of her boot.

We start to pull away.
We pick up speed.
Shadow runs and grows stronger as we move toward the horizon.

Soot.
Smooth are the hands that turn black.
The Priest outlines his face with his own fingertips.
Sharp nose. Hollow cheeks that swerve into thin-line lips.
Black gown topped with a white collar.
White collar topped with a black face, once white.
He is still smiling and rolling his eyes.
He turns to the window and places his finger against the glass.
Writes:

Messy in dust & dirt I am born.
I am alive.

The words are made of strokes.
Symbols that go up. Down. Quick. Slow. Down.

The sun is a sinking dot.
Shadow becomes longer and more certain of herself.
She can almost reach through the spaces between cars.
I slide lower in my seat.
Her scent creeps around my legs and my eyes start to close.
Drake flaps the cover of his book to startle me.
Don't go, he thinks.
Mink writes it for him and passes the paper to me.
I crumple it and throw it on the floor.
The Priest picks it up and puts it in his mouth.
He chews slowly.

Outside, Shadow extends her hand to me.
How perfectly she runs.
One rubber boot lands rhythmically after the other.
Flat on the earth.
She is winning now.

It occurs to me that it would be easy to lure Drake from Mink's side.
All I have to do is curl my index finger.
Like this. Three times.
Mink is too engrossed in her blank pages to realize what is happening.
Soon Drake is holding my hand.
He strokes it.
Up. Down. Up. Down. Quick. Slow. Quick.
In his other hand he holds a book.
Tattered. Opened to page six.
I stare down at the table. The pen. The paper.
It is true that I have replaced Mink.
All sleek and skimming.

Now it is me breathing hard.
I close my eyes to get a perspective.
Against my eyelids the train slows
  and the faces of the others grow dim.
When did I get on?
Where am I traveling to?
No answer.
A black dot eclipses me and I open my eyes.
Shadow is before me.
All around me.
I hear breathing.

Alone in her seat, Mink has given up on words.
Now she draws.
Quick dark marks, an outline on white.
When she finishes, she tapes it to the window.
Instead of the landscape, there is a picture.
Not surprisingly, it is a dragon composed
  entirely of black strokes and dots.

It is night behind the window.
The Conductor appears, reflected in the glass.
I wave at his image.
He waves back.
I blink and smile.

So does he.
When I turn around to speak, his back is already to me.

Mink draws again. A picture of us:
SheandDrake merge into one.
The Priest is a bundle of paper held together with a string.
The Conductor has dripped out of the pen,
now just a drop of ink beside the word: train.
Shadow can only be seen from my window.
She does not ride, so is not in Mink's picture.

Outside, both of us are running.
She has me.
We each wear one boot.
Our legs move in unison,
in time to the rhythm of the train.
Shadow says:
If we speed up our pace a little every day,
soon we will be able to look inside the window.
She says:
  There are many passengers aboard the train,
  all very interesting and real.
I look at her ear.
She wears one glass earring.
It is a dragon and I can see my reflection.

Dawn

Tim Wynne-Jones

Barnsey met Dawn on the night bus to North Bay. His mother put him on at Ottawa, just after supper. His parents owned a store and the Christmas season was frantic, so for the third year in a row, Barnsey was going up to Grandma Barrymore's, and his parents would follow Christmas Day. He had cousins in North Bay, so it was fine with Barnsey, as long as he didn't have to sit beside someone weird the whole way.

"What if I have to sit beside someone weird the whole way?" he asked his mother in the bus terminal. She cast him a warning look. A let's-not-make-a-scene look. Barnsey figured she was in a hurry to get back to the store.

"You are thirteen, Matthew," she said. There was an edge in her voice that hadn't been there before. "Has anything bad happened to you yet?"

Barnsey was picking out a couple of magazines for the trip: *Guitar World* and *Sports Illustrated.* "I didn't say anything *bad* was going to happen. If anything *bad* happens, I make a racket and the bus driver deals with it. I know all that. I'm just talking about someone weird."

"For instance?" said his mother.

"Someone who smells. Someone really, really fat who spills over onto my seat. Someone who wants to talk about her liver operation."

His mother paid for the magazines and threw in a Kit Kat too. Barnsey didn't remind her that she'd already bought him a Kit Kat, and let him buy a Coke, sour cream and onion chips and some gum. And this was apart from the healthy stuff she had already packed at home. She was usually pretty strict about junk food.

"I just asked," said Barnsey.

"Come on," said his mother, giving his shoulder a bit of a squeeze. "Or the only weird person you're going to be sitting beside is your mother on the way back to the store."

Barnsey didn't bother to ask if that was an option. His parents put a lot of stock in planning. They didn't put much stock in spontaneity.

"What if I end up in Thunder Bay by mistake?"

His mother put her arm around him. He was almost as tall as she was now. "Matthew," she said in her let's-be-rational voice. "That would require quite a mistake on your part. But, if it were to happen, you have a good head on your shoulders *and* your own bank card."

His mother almost looked as if she was going to say something about how they had always encouraged him to be independent, but luckily she noticed it was boarding time.

They were at Bay 6 and his mother suddenly gave him a very uncharacteristic hug. A bear hug. They weren't a hugging kind of a family. She looked him in the eyes.

"Matthew," she said. "It's not so long. Remember that."

"I know," said Barnsey. But he wasn't sure if his mother meant the trip or the time before he'd see her again. He couldn't tell.

They moved through the line toward the driver, who was taking tickets at the door of the bus.

"Don't do the thing with the money," Barnsey whispered to his mother.

"Why not?" she said. Barnsey didn't answer. "It's just good business. And besides, young man, I'll do what I please."

And she did. As Barnsey gave the driver his ticket, Barnsey's mother ripped a twenty-dollar bill in half ceremoniously in front of the driver's face. She gave half the bill to Barnsey, who shoved it quickly in his pocket.

"Here, my good man," said his mother to the bus driver in her store voice. "My son will give you the other half upon arrival in North Bay. Merry Christmas."

The driver thanked her. But he gave Barnsey a secret kind of cockeyed look, as if to say, Does she pull this kind of stunt all the time?

Then Barnsey was on board the bus, and there was Dawn.

There was no other seat. His mother had once told him that if there weren't any seats left, the bus company would have to get a bus just for him. That was the way they did business. So Barnsey shuffled up and down the bus a couple of times, even after he'd put his bag up top, looking—hoping that someone would take the seat beside Dawn so he could triumphantly demand a bus of his own. But there were no other seats and no other passengers.

He suddenly wanted very much to go back out to his mother, even though she would say he was being irrational. But then when he caught a glimpse of her through the window, she looked almost as miserable as he felt. He remembered the bear hug with a shiver. It shook his resolve. Timidly he turned to Dawn.

"Is this seat taken?" he asked.

The girl took off her Walkman earphones and stared at the seat a bit, as if looking for someone. She took a long time.

"Doesn't look like it."

Barnsey sat down and made himself comfortable. He got out his own Walkman and arranged his tapes on his lap and thought about which order he was going to eat all the junk he had or whether he'd eat a bit of each thing—the chocolate bars, the chips, the Coke—in some kind of order so they all came out even. At home his mother had packed a loganberry soda and some trail mix. He'd keep those for last. Strictly emergency stuff.

Then the bus driver came on board and they were off.

"There's talk of big snow up the valley a way, so I'm gonna light a nice cozy fire," he said. People chuckled. There was already a cozy kind of nighttime we're-stuck-in-this-together mood on the bus. Nobody was drunk or too loud. And the girl beside Barnsey seemed to be completely engrossed in whatever was coming through her earphones.

It was only the way she looked that he had any problem with. The nine earrings, the nose rings and the Mohawk in particular—orange along the scalp and purple along the crest as if her skull was a planet and the sun was coming up on the horizon of her head. She was about twenty and dressed all in black, with clunky black Doc Martens. But as long as she was just going to listen to her music, then Barnsey would listen to his and everything would be fine.

And it was for the first hour or so. By then the bus had truly slipped into a comfortable humming silence. It was about nine and some people were sleeping. Others were talking softly as if they didn't want to wake a baby in the next room. That's when the mix-up occurred.

There isn't much room in a bus seat. And there wasn't much room on Barnsey's lap. Somehow a couple of his tapes slid off him into the space between him and Dawn, the girl with the horizon on her head, though he didn't know her name yet. The weird thing was, the same thing had happened to her tapes. And the weirdest thing of all was that they both found out at just about the same time.

Barnsey shoved the new Xiphoid Process tape into his machine and punched it on. While he was waiting for the music to start, he looked again at the hologram cassette cover. The band was standing under lowering skies around an eerie-looking gravestone. Then if you tipped the cover just right, the guys all seemed to pull back, and there was a hideous ghoul all covered with dirt and worms standing right in the middle of them where the grave marker had been. It was great.

Barnsey pulled a bag of chips from the backpack at his feet, squeezed it so that the pressure in the bag made it pop open, and crunched on a couple of chips as quietly as he could. He was busy enjoying the way the first sour cream and onion chip tastes, and it took him a minute to notice he wasn't hearing anything.

He turned the volume up a bit. Nothing. Then he realized there *was* something. A tinkling noise and a bit of a whooshing noise, and a bit of what sounded like rain and some dripping and more tinkling.

Barnsey banged his Walkman. He thought the batteries were dying. Then Dawn changed tapes as well and yelled, as if she'd just touched a hot frying pan. Some people looked around angrily. The looks on their faces made Barnsey think they had just been waiting for a chance to glare at her. One lady glanced at him too, in a pitying kind of way, as if to say, Poor young thing. Having to sit beside a banshee like that.

Meanwhile, both of them opened up their Walkmans like Christmas presents. They held their tapes up to the little lights above their heads to check the titles.

"*Rain Forest with Temple Bells*?" Barnsey read out loud.

"*Scream for Your Supper*!" Dawn read out loud.

Then they both laughed. They made the switch, but before Barnsey could even say thank you, the girl took his tape back.

"Tell you what," she said. "You listen to that fer 'alf a mo, and I'll give this a try. 'kay?"

She had a thick accent, British.

"Okay," said Barnsey, "but I think yours is broken or something."

She took her tape back and tried it. She smiled and her smile was good. It kind of stretched across her face and curled up at the end.

"Naa," she said. "Ya just 'av ta listen, mate. Closely, like."

So Barnsey listened closely. He turned it up. There was a rain forest. There were ravens croaking and other birds twittering away. And there were bells. He thought someone was playing them, but after a while he realized that it was just the rain playing them, the wind. He kept waiting for the music to start. He didn't know what the music would be. Any moment a drum would kick in, he thought, then a synth all warbly and a guitar keening high and distorted and a thumping bass and, last of all, a voice, altered, maybe, phase-shifted. Maybe singing about trees. About saving them.

No drum kicked in. Maybe the tape *was* broken?

It took him a minute to realize Dawn was tapping him on the shoulder. She had his Xiphoid Process tape in her hand and a cranky look on her face.

"This is killer-diller," she said.

"You like X.P.?" he asked.

"It's rubbish."

Barnsey laughed. Rubbish. What a great word. He pulled out *Rain Forest with Temple Bells.*

"What ya think?" she asked.

"It's rubbish."

Then they both started to giggle. And now people stared at them as if they were in cahoots and going to ruin the whole trip for everyone. Dawn hit him on the arm to shush him up.

He showed her the hologram cover of the X.P. tape.

"You think it's their mum?" she asked.

"Maybe," he said. He wished he could think of something to say. He just flipped the picture a few times. She leaned toward him. Her hand out.

"Dawn," she whispered.

It took him a minute to realize she was introducing herself. "Barnsey," he whispered back, as if it was a code. He shook her hand.

He offered her some chips. She took the whole bag and made a big deal of holding it up to the light so she could read the ingredients. She shuddered.

"It's a bleedin' chemical plant in 'ere," she said.

"Rubbish," said Barnsey. Then he dug out the trail mix and they both settled down to listen to their own tapes. Barnsey turned X.P. down to two, because there was no way Dawn would be able to hear her forest with Spice-box wailing on the guitar and Mickey Slick pounding on the drums. After a couple of cuts he switched it off altogether.

He found himself thinking of the time he had traveled with his father out to British Columbia, where his dad was from, to Denman Island. He remembered the forest there, like nothing he'd ever seen in southern Ontario. Vast and high. It had been a lovely summer day with the light sifting down through the trees. But, he thought, if it rained there, it would sound like Dawn's tape.

He didn't put a tape in his cassette. He left the earphones on and listened to the hum of the bus instead.

"It's not so long."

It was the bus driver. Barnsey woke up with his mouth feeling like the inside of a bread bin.

There was a stirring all around. People waking, stretching, chattering sleepily and my-my-ing as they looked out the windows. The bus was stopped.

"Will ya lookit that," said Dawn. Her nose was pressed up against the window. Outside was a nothingness of white.

They had pulled off the highway into a football field–sized parking lot. Another bus was parked up ahead. Through the swirling blizzard they could see lots of trucks and cars in the lot. It wasn't the stop Barnsey remembered from previous trips.

Barnsey could see the driver standing outside without his jacket, his shoulders hunched against the driving snow. He was talking to another bus driver, nodding his head a lot and stamping his feet to keep warm. Then he hopped back on the bus and closed the door behind him.

"Seems like we've got ourselves a little unscheduled stop," he said. "The road's bunged up clear through to Mattawa."

Someone asked him a question. Somebody interrupted with another question. The driver did a lot of answering and nodding and shaking his head and reassuring. Barnsey just looked over Dawn's shoulder at the outside, shivering a bit from sleepiness and the sight of all that whirling snow. Dawn smelled nice. Not exotic like the perfume his mother wore, but kind of bracing and clean.

"This here place doesn't have a name," said the driver. People laughed. He was making it all sound like fun. "But the barn there with all the blinking lights is called the Cattle Yard, and the owner says y'all welcome to come on down and warm yerself up a spell."

Passengers immediately started to get up and stretch and fish around for handbags and sweaters and things. There was an air of excitement on the bus. The Cattle Yard was a big roadhouse painted fire-engine red and lit up with spotlights. It was no ordinary way station.

Still sleepy, Barnsey made no effort to move as people started to file past him pulling on their coats. Dawn still had her nose pressed up against the glass.

"D'ya know where I spent last Christmas?" she said. Barnsey thought for a moment, as if maybe she'd told him and he'd forgotten.

"In Bethlehem," she said.

"*The* Bethlehem?"

"That's right," she said. "In a bar."

Barnsey looked at Dawn. She was smiling but not like she was fooling. "There are bars in Bethlehem?"

She laughed. "Brilliant bars. Smashing litt'l town is Bethlehem."

Barnsey tried to imagine it.

Then the bus driver was beside him. "Here, you might need this," he said. And with a click of his fingers he produced the half a twenty Barnsey's mother had given him. Barnsey was about to explain that it was meant to be a tip, but the driver waved his hand in protest. "Just don't get yourself all liquored up, son," he said, and then, laughing and clapping Barnsey on the back, he headed out of the bus.

"Wha's that then?" asked Dawn, looking at the half a twenty-dollar bill. Barnsey pulled the other half out of his pants pocket and held them side by side.

"Hungry?" he said.

And she was hungry. He hadn't realized how skinny she was, but she stored away a grilled cheese sandwich in no time and two pieces of apple pie with ice cream. She ordered hot water and fished a tea bag from deep in her ratty black leather jacket.

"Ginseng, mate," she said. "Nothing illegal."

But Barnsey had only been noticing how stained the tea bag was and the little tab at the end of the string, which had strange characters written on it.

It was all so strange. Strange for Barnsey to walk into a place with her, as if they were on a date—a thirteen-year-old and a twenty-year-old. He wondered if people thought she was his sister. He couldn't imagine his parents putting up with the way Dawn looked. She sure turned heads at the Cattle Yard. He wasn't sure if he minded or not. In his burgundy L.L. Bean coat, he didn't exactly look like he belonged in the place either.

It was a huge smoke-filled bar with moose antlers on the knotty pine walls and two or three big TVs around the room tuned into the Nashville Network. There was a Leafs game on the TV over the bar. Just about everyone was wearing a trucker's hat and nobody looked like they were leaving until maybe Christmas.

The bus passengers were herded down to one end where a section had been closed off but was now reopened. The bus drivers smoked and made phone calls and made jokes to their passengers about not getting on the wrong bus when they left and ending up in Timbuktu. Through the window and the blizzard of snow, Barnsey watched another bus roll in.

"I saw three ships cum sailin' in," sang Dawn. She was picking at Barnsey's leftover French fries—chips, she called them—trying to find ones that didn't have any gravy on them. She was a vegetarian.

"Bloody heathen," she'd called him when he'd ordered a bacon burger and fries. He loved that.

"I've gotta go find the loo," she said.

"Bloody heathen," he said.

She flicked him on the nose with a chip as she clomped by in her Doc Martens. He wondered if it was possible to walk quietly in them.

"Rubbish," he said. He watched her walk through the bar toward the washrooms. Somebody must have said something to her because she suddenly stopped and turned back to a table where five guys in trucking caps were sitting. They looked like all together they probably weighed a ton, but that didn't seem to bother Dawn. She leaned up close to one of them, her fists curled menacingly, and snarled something right at his face.

Barnsey watched in horror, imagining a scene from some movie where the whole place would erupt into a beer-flinging, window-smashing brawl. Instead, the guy whose face she was talking at suddenly roared with laughter and slapped the tabletop. The other four guys laughed too. One of them ended up spitting half a mug of beer all over his friends. Then Dawn shook hands with her tormentors and sauntered off to the loo, as she called it.

Barnsey felt like he would burst with admiration. He picked up her teacup and smelled the ginseng. It smelled deadly. The writing on the little tab was Indian, he guessed. From India.

He looked around. On the big TV a country songstress with big country hair and dressed in a beautiful country blue dress was draping silver tinsel on a Christmas tree while she sang about somebody being home for Christmas. Then the image would cut to that somebody in a half-ton truck fighting his way through a blizzard. Same boat we're in, thought Barnsey. Then the image would cut back to the Christmas tree and then to a flashback of the couple walking up a country road with a bouncy dog, having an argument in the rain and so on. Then back to the guy in the truck, the girl by the tree. It was a whole little mini-movie.

Barnsey found himself trying to imagine X.P. dressing that same tinselly Christmas tree in that nice living room. But of course the guy in the truck trying to get home for Christmas would be the grim reaper or something with worms crawling out of its eyes.

Then Dawn came back.

"What did you say to that guy?" Barnsey asked.

She smiled mysteriously. "I told 'im that if he'd said what he said to me in Afghanistan, 'e'd 'ave to marry me on the spot."

It was around eleven before word came through that it was safe to leave. The drivers got everybody sorted out and back on board. Everyone at the Cattle Yard yelled Merry Christmas and held up their beer glasses in a toast. The guy who had been rude to Dawn stood and bowed as she passed by, and she curtsied. Then she made as if she was going to bite off his nose, which made his ton of friends roar again, their fat guts shaking with laughter.

By then Barnsey knew Dawn had just got back from Nepal, where she'd been traveling with " 'er mate," ever since she left Israel, where she'd been working on a kibbutz after arriving there from Bloody Cairo, where she'd had all her kit stolen. Before that she'd been in Ghana and before that art school. Barnsey didn't know what a kit was or a kibbutz. He wasn't sure where Nepal was either, or what or who 'er mate might be. But he didn't ask. She'd called him mate too.

On the bus the excitement of the unscheduled stop soon died down. The roads were only passable so it was slow going. It was kind of nice that the three buses were traveling together. In a convoy, the driver had called it. It sounded reassuring. Soon people were falling asleep, snoring. But not Barnsey. He sat thinking. Trying to imagine working on a flower farm in Israel, the heat, and the fragrance of it. Trying to imagine Bethlehem.

"Was it cold?"

"Freezin' at night," she said.

"See any stables?"

She laughed. "No, but I did see a good-sized shed behind a McDonald's."

Barnsey laughed. He tried to imagine the holy family pulling into Bethlehem today and huddling down in a shed out back of a McDonald's. Maybe Joseph would have a Big Mac. But Mary? Probably a vegetarian, he decided.

Quietness again.

"What kind of a store is it your people 'ave, master Barnsey?"

"A gift store," he said.

"Ah, well," said Dawn. "I can imagine a gift store would be busy at Christmas."

Finally Barnsey dozed off. And the next thing he knew, the bus was slowing down and driving through the deserted streets of North Bay. It was past 2:00 AM.

"That'll be 'er," said Dawn as they pulled into the bus terminal. Somehow she had recognized his grandma Barrymore in the little knot of worried folks waiting.

Barnsey just sat drowsily for a minute while people stirred around him. He felt like he weighed a ton.

"Get on with ya," said Dawn in a cheery voice. And she made a big joke of shoving him and roughhousing him out of his seat as if he was Dumbo the elephant. Then she gathered up all his wrappers and cans and threw them at him, saying, "'Ere—lookit this! Yer not leavin' this for me, I 'ope." Barnsey found himself, weak with laughter, herded down the aisle. At the door he said goodbye and hoped that her trip to Vancouver would be nothing but rubbish the whole way. Grandma Barrymore was standing at the foot of the bus stairs. Much to her surprise, Dawn grabbed Barnsey by the head and scrubbed it hard with her knuckle.

"In Afghanistan, you'd have to marry me for that," said Barnsey.

"Toodle-oo, mate," said Dawn, blowing him a kiss. She blew one at Grandma Barrymore too.

Dawn would arrive in Vancouver on Christmas Eve. Barnsey thought of her often over the next couple of days. He'd check his watch and imagine her arriving in Winnipeg, although all he knew of Winnipeg was the Blue Bombers football stadium, which he'd seen on TV. And then Regina and Calgary. He imagined the three buses like wise men still traveling across the country in a convoy. But as much as Barnsey thought about Dawn, he gave up trying to talk to anyone about her. Grandma had seen her but only long enough to get the wrong impression. And when Barnsey tried to tell his cousins about her, it came out like a cartoon, with her wacky hair and her fat black boots. He couldn't get Dawn across to them—the *life* of her—only the image of her, so he stopped trying.

There was a lot to do, anyway. His cousins had arranged a skating party and Grandma wanted him to go shopping with her and help with some chores around the house. He enjoyed all the attention she showered on him. She spoiled him rotten just the way she'd spoiled his father rotten, she liked to say. But he'd never noticed it quite so much as this year. Anything he looked at, she asked him if he wanted it. It was spooky.

Then it was Christmas morning. It was a four-hour drive from Ottawa. His parents would arrive by 1:00 PM and that's when the celebration would start. When he saw his father's Mustang coming up the driveway at 10:30 AM, Barnsey knew something was wrong.

He didn't go to the door. He watched from the window. They should have come in the big car. But there wasn't any *they*. Just his dad.

"Matthew, go help your dad with his parcels," said Grandma.

"No," said Barnsey. He was remembering the last time he had looked at his mother in the bus terminal, through the window. The look on her face. "It won't be so long," she had said.

It wasn't that his mother was sick or there was some problem at the store; they would have phoned. Barnsey's mind grew icy sharp. Everything was suddenly clear to him. He could see a trail of incidents leading to this if he thought about it. You just had to tilt life a bit, and there was a whole other picture.

His parents weren't very talkative. They didn't chatter; they didn't argue. And yet in the moments while his father unpacked the trunk of his salt-stained Mustang and made his way back and forth up the path Barnsey had shoveled so clean just the night before, Barnsey could hear in his head all the signs and hints stretching back through the months—how far, he wasn't sure. Right up to now, the past few days, with Grandma so attentive. Spoiling him rotten.

Then his father was in the living room, still in his coat, waiting for Barnsey to say something. His face didn't look good but to Barnsey he didn't look anywhere near bad enough, all things considered. Grandma Barrymore was standing behind him with her hand on her son's shoulder. She looked very sad. They waited. Barnsey looked out the window. Old-fashioned lace curtains hung across the living-room window. They were always there, even when the drapes were open. Barnsey stood between the lace and the cold glass. He turned and looked at his grandma through the veil of the curtain.

"I wish you'd told me," he said.

"She didn't know, Matthew," said his father. "Not for sure."

The ball was back in his court. That was the way his parents were with him. Lots of room. His father would not press him. He could wait forever and his father would never start saying stuff like "I'm sorry, honey," or "It's all for the better," or "Your mother still loves you, Matthew." Barnsey could wait forever and he wouldn't see his father cry. He would have done his crying already, if he had any crying to do. His parents didn't hold much with spontaneity.

He glanced at his father in his black coat and white silk scarf. He wanted him to do something.

Barnsey stared out the window.

"When did you get the ski rack?" he said.

"When I needed something to carry skis."

There was a pair of skis on the top of the car. Rossignols.

"They're yours," said his father. "I couldn't exactly wrap them."

Barnsey had been wanting downhill skis. And one of the large boxes piled in the hall was probably a good pair of ski boots. His parents would have read consumer reports about this. Even while they were breaking up.

"Your mother is hoping maybe you'll go on a skiing trip with her later in the holidays. Maybe Vermont."

"That would be nice," said Barnsey. Then he left the window and went to his room. His father didn't follow. It was his way of showing respect. He didn't say that; he didn't have to. He was there for him. He didn't say that either, but it was something Barnsey had heard often. "We're here for you, chum."

Barnsey stayed in his room a long time, long enough to hear both sides of the new X.P. tape he hadn't had time to listen to on the bus. He flipped the cassette cover again and again. The ghoul glowed and vanished. Glowed and vanished.

Then his mother phoned. They had probably worked all this out too.

"Must have been a terrible shock . . . "

"Decided it was the best way . . . "

"We couldn't dissolve the partnership in time for the shopping season . . . "

"Couldn't see us playacting our way through Christmas . . . "

Barnsey listened. Said the right things.

"Do you think we could head down to Mount Washington for a long weekend?" said his mother. "Give those new skis a workout?"

"They aren't new," said Barnsey.

"They sure are," said his mother. "They're the best."

"There's a lot of snow between here and Ottawa," said Barnsey. It took his mother a minute to realize it was a joke. A lame kind of joke.

Then, with plans tentatively set and the call over and his mother's voice gone, Barnsey joined his father and his father's mother in the living room. They both gave him hugs.

"You okay?" his father asked.

"Yes."

"You want to talk now? Or later?"

"Later," he said.

"I think we all need a sherry," said Grandma. She poured Barnsey a glass. He liked the idea of drinking sherry better than the sherry.

They ate lunch and then, since it was Christmas, they sat in the living room opening presents. Barnsey kept glancing at his father, expecting to see a little telltale tear or something. But all he ever glimpsed were the concerned looks his father was giving him.

He took his father's place as the hander-outer. When he came to his own present for his mother, he said, "Where should I put this?" His father piled the package on a chair in the hall.

Barnsey wasn't looking forward to Christmas dinner at his aunt's. His father had already taken that into consideration and would stay with him at Grandma's, if he liked. They'd make something special, just the two of them. But when he phoned to explain things, his sister wouldn't hear of them not coming, and his cousins got on the phone and begged Barnsey to come and try out their new computer game. In the end he went. Nobody talked about his mother not being there, at least not while Barnsey was around. Everyone was really considerate.

In bed he lay thinking about what kind of a place his mother would live in. She was the one leaving the relationship, so she was the one leaving the house. Barnsey wondered whether there would be a room for him or whether she'd just make up a couch when he came to visit. Then he wondered if his father would stay in Ottawa or move back to the West Coast. He lay trying to think of all the many things that could possibly go wrong so that he wouldn't be surprised by anything.

"I just wish someone had told me," he said.

"We'll turn it around, Matthew," his father had said when he came to say goodnight. "We'll make this into a beginning."

Was that from some kind of a book? How could he say that? Couldn't he tell the difference between a beginning and an ending?

There wasn't another man in his mother's life. His father hadn't found another woman.

"At least it isn't messy," his father said. He needn't have bothered. Nothing they ever did was messy.

In his sleep, Barnsey escaped. He found himself back on the bus.

"Rubbish," Dawn kept saying, and she pounded her fist into her palm every time she said it. Then the man in the seat ahead of them turned around, and it was the guy who had been in the country video heading home in his half-ton through a blizzard to his tinsel-happy lady.

"Rubbish," he said. And then all of Xiphoid Process who were *also* on the bus turned around in their seats, pounding their fists and saying, "Rubbish. Rubbish. Rubbish." Soon the bus driver joined in and the whole bus sang an alleluia chorus of "rubbish, rubbish, rubbish."

Barnsey woke up, his head spinning. All he could think about was rubbish. He thought about the talk he had to have with his father that day. His father wouldn't insist, but he would be expecting it. He would say all the right things and, before Barnsey knew it, *he* would be saying all the right things too. They'd talk it out. Get things out in the open. It would all make perfect sense.

Rubbish.

So he left.

He didn't pack a bag, only stuffed a couple of extra things in his backpack. He wasn't sure what a ticket to Vancouver cost, but it didn't matter. He had his bank card. He had no idea what he was going to do and he didn't care. He would not run away like his mother, carefully planning it all out first. How far did that get you?

And so, by nine o'clock Boxing Day morning, he was at the bus terminal, a ticket in his pocket, sitting, waiting. He had his Walkman with him and he rooted around in his backpack for a tape other than X.P. He didn't think he could take that right now.

He had five or six tapes in the bottom of his bag. He hadn't emptied it since the trip. He pulled them out one by one: Alice in Chains, Guns N' Roses, Nirvana, *Rain Forest with Temple Bells*—

Rain Forest with Temple Bells?

Barnsey stared at the tape. He must have packed it up in the dark of the bus without noticing. Then he saw a piece of paper sticking out of the edge of the cassette. He opened the cassette and took out a folded-up note written in pencil.

> *dear barnsey this is for the meal and for the fun and for when the rubbish gets to be too much but you're snoring while i write this so maybe i'll shove the note in your gob!!! no i won't i'll hide it and it'll be your xmas present from dawn xox*

Barnsey found himself shaking. He read the note again and again. He smelled it—trying to catch her scent—and held it and then folded it up carefully and put it back in the cassette. He took out the tape and put it on.

He closed his eyes and let the rain on the bells and the ravens and the smaller birds and the ferns and the trees and the wind fill his ears.

How crazy it had been to wait for the music to start. You had to supply your own. Make it out of what was there. Because there was more than the rain forest. Beyond his earphones there were people talking, departure announcements, a man waxing the floor—they were all part of the music.

Then suddenly there was a voice much closer.

"Matthew," said the voice, and Matthew became part of the music. "Matthew." Barnsey opened his eyes and his father was sitting there beside him. He touched his son's knee so tentatively; it was as if he was afraid the boy might break, like some fragile ornament from the gift store. Barnsey wondered if he would break, but he wouldn't. He was going to Vancouver to find Dawn. He stared at his father, who could not know this.

His father was in his black coat and white scarf, but his hair was a complete mess. Barnsey had never seen his father out of the house unshaven and looking such a mess. His eyes were the worst mess of all.

"You look scared," said Barnsey. His father nodded. He didn't speak. He was waiting, giving Barnsey space. Then Barnsey looked closer into those wrecked eyes and suddenly it occurred to him that his father wasn't giving him space. He just didn't have any idea what to say or do. He was a million miles from the safe world of the gift store. He looked as if all his careful plans had fallen through.

Barnsey wanted to shake him, to knuckle his head, to throw stuff at him, laughing and shoving. To wake him up.

"Here," he said. He took off his earphones and put them on his father.

"What is it?" his father asked. "Is it broken?"

"No," said Barnsey. "Listen closely."

He watched his father listening to the music. Barnsey listened too. He didn't need earphones to hear it.

Fish-Sitting
Gil Adamson

My brother has stopped talking. All he does now is read: kids' books, adult books, newspapers, the cereal box, pill bottles, signs, advertisements and scrawls on the sidewalk. He's the best reader in his class, but they can't make him talk. I'm looking at him now, lying on his stomach on the living-room rug.

"What're you reading, Andrew?" I say. But he just holds it up: Asterix.

I go back to spying on the new neighbors with the binoculars. The new neighbor lady, Mrs. Draper, is out, drinking on the grass of her backyard with someone who isn't her husband. In this way, she is just like the previous neighbor lady. My mother says that maybe it's something about the house itself, like a gas that comes out of the basement and makes people crazy. She's convinced Mrs. Draper is having an affair with this man, and it looks like she's right. Mrs. Draper has her foot up on his thigh and she lets her head fall back, sun beaming on her neck. He's rubbing her ankle and touching her leg. He's got his back turned to me, but I can see the orange hair under his baseball cap and on his forearm. He leans over and retrieves the bottle from under her chair. With Mr. Draper the way he is, I'm not surprised she's opted for an affair.

I can also see my father out there, talking to the Bison. I call him the Bison because he's got this huge head with woolly hair that starts too far back. I imagine a sci-fi world where everybody looks like that. He's kind of shuffling around on his front mat, the blare of sunset throwing his lumpy shadow across the front door. My dad's at it again, I can tell by his expression: open, fatherly. The Bison is spilling his guts.

When Dad comes in I say, "What did he tell you?" Andrew glances up at Dad, wiggles his nose to adjust his glasses.

"The Bison? Oh, well, he's worried about selling junk bonds, mostly because it's just a disgusting thing to do, he's attracted to Mrs. Shiffler down at the corner, and … um, I think that's all. Oh, ya, his first sexual encounter was with his cousin."

That's my father these days. He's spending more time talking to people, mostly because he can't talk to Mum, and as time goes by, he's getting better at it. People seem to trust him, to want to confide in him; he's the stranger on a train. They take one look at him and decide it would be much better to get that niggling little secret out in the open. Men confess to impotence, cheating on their taxes, a desire to drive into oncoming traffic. One lady confessed to poisoning her husband's dog because he always kissed it on the lips. "It was repulsive," she said.

It was good to find out how really warped other people were, because our own home life was a mess. My parents had decided to separate and my mother was moving out. We were all kind of floating because, even though the change had come, nothing had happened yet. This was a time when I wasn't doing too well in school. I don't know what it was, but I felt like summer had come all of a sudden and I had nowhere to go and nothing important to do. My dad would take me aside and do his best to scare the shit out of me about what happens when you let yourself go, but I still felt like it was something other people had to care about, not me. I'd sit in class and enjoy the sound of talking, but I wasn't really there. Some of my teachers worried about me. I saw their mouths move, but it didn't occur to me to wonder what they were saying. And then at night I'd stay up late and stare through the binoculars.

Sometimes, walking along the street, I'd pass by a face I'd been spying on, and it was hard not to say hello. Or worse, to say something like: "How's the zit cream coming?" or "Why do you let that cat lick your toes?" It's true, there was a woman who put her feet out on the coffee table and her cat got up and licked her toes. I'd go through the roof.

It's ten o'clock at night, and I see Mr. Draper coming up the drive to his house. He swaggers, fumbles with the key. In the dark he lets a bottle drop on the stoop. She's locked him out again. I can see his shape from where I sit in my room with the lights off, and I watch as he disappears into the house leaving the door ajar. In a minute she comes out with a dustpan and pokes the shards of glass onto it with a fingernail. Then she's gone and the door is still open, the light from inside glistening in the pool of booze. I can tell something's going on downstairs. It's pretty quiet as usual, no raised voices. My brother comes in and sits on my bed with a book; sometimes he crawls under the bed and reads with only his head and shoulders sticking out.

My midterm report is a wall of rejection, and what's worse is my dad can see I don't care. My parents are like wolves working as a team to pull something down. This is one of the rare moments when they cooperate in anything, and I sit there mostly admiring their self-control. I know I'm a pain in the ass. I know I should be promising things, acknowledging faults or at least trying to look worried. But I can't even manage that.

We're in the kitchen, with the back door open and a lawn mower droning away somewhere. I sit there on autopilot, as usual, watching their mouths move, listening to the grinding machine like it might tell me something useful. When I come back into focus my father is sitting back, looking satisfied. My mother gives me a kiss on the forehead and then leaves the room. I realize that I've agreed to something, but I have no idea what it is. Two days later, Mum gives me a book from the library on tropical fish. "I thought this might help," she says. I tell her thanks. Apparently, I've agreed to do something about fish.

I've always hated school, but now even my girlfriends there are acting like I've got some illness they don't want to catch. We're sitting at a greasy spoon eating fries and gravy, drinking coffee.

"You know," Ginger says, "you used to be a lot more fun." I can tell she's angry for some reason, glaring at me, stabbing her fries in Rosalie's gravy. It's obvious they've been talking about this, because Rosalie looks panicked, like she's thinking maybe it'd be good to hurry away to the washroom right about now.

"You spend too much time with Marty. I don't know what you think is so great about Marty. She's not a normal person."

"What do you want me to say?" I ask, and it's a real question. But Ginger doesn't take it that way.

"See? That's what I mean. You think it's everybody else's problem. You totally change, and it's everybody else that's screwed up, right?"

Rosalie jumps in to save me and tells Ginger to lighten up, what's the point in getting upset, and those are the last words I hear, because I tune out again. I know that if Rosalie wasn't here, Ginger would be pulling out the big guns and talking about my parents, maybe saying I'm unbalanced because of it, or maybe that it's my fault what's happening to them, and to me. Everything she says is familiar, and it all translates into: You are getting on people's nerves. I watch the cook scrape the grill with a spatula, the oil rolling up under it, the thin hiss of metal on metal.

My mother comes into the living room and looks at us. Andrew is reading the *TV Guide*, sequentially, like it is a novel, and I'm spying on the Drapers. Mr. Draper is home and I can see he's throwing sofa cushions around. I wonder why a man would come home early from work to do that. I stop and look up at my mum. She has another fish book.

"This is for when you fish-sit."

"Oh... ya," I say, "when is that?" I have no idea yet what she's talking about.

"I can't remember, but I'll call her and ask." There is a sound of something smashing next door. Mum bends down and looks through the curtains.

"Maybe I'll wait a while," she says.

I stare at my mother in disbelief. It's incredible.

"I have to fish-sit for the Drapers!?!" I yell. But she's looking at Andrew where he sits, his face four inches from Thursday night. "What are you reading, dear?" she asks and strokes his hair. Without looking up, Andrew raises the *TV Guide.*

It's night. On top of being a zombie all day, I can't sleep properly either. I wake up every hour or so and just seethe with frustration. I look out with the binoculars but there is never anything to see. Why can't these people do something interesting—aren't there neighborhoods where people are up all night killing each other? Tonight, I decide to get up and do something useful. I read about fish.

They are pitiful pets, really, but I can see why someone might want a tank in their house; some of them are lovely. There are Japanese fighting fish with their long tails and mutating colors. Glass catfish that are completely see-through. Mollies. Tetras. They have sharks the size of a stick of gum. Hatchetfish with their fat bellies. Piranhas with under-slung jaws, which can grow to the size of trash can lids. I gaze at the pictures of iridescent scales and emotionless eyes and small snapping mouths. I gaze, half dreaming, at the photos of dissected fish, the mushroom-like frill of gills, the strange little sacks and organs all balled up together. There is a plastic ruler, measuring the wreckage; a white pointer, indicating nothing.

Andrew still won't talk. My mother kisses his hair; my father squats and whispers to him and presses his forehead to Andrew's; nothing works. He comes in to my room and we sit together on my bed with our backs against the wall, reading. Neither of us turn a page for half an hour, but our eyes move, wandering over lines of print.

Tuesday, 9:00 AM: excellent. The most excellent things about today are that my mother is calling the movers, and I have the twelve-minute run. Ginger claims she has her period, but the two phys-ed teachers stand in the door to their office, not buying it. They're both huge, spongy and blond, and they wear stopwatches that hang to their groins. One is a man, the other a woman, and no one could ever see the difference between them. Rosalie and I go and get dressed while Ginger begs for her life. In the end, she's just going to have to hurry and get dressed like the rest of us. Marty comes in then, her jean vest looking even tighter, and we all stare at her as we struggle into our gym clothes. She strips quickly, and a dozen pairs of eyes gaze openly at her body, knowing she will start last and finish first. With a body like that she could walk through walls. Marty is my friend these days because, as she puts it, I'm a freak like her.

Lilac bushes and mock orange float by on an undulating field of nausea. I feel like I have needles in my lungs. Every time I come out into the sun I feel ten pounds heavier, and every time I pass under a tree I feel human again. When it's over I sit in the change room and sleep with my eyes open. As people dress and leave, the two doors swing open, then swing closed and a sliver of the hallway can be seen. Marty is out there waiting for me, smoking.

When I'm ready, we go for fries and gravy. We smoke and eat at the same time, which grosses the waiter out. As usual when I am with Marty, I chatter like an idiot and she listens to me in amused silence. I make up weird facts and theories about things, like that curly hair means your mother didn't get enough sleep; things that would bug Ginger. Marty almost never talks, she gives me room. Marty has failed two years already; she's older than any of my friends and she lives by herself in an apartment. Once in a while her twin brother, who looks nothing like her, pulls into town on his bike and she disappears for a week or two with him.

I grab Marty's cigarette and finish it while she fishes another out of the pack and lights it. No one has seen Marty for quite a while, and she's made no mention of her brother, which is intriguing. When I ask her where she's been lately, she grabs the butt out of my mouth, stubs it out.

"You're tired," she says, "go home and sleep."

But I can't go to sleep. Today is the day I have to go over and meet the Drapers, get instructions about their stupid fish, and my mother has made me promise to thank them for the jam Mrs. Draper made. I drag Andrew along for moral support, and he follows me like a sleepwalker. When Mrs. Draper meets me at the door her face jumps out at me, younger than I thought and more friendly too. I'd stared at that face many times, but never really seen it clearly. Andrew stands there in silence and glares at her through his glasses until she invites us in and takes us around the house, looking at what she calls "her babies."

There are tanks everywhere, built into walls, standing in hallways, a big long one that separates the living room from the dining room, and all of them have sheets of paper taped to the glass. On the papers are written instructions, the names of the species of fish, and pet names with quote marks around them. "Dingus." "Ralphy." "Slow Learner." In the fridge they keep a canister of brine shrimp and lettuce for the shark, Arnie, and a shallow dish of larvae for the rest of them. I look at the larvae lying inert beside the Parmesan cheese. I make a mental note to throw out the jam Mrs. Draper gave us.

The husband keeps his distance from me but I can smell it on him from where I am, like orange juice that has been left in the sun. Andrew, whom they've tried in vain to butter up, is staring now at the lists of names, dates, and the feeding and saline instructions like he's committing them to memory. I have to drag him by the elbow as we go from tank to tank. I keep looking at Mr. Draper and he keeps looking at his wife with a shallow, wary grin. She's leaning close to the bright blue tanks and gazing intently at the fish where they swim in slow, pointless patterns. Then she tries to show me a sick crab, which I can't find among all the greenery and pebbles and toy castles; everything I look at turns out to be a rock. She tells me that if the crab dies while they are away, I shouldn't blame myself.

A car horn goes off in the driveway and Mr. Draper says "Jeff." The woman gets this furious look on her face and hustles us out the door, making me promise to thank my parents for offering my services. Andrew doesn't need to be pushed and is already halfway back into our house. They wave goodbye to us and wave hello to Jeff, who is coming up the walk. I recognize him; he has red hair, not as thin as I'd thought, and sandals on, and he has a pair of mean blue eyes. I pause on our porch to see Mr. Draper give Jeff a long, affectionate bear hug and slap him on the back.

"I think that man is their son," I say to my mother. She's in the living room, tossing the cat in the air and saying "Yikes!" over and over. The cat is just as limp as a doll and he's purring.

"What man?"

"The one you thought was having an affair with her," I say.

"Shh!" she looks absurdly at the wall. "Really?"

"The husband gave him a big hug."

"Well, they could all three be... you know... "

Marty is whistling into the empty hallway. She says the only way to find out is to come right out and ask Mrs. Draper. This is typical of Marty, who has the social graces of a snake. I can picture Mrs. Draper just standing there, and then fainting. The only sure-fire way is to sic my dad on them, but my dad has opinions about who he will bother pumping for info, and he thinks the Drapers are creepy.

"Fish," he says. "I hope they move out. Fish is typical of that couple."

I'm thinking about that when Mr. Butcher comes down the hall, and I elbow Marty. She lowers her arm, in which she has a cigarette. A NO SMOKING sign hangs in the cloud over our heads. Marty stands eight inches higher than me so Butcher doesn't see me until he is quite close. The look on his face changes, then, from nervous to blank.

"No smoking, ladies," he says as he passes us, and after a second Marty snorts two pencils of smoke from her nostrils.

By the next morning I understand that I'm disappearing again, like a TV signal bizzing into a simple white dot. One minute I'm by the window in room G44 with an untouched test in front of me and the sun is coming through and I can see my hands lit up on my lap. The next minute I am in the basement, looking at a pipe. Rosalie grabs my belt loop and drags me to art class. She got bored waiting as I stared at a pair of initials gouged in the drywall next to the pipe. I don't know whose initials they are. Just two people. Maybe it's all over between them, maybe they aren't even in school anymore. I tell Rosalie we should scratch a date in there, 1902, and see if anyone notices. It's exactly the kind of anal little thing that drives her crazy about me. She shoves me into a chair, then crosses the room to get away from me. I watch the art teacher's legs come out of her shorts and her elbows that never straighten.

It's the second night I have to feed the fish, and already I've gotten into the habit of leaving the lights off when I walk through the house. I like the way the blue tanks light everything up and shadows of fish move like clouds over the walls and carpet. The tank lights are on timers and the water is heated, so all I have to do is check the temperature, use the saline meter to make sure the water is salty enough, and give them a tiny amount of food. Fish eat practically nothing. I open the wall units at the top, slide back the grill and drop in a pinch of food. It's a foul-smelling kind of lumpy mess. Some of it floats on the surface and some of it drifts down through the water in clots. When I get up on the chair, the fish go wild and they dart at each other, stab right into the air at my fingers, and shoot from the top of the tank to the bottom, scattering the little blue stones. The crabs tuck in under their shells and the snails sucker themselves tight against the glass, as if a bomb was going off.

Arnie the shark stops moving when I come upstairs and into the hallway, his lidless eye looking at me sideways. He's only as big as my thumb, but I think of him as potentially dangerous. The books say sharks simply refuse to mate in tanks, they'd rather chew each other up. Arnie drifts closer to the glass, staring out at my white T-shirt suspended in the gloomy hall. I drop a lettuce leaf in and he stabs and nips at it. The leaf flips and drifts in the lighted water like a sheet carried away on the wind.

Later I sit with my feet up on the dining-room table and watch the fish, or spy through the front window with my binoculars. I have a whole different perspective on the neighborhood from this house—I can see clearly into different rooms. At about nine-thirty, the lady with the cat usually calls someone on the phone. She pulls her hair around and looks at the split ends up close. She points her finger at the air like she's giving an invisible person a lecture. My guess is it's her sister on the phone. I bet there's a lot of fibbing going on, sentences that start with: "And I told him, I said: 'Look! …' " Soon she hangs up, eats out of a small tub of ice cream and watches TV. Then her cat gets up on the coffee table and licks her toes. It hunches over, looking urgent. I can hardly stand it—I have to get up and scratch my scalp and walk around the room in the dark. I also learn that zit cream boy shaves his armpits. Maybe he's a speed swimmer or something. Maybe not. Then there's a teenager, who I think is the Bison's daughter. She smokes leaning out her window, stubs the butts out on the shingles and lets them roll into the eaves trough. And downstairs you can see Mrs. Bison cutting things up: fish, carrots, sausages, frozen lasagna, hunks of gray meat. Mrs. Bison is good with a knife.

But it's all so dull, really. And so it occurs to me to look around inside the Drapers' house, see if I can find anything incriminating. They have a few sexy books on the shelf above the bed, books with creative suggestions to make sex more fun, but they've kept these next to a medical dictionary with horror-show diagrams and photos. It's a combination guaranteed to put the idea of sex right out of your head. I look in all the drawers, open the bathroom cabinet and inspect all the bottles and clippers and foams. But it's a bleak search. No rubbers or sex devices. No drugs. No embarrassing poems or letters. No medications for anything gross or sad. I spend a long time and come up with nothing.

I make my way downstairs in the dark, Arnie whipping back and forth in a panic as I pass, and I grab my binoculars and head for the door. But something stops me. I don't really want to go home at all these days; I just don't know what to expect when I come in the door—maybe one of them fuming silently, or maybe talking to Andrew, trying to communicate with Mars. I stand in the Drapers' hall and look through the binoculars to our front door. The doorknob appears, big as a pumpkin, motionless and strange. I swing the binoculars round, trees dissolving, colors and shapes blurring and re-forming to the outline of my father.

"Dad," I say, out loud.

He is standing in the backyard of our house, in the dark, with his hands in his pockets. If I'd never seen this man before in my life, I would have understood him to be what he is: kind, confused, and moving day by day into a future he can no longer elude.

This Is the Story of My Family
Stuart Ross

There will be no barbecue today.

I'm sitting in my father's fading blue Valiant in the driveway in front of our house, and it's raining. I love the sound of the rain hitting the roof of the car, and there's no place I'd rather be when it's raining. I sit in the backseat for a while, then tumble over into the front seat, clutch the steering wheel, flick around with the headlights, switch the radio on and off. If I leave the radio playing, the battery will die. As I swing the wheel back and forth, I go "errrrk!" I'm Napoleon Solo in *The Man from U.N.C.L.E.* and I'm taking the corners sharp. Then I tumble back into the backseat and sit right in the middle, fold my hands on the back of the seat in front of me and rest my chin on them.

It's getting on toward evening, so it's not really dark yet, but you couldn't call it day either. The rain drills the car roof relentlessly and I close my eyes and listen. Listen to the rain splashing off the roof and the windshield and the windows. The tree on our front lawn, and the bushes, are beginning to sway violently. The car is rocking gently. It's good to be in the car.

The curtains are pulled closed at our living-room window, but I can make out the glow of a lamp inside. I watch for a while, and then a dark shadow blots out the lamplight for a moment and disappears. This is my father. I can tell because the shadow was so large. In a few moments, he'll be sitting on the sofa and reading the newspaper. He'll cough a couple of times and fish for the sports section.

Through the noise of the rain hitting the car, I think I can hear another steady, rhythmic sputtering. In a room on the other side of the garage, my grandfather's foot is going up and down on a pedal, a heavy iron pedal with intricate designs. There's always something to sew, always a pair of pants to take up or take down, a leg to taper, a waist to take in. The needle jumps up and down between his dry thin fingers, tugging at the spool of black thread on top of the machine. Between his teeth, the teeth that he places in his mouth every morning, he clenches a smaller needle with a bit of brown thread dangling from it.

I turn and peer down the block. At the corner, a woman is running up the steps of her porch, pressing close against the door to avoid the rain while she rifles for her keys. I was in that house once and it smelled like fried fish. It didn't smell normal, like my house.

Mist has formed on the inside of the car windows, and I draw a little face with my index finger. Then I rub it out with the side of my hand, and my hand is all wet with a dirty kind of water.

There will be no barbecue today because we only have one of those old metal tripod barbecues, rusted and unsteady, and it doesn't have a cover. Do you think my dad would stand out and barbecue in the rain, holding a newspaper over the barbecue and over his head? He wouldn't do that; that would be crazy.

The room above the garage is my oldest brother's room. The drapes are open, but there's no light on. He's over at his girlfriend's, probably, a couple of blocks away. His room smells like smoke because he smokes a pack of Rothmans every day. I imagine that I'm up in his room, peering out his window down at the car in the driveway, wishing that I were in it, watching the rain splash against the windows, streaming down in jerking rivulets.

My other brother isn't home either. He went to coach a baseball game that I'm sure has been canceled, unless it's in another city.

I look at the living-room window again, and now the light is off. It's pitch-black in the house, but I know they're in there. A face appears at the tiny window in the front door, and it is my mother. I duck down in the back of the car and hold my breath.

Soon I hear her voice.

The Legacy
James Heneghan

When Danny got home from school late on Friday afternoon he found his mam and Mary clinging together on the front room sofa. Their faces were raw from crying.

Father Coughlin and Uncle Matt sat opposite. When they saw Danny, the two men stood.

Uncle Matt said, "Ah, Danny, it's the terrible thing." His face was white. "They've murdered your da."

Danny's heart stumbled.

Father Coughlin bowed his head. "Yes, boy, it's the sad fact, so it is. May the Lord have mercy on your father's poor soul."

Mam sobbed quietly into her pinafore. Mary sat in her lap, arms locked about her neck.

"Let us all kneel and pray." Father Coughlin kneeled on the worn carpet and began praying in a soft murmur. The others made no move to kneel or pray but sat or stood in silence.

Mary was six. She slipped from her mam's neck and ran to her big brother and clasped him about the hips. Danny would be fifteen next month. He stroked his sister's head. Over the murmur of the priest's prayers, he whispered to his uncle, "What happened?"

Uncle Matt shook his head. "Ah, wasn't I there?" he whispered. "Sitting at the bar in Murphy's I was, with Joe Corrigan and Con Gillespie. There was three of them, big bastards with masks. May the devil take their black souls. Rushed in past me and the boys in the bar and into the snug, the guns in their fists exploding like bombs—I swear to God I counted more than a dozen shots, and the walls covered in blood. They knew just where to find them, so they did. They murdered three of them: your da and Tim Reilly and John Lynch. Simon Begley was shot also; he is lying in the hospital, not expected to last the night. Then the gunmen were gone out the back door and down the alley before you could say Sweet Sacred Heart of Jaysus."

Danny could picture it: his da in the snug with his cronies—not one of them with a day's work in five years of looking—and Murphy serving them porter and trying not to listen to their plotting and scheming against their two mortal enemies, Belfast's British army of occupation and the Protestants.

"It's terrible cruel, so it is," said Uncle Matt to himself.

"Cruel and senseless," said the priest, looking up from his prayers. "Irish people killing each other like savages." He grasped the arm of the chair and pulled himself up off his knees and stood peering at Danny through thick spectacles. "The saints are weeping in Heaven this black day. It's the man of the house you are now, Danny. You're the one will be taking care of your mother and sister. God help you in your time of trouble." He made a sign of the cross.

"Who did it?" Danny's pale blue eyes found his uncle's dark ones.

Uncle Matt shrugged helplessly and looked down at his shoes.

Danny turned to the priest. "Who killed him?"

"What's done is done, boy," said Father Coughlin. "There will be no talk of hatred or revenge; isn't the country cursed with it! Isn't hatred the mortal sin of Northern Ireland? Any revenge there is will be God's own, you know that well enough. You'll not suffer the loss of your own soul if any of us can help it, isn't that right, Matthew?"

"That's right, Father."

"'That's right, Father'!" Danny mimicked his uncle's subservient tone.

Danny's mother, a small woman with hollow cheeks and hair more gray than black, wailed anew, her hands pressing to her swollen eyes the faded pink pinafore she wore over her white shirt and brown frock.

"And lose your soul you will," said the priest sternly, "if ye don't mind the holy gospel." He reached to lay his hand on Danny's shoulder, but the boy pulled away. Father Coughlin shook his head. "You've always been the good boy, Danny. Your father was proud of you, the best young scholar in the school—"

Uncle Matt said, "Ah, he was proud, right enough."

"—never missed a day, highest math scores in the whole of Belfast, and your dear mother—"

"Oh, sweet Jesus!" Danny's mother wailed through the pinafore. "Didn't I tell him this day would come. It was only a matter of time. Wasn't I tired telling him! And him sitting above in Murphy's every afternoon like King Dick with his eejit cronies about him, and them forever making fine airy plans for the united Ireland that will never be? Sitting ducks! Ah, sure couldn't any child who had a gun walk in and shoot them all down?"

Danny left them talking. He climbed upstairs to the tiny room he shared with his sister, closed the door, and fell onto the bed where he lay with his eyes shut.

It was January and the room was cold.

After a while he opened his eyes and stared at the picture on the chest of drawers of the four of them on the beach at Bangor, taken five years ago by one of the guests at the Seacliff Road B&B where they had stayed that summer. His own nine-year-old face smiled shyly back at him. His mam cradled the baby in one arm and held her white hat with the other as the wind played with her black hair. And there was his da in his bathing suit, grinning like an eejit, his big hand resting fondly on the top of Danny's head and his red curling hair blowing in his eyes.

He closed his eyes again and remembered Brendan Fogarty, a week before, coming up to him in the street as Danny came out of school. Brendan had been blowing on his hands in the cold air.

"Hello to ye, Danny Dolan," he'd said with a foxy grin on his face.

Brendan, a year older than Danny, had dropped out of school the year before to hang around with a gang of Brit bashers, kids who threw bottles and rocks and apples with nails in them at the English soldiers on the Falls Road.

"Hello yourself," said Danny, wary of the rough-tough Brendan.

"Sean Connor was asking after you."

"After me?" Danny pushed his red hair from his eyes. "Was he now?" Sean Connor was in the IRA, the Irish Republican Army, Catholic freedom fighters. Sean Connor was a bomb-maker, everyone knew that.

"He's recruiting for the Fianna."

"Fianna wouldn't want me," said Danny.

"Sean has his eye on you, right enough."

"He has?" Danny had felt a buzz of pleasure even though he would never join Fianna, the IRA youth auxiliary, not in a million years. He wanted no part of that, the fighting and the killing. Besides, if his da ever found out, he'd leather him black and blue and he wouldn't walk for a week. "What about you then, Brendan—are you a member of Fianna?"

Brendan grinned. "That would be telling, now, wouldn't it."

Danny shrugged and started up the hill away from the school.

Brendan fell in beside him. "Sean said if I taught you a few things he might take you."

"What things?"

"Like how to make a petrol bomb—the right mix of sugar and flour and petrol, the right kind of bedsheets that make good fuses, the right kind of containers."

"Milk bottles," said Danny. "I know all that."

Brendan laughed. "Did ye hear the one about the IRA woman who asked the milkman to leave her one bottle of milk and two empties?"

"Funny."

"I could show you how to make a nail bomb."

"Gelignite and razors. Nails and ball-bearings," said Danny.

"Aren't you the clever little fucker then."

"Not interested," said Danny.

Brendan gave him a push, trying to start a fight, but Danny had laughed and shrugged him off, leaving him standing in the street blowing on his fists.

That was last weekend.

Now, lying on his bed, he opened his eyes. On the wall over the family beach picture there was a picture of the Sacred Heart, Jesus with his long sad suffering face, one hand pointing to his burning heart.

Danny had to get out of the room and away from the pictures. He jumped up off the bed and crept downstairs to the kitchen. They were still in the front room, talking and praying. His mother had stopped crying. He grabbed his thick coat and cap off the peg in the hallway and slipped out the back and along the alley until he came to a cross street, and then he walked.

The cold was numbing. It had come after the snow was almost gone off the streets. Icicles hung under the gutters of the houses. He pulled his cap down over his ears and thrust his hands deep into the pockets of his coat and walked quickly in no particular direction, through the frozen landscape, along Ballymurphy to Cavendish, taking whichever street happened to be there, avoiding the patches of snow turned to ice. He walked through the bleak streets and alleys with their barricades of rusty corrugated tin, brick and barbed wire. There was no grass or greenery, only broken pavement. Starving dogs shivered with the cold. He walked through frozen air hazy with soot and smoke from coal and turf fires, past the houses of blackened red brick, many of them derelict, with bricked-up windows, gable ends screaming FUCK THE POPE! KILL KILL KILL! BLOOD DEBTS REPAID IN BLOOD!

He walked for a long time, up and down and round about, until his feet and calves ached and his face was numb with the cold, until eventually he found himself at Murphy's pub. A sign in the window said CLOSED TILL FURTHER NOTICE.

He kicked on the door and Murphy opened it and stood looking down at him, not saying anything. When the boy didn't speak, he said, "The pub's closed, Danny."

Still he did not speak.

Murphy opened the door wider and stepped back and Danny went in past him into the empty bar and the back room beyond, the snug as it was called, and stood looking at overturned tables and chairs, spilled ashtrays, fragments of broken plaster, shards of glass, shattered pictures of Irish soccer players, cream-gloss walls splattered with blood.

"I'm terrible sorry for your trouble, boy. God rest their souls," said Murphy quietly as Danny pushed his way past him and out the door back onto the cold street.

Undertaker Logan supervised the delivery of the coffin that same night, directing it be laid on the bier placed near the window in the small front room. Danny looked down at his pale da, calmly sleeping, and his mam clutched her beads and cried again. Mary, clinging, cried and would not let go of her brother's arm. Father Coughlin came and said some prayers, and on Saturday there was a steady stream of neighbors who looked in the coffin and were given tea and shortbread biscuits.

His da's funeral was on Monday, following the requiem Mass. Danny shined his brown shoes, the only ones he had, and wore a black band on the arm of his school blazer. He had no best shirt—his two school shirts, no longer white, were worn at the collars—so his mam fetched one of his da's white ones and made him put it on, weeping softly as she helped him roll up the sleeves, which were too long.

After the Mass, he put his coat on over the blazer and stood by the open grave with his mam and his sister and his Uncle Matt. Mary wore her navy-blue wool coat and blue wool cap, and his mam wore a black coat and hat loaned by Mrs. Fitzgerald from next door, whose own husband had died in a bomb blast two years before. The ground was frozen, and the freshly dug earth glistened white. Four coffins—Simon Begley had died in the night. The IRA contingent, a small army of men, were there with their masked faces and their guns and their black berets.

Uncle Matt growled, "If the police try to arrest them there'll be a riot for sure."

The police were out in full force. The British soldiers were there too in their armored Saracen cars. Schools were closed. Milltown cemetery was crowded. Not a blade of grass could be seen, only the hundreds of mourners and their breathy vapor in the cold air.

It was the last Danny ever saw of his da, a dark wooden box on the shoulders of the IRA pallbearers. He watched, dry-eyed, his face pale in the cold sooty air as the coffins were lowered into the consecrated ground and his mam and Mary and his uncle wept.

The IRA pallbearers lined up along the sides of the graves. The priest murmured the prayers.

Whispers carried in the cold. A woman in the crowd behind Danny muttered, "Ah, and I don't suppose there's the bit of insurance left the poor family."

"There's nothing," said another woman's voice. "Tom Dolan had nothing to leave but heartache and tears."

When the prayers were finished the IRA men marched away. The police and the British soldiers held back, watching them go. "There will be no riot, thanks be to God," the woman muttered. "Not this time," said her companion.

Danny watched his mam stoop and gather up a fistful of dirt and drop it into the grave. Mary copied her mother, letting the dirt trickle through her fingers. Father Doyle, the parish priest, made the sign of the cross. Danny turned and walked quickly away.

When he got home he couldn't get in: his mam had locked the door. He walked around to the back, climbed over the wall and sat in the outside lavatory with the door closed, and there, for the first time since his da had been killed, he cried.

The lavatory, like the house itself, was old, with a not unpleasant smell of rot and rust. Toilet paper was a stack of newspapers on a wide pine seat that gathered dust and spiders and flakes of rust from the ancient cistern tucked under the roof. To flush the tank you pulled the chain, which had a wooden handle polished black through years of use.

Danny dried his eyes and nose on the pulled-down sleeves of his da's white shirt. When he had stopped sniffling, he stood on the pine seat and thrust his hand into the dark recess above the cistern, groping around the rusty mechanism to pull out a bundle wrapped in burlap. He jumped down and looked at the thing in his hand. It was his da's gun, heavy, like a lump of iron. The burlap was oily. He unwrapped it and held the gun in his hands, surprised at its heaviness, its deadly blackness gleaming at him like a snake. He stroked the handle with his fingers. How many Protestants had it killed?

He knew his father had been a member of the IRA not that his da ever said anything, there was no need, but Danny had eyes. And he'd known for months about the gun; hadn't he searched every inch of the house and yard until he'd found it. He put the gun down on the seat and climbed up again and felt around the top of the tank. At the back near the wall, he found a box of ammunition. He opened the cardboard box and examined the bullets, then put it back. He looked at the gun again. It gave back a feeling of power. He wrapped it carefully in the burlap and returned it to its hiding place behind the cistern.

He didn't go to school the next day. Instead he took the gun down from behind the cistern, loaded it with ammunition and stuffed it into his belt. Then he pulled on his warm coat and cap, and set off in the cold gray gloom, looking for Brendan Fogarty.

Rock Paper Scissors
Susan Kernohan

"I'm saving it, man." Russ shoved Greg away from the open pizza box. "It's for Tara."

Greg shrugged and lit a cigarette. He bent his head and cupped his hand intently around the flame as if a strong wind might blow through the living room.

"Do you want an apple or something?" Russ asked doubtfully.

Greg's face twitched like he'd just noticed a stench in the room. "I don't want a fuckin' apple, man. When's the last time *you* had an apple?" He shook his head, a shiver of disgust constricting his face. The freckles and unruly hair that had given him a reckless air as a kid were a liability to him at nineteen.

"Well, *Tara*. You know. She's gotta eat." Russ spread his hands to show how blameless he was, how he was a victim.

"Where is she, anyway?" asked Greg.

"At school."

"I'm surprised they let the dumb shit go back. She'll be doing someone else damage next."

"She's not doing woodworking anymore, just math and stuff. And it's the last day tomorrow." Russ was both defensive and dismissive. Tara was his, but he knew it was sort of dopey that she'd cut off her finger. He lit a cigarette and let the smoke rise up between him and Greg.

Tara was putting her new shirt on. It was the same mauve color as the faint thumbprint blotches under her eyes. Russ saw how the bandage on her injured finger was making her fumble with the buttons but already knew she wouldn't want his help. The shirt fit nice and tight around her, had long sleeves and a fold-down collar with a butterfly embroidered on it. Russ had never seen Tara wear anything but T-shirts and sweatshirts. Some aunt had seen the small mention of Tara's accident in the paper and shown up a few days ago with a check and the shirt in an Eatons box. Russ watched *Oprah* while Tara and her aunt talked in the kitchen. When she was gone, Tara had come and sat on the floor near his chair.

"Did you tell her?" he asked during a commercial.

"She already knew. That's why she came."

"I don't mean your finger."

"Oh." Her ink blot eyes had shot up at him. "Not that, no. Why would she care?"

Once she had the last button through its hole, they headed out to Beckers. When they first started hanging out back in December, it was so cold that neither of them ever wanted to go out to the store when they ran out of smokes. Russ taught Tara how to do Rock Paper Scissors, and for a long while there was no dispute they couldn't settle.

"How come you never heard of Rock Paper Scissors before?"

"I'm a freakin' orphan, Russ. Orphans don't get to play games."

Sometimes there'd be a blue spark in her dark eyes that let him know she was joking with him. Sometimes she rubbed and worried the skin on her elbow until it was broken and raw. Her parents died in a motorcycle accident when she was a kid, and she'd lived with different aunts and uncles until she was sixteen and threatened to drop out of school unless they let her live by herself. She moved into the little house near the lake that she'd lived in with her parents and would legally own when she came of age. She kicked out the people who'd been renting it and moved in with her garbage bags of clothes and a rolled-up tube of posters. The house used to be a cottage and it still had a sandy, gritty feel underfoot and windows that let in a lot of winter. Tara left it as it was, and the aunts and uncles would show up from time to time with cast-off Arborite coffee tables and chunks of carpet that slowly filled the house.

The windows at Beckers were covered with skinny winged insects. Millions of them shifting slightly this way and that so the glass itself seemed mobile. Russ and Tara stopped and looked at each other. "Gross," said Tara. "They're just mayflies," said Russ. "They only live for a day or something. I remember them from when I was a kid." He sounded cool, but he was flapping his hands around in front of his face.

"Mayflies? But it's June." Tara opened her mouth a bit the way she did when considering a puzzle. "They must be June bugs." Without giving Russ a chance to respond, she went into the store, unconcerned by the zinging cloud of insects she stirred up. Russ pulled his T-shirt up over his mouth, held his breath and darted in after her.

Russ knew that his friends, especially Greg, thought he was crazy to be with Tara. They thought she was dumb. She'd failed a bunch of grades in elementary school and screwed up her high school classes too. Greg's favorite argument, always delivered with his arms spread wide by outrage, was "For Christ's sake, she got herself fired from packing fish at Purdy's. What kind of a moron can't put dead fish in a box?"

Cutting off her index finger nearly to the second knuckle in woodshop had absolutely sealed Greg's opinion of Tara. He came over the night of the accident and hung out with Russ while Tara slept off the painkillers they'd given her at the hospital. When Russ blushingly told Greg that the doctors who looked after her finger had also announced that Tara was pregnant, and not just fighting off the flu, Greg was hardly even surprised. They were sitting in the backyard at the picnic table and Greg shook his beer bottle so the last few drops fell into the grass.

"Figures," he said. "At least she can get an abortion. There's no way she can get her finger back."

Russ had hesitated before he said, "Actually, thing is, she's thinking she might have the baby. The doctor said she had to make up her mind pretty quick because she's, uh, pretty far along." He glanced at Greg to see if he was following. "It really could go either way. She only has a week or something to think about it."

"Holy shit. What are you gonna do?" Now Greg was surprised.

"Well, this nurse at the hospital gave us a booklet about what Tara should eat and stuff. And…" Russ trailed off. He had just remembered that Tara was supposed to quit smoking. "Yeah," he continued. "So I guess it'll be okay and everything. We'll be careful about food while she thinks about it and then, whatever she decides … " He trailed off again and tried to grin.

"God, you're such a fucking wimp." Greg shook his head in exasperation and lit a cigarette. "You'll be stuck for life if she has a kid, you know. They have kids and then they've got you by the short and curlies." Greg was getting agitated, searching for something to prove he was right. "I saw this thing on TV about men having rights in this kind of scenario. You've got a right to say she should have an abortion. It's the rest of your life, you dipshit." Russ just kept smiling at him uneasily and helplessly. Greg gave Russ a new look, a look that said he deserved to be with Tara. With her mangled finger and lousy luck. Russ felt like he was part of a clumsy two-headed Russ-and-Tara monster that didn't know its asshole from its elbow.

They first met at Huron Lanes bowling alley near Tara's house. Not bowling, but drinking coffee at the tables set up beside the shoe counter. Russ had been hanging out a lot with Kevin Cooper, who lived out by the lake too. Coop was a big guy, kind of slow, but his periodic construction jobs kept him well stocked with beer and cigarettes, which he didn't mind sharing. Russ, and sometimes Greg, would go over to where Coop lived with his mom in the tucked away cluster of mobile homes off Lakeshore Road. Coop's mom asked Russ to call her Barb, and she didn't care about them smoking and drinking. She'd talk with them and remind them to be gentlemen and pour her beer into a glass for her, but sometimes she'd say "I'm sick of looking at you. Don't you have somewhere to go?"

They didn't, so they went to Huron Lanes to nurse coffees and smoke. If Coop had been working, he'd pay for everyone, even insisting that they have pieces of pie left over from league tournaments. Coop's dad was Lou Gualtieri, who controlled most of the construction jobs in town. Lou felt he did his duty by his son by giving him work. He once said to Coop, "If I'd married your mother, life would be very different for you. You'd have anything you want. But she's a whore, your mother. You can thank her for the filthy life you have. Nothing personal, of course." Lou was married with four daughters and lived in a big house with beachfront. All the work on the house was custom: the brick, the tile roof, the interlocking stones in the driveway. Coop's mom would laugh when she talked about him. "Poor Lou, all he wants is a son to give his business to, but his little wifey only gives him girls. If he had any brains in his head, he'd tell everyone he already has a son. You should tell him to go stick his jobs, honey." And she'd pat Coop's head and he'd lap it up like a big Labrador dog.

Tara was usually at Huron Lanes with her friend Cheryl. It was Cheryl that Russ noticed at first. She was stacked, and even from two tables away Russ could smell her fruity soda pop girl smell. But after Russ and Coop had managed to sit with her and Tara a few times, Cheryl stopped coming. "Where's your friend?" Russ asked Tara, trying to sound gruff. Tara gave him a surprisingly shrewd glance through narrowed eyes, but looked away before she said, "There's this stereo salesman downtown she's been after and his wife's away right now." Tara shrugged and butted out her cigarette on her plastic pie plate. "I told her it's stupid, but she won't listen."

So for a while it was Russ and Coop and Tara who hung out at the bowling alley. Coop started working overtime and it was just Tara and Russ. Then Russ started going over to Tara's house, and eventually he lived there. Russ found out he liked lots of things about being with Tara. He liked living away from his stepdad, who he'd never got along with. He liked Tara's stereo and music collection she'd inherited from her dead father. He also found he liked Tara. She profoundly didn't mind most things. When Coop and Greg came over, they could all watch TV together or play Risk or euchre, and Tara would be fine with that. Even if no one else was there, Russ liked being with Tara. She had a habit of humming bits of songs that he grew very used to, the way people living near train tracks will come to rely on the sound of passing trains. She'd add in a few words—half sung, half spoken—and then return to the wandering hum. She even hummed when she was on the toilet, and he could hear her through the walls. She didn't talk a lot, she didn't expect him to take care of her, she was more into sex than any other girl he'd been with, and she didn't bug him about getting a job. So Russ didn't mind that Greg thought Tara was dumb and even Coop once said she was "kinda spacey"; he would point out that neither of them had finished their grade twelve and he would leave it at that.

Russ and Tara went shopping at the pricey new fruit and vegetable store that had opened on the corner across from Beckers. The nurse had told them that Tara should eat fruit, green vegetables and liver and had drawn a box around a sample grocery list in the information booklet. They picked out Granny Smith apples, green beans, iceberg lettuce, green peppers and a bag of frozen peas. At the meat counter Russ said, "I had liver once and it was really gross, man." Tara looked concerned. "Try it though," he went on. "I mean, maybe you'll like it." She held up the Styrofoam tray and examined the shiny purplish meat pressed against the plastic wrapper.

"It's not like I'm going to have the baby for sure," she said and put the liver back.

By the dairy display, Russ said, "I been thinking. If you have a baby, it's my baby too, right?" Tara looked at him blankly.

"What I mean is, I have rights. I have a say in this. It's my baby too." It came out haltingly, when he'd meant to sound sharp and sure, like Greg. Tara was staring straight into his face as if she were trying to lip-read. Russ shifted from one leg to the other and pushed at a wilted lettuce leaf with the toe of his running shoe.

"What?" Tara finally asked.

"Well, it's not like you got yourself pregnant, you know. I was kinda *involved*, I mean, jeez, Tara … " He gestured lamely with one hand.

Tara pushed her long bangs out of her eyes. She looked tired and shrunken. "All I know is I only have a week to decide if I'm gonna have a baby or not. What's it matter if it's your baby or my baby? I still have to make up my mind, and while I make up my mind, I have to eat all this stuff I never had before." She awkwardly picked up a container of cottage cheese with her bad hand, put it in the shopping cart and walked off toward the checkout.

Russ hung back in the store and met up with her again outside, where she was sitting on a parking divider waiting for him. He held up a plastic shopping bag. "I got some liver anyway. I figured I could eat it too, and I bet it won't be that bad. We'll put ketchup on it." Tara was looking back at him over her shoulder.

"Okay," she said, "it's only for a week, right?"

Later that afternoon, Russ sat Tara down and told her she really had to quit smoking. She said if she had to quit, then so did he. They went cold turkey. The first few days they ate three bags of chocolate chip cookies between them and drank a case of beer. On the third day Tara caught Russ smoking in the backyard. She lit up too and they sat at the picnic table, their feet in the long grass, and breathed in big lungfuls of smoke. As the buzz spread through him, Russ felt like he was returning to his body from very, very far away.

"It's better for me than drinking beer," Tara said as she blew out a happy gray breath. Russ knew this to be true—the nurse had said repeatedly that Tara shouldn't drink. Tara wasn't normally a big drinker, since an aunt once told her she was bad at school because her mother was a drinker and that her parents were dead because her father was a drinker. Russ and Tara sat and talked for a long time at the picnic table. They decided that they could each have seven cigarettes a day, at seven necessary times. Number one when they first woke up, because you have to have a smoke then or you'll feel like crap all day. Number two after breakfast just to get ready for the day. They decided they could likely make it through the morning and have number three after lunch, though Russ only agreed to this reluctantly. Number four had to be in the middle of the afternoon. "It's the longest part of the day," Tara said. "I need something to do." Number five was the sacred after-supper cigarette. That's when they had coffee, and they couldn't imagine drinking coffee without smoking. Number six was for relaxing in the evening, and they threw in number seven as a reward for having smoked only six cigarettes the whole day.

"I'll take little hauls," Tara promised.

"But if you keep it, you'll quit, right?" Russ asked.

"If I keep it," Tara repeated as if she didn't know what he meant. "The baby." There was a pause. "Oh, yeah, I'd definitely quit if I had a baby."

Coop hadn't been around and no one had told him that Tara was pregnant. He came by one night to show them the Z28 he'd bought off a guy at work. Greg was there too and Coop wanted to take them all out for a drive, but no one wanted to go. "C'mon guys, it might rain in a while and I want to have the sunroof open for you," Coop pleaded. Greg and Russ were sitting at the kitchen table eating a bag of chips, and Tara was leaning against the counter waiting for toast to pop up. They had all trooped out to the driveway when he first arrived and circled around the car admiringly, but that wasn't enough for Coop. He was high on the sleek black machine and wanted his friends to know that feeling too.

"What's up with you guys? Are you pissed that I have a car?"

"Tara's got a bun in the oven." Greg was the one who said it. What no one said was that Tara would see a doctor the next day to give her decision. And no one was sure what that decision was going to be.

"Hey, congratulations, man." Coop knocked Russ on the shoulder and gave Tara a smile. "My cousin Danielle had a baby a while ago, and I bet she'll give you clothes and all that stuff. She's cool, you'd like her."

"Thanks," said Tara as she tugged at the plastic wrap on a cheese slice, her bandaged finger bobbing uselessly. Russ nodded and shrugged at the same time. He was relieved that Coop was being nice, but he didn't want to let on to Greg. Russ had spent a restless day wishing he could smoke more, and Greg had only made him feel worse. When Greg arrived, he'd asked Russ straight out whether Tara was going to have the baby and Russ had to admit he hadn't exactly asked Tara. Greg had called him a turd and was smoking more than usual, Russ was sure, just to be an asshole. Tara had spent most of the day tanning in the backyard. Anytime she was in the house she didn't pay any attention to Russ at all.

Coop joined Russ and Greg at the table and started going on about his car. Tara was spreading margarine and mustard on her toast and she began to hum to herself, a slow, quiet hum. Russ was glad to hear her and he relaxed enough to really listen to Coop. Greg asked about mileage and bodywork and paint jobs, and Coop's voice was earnest and low as he answered. Russ didn't know the first thing about cars, but listening to his friends made him feel like he did. He lit up his final cigarette of the day—what the hell?—it would be his way of celebrating Coop's car. And maybe tomorrow he could smoke as much as he wanted. There was a pause in the car talk and they all heard Tara singing. She became a bit quieter when she noticed she was singing into a silence, but she went on:

I believe He healed the lame man and He made the blind man see,
and He washed away our sins that day He died in Calgary.

Greg turned to Tara, smirking. "Did you say Calgary? A song about Jesus in fucking Calgary?"

"It's just a song I remember, okay?" Tara said, waving her cheese and mustard toast at him.

"Well, you remember it incorrectly, then, 'cause Jesus never went to Calgary."

"I went to church, you know, with my nana. She taught me that song and she was really religious. It's Calgary, that's what the song says." Tara looked to Russ and Coop, but they both shrugged. It was the first Russ had heard of Tara going to church and having a nana.

"I hardly think so." Greg was enjoying himself. There was nothing he liked better than being sure. "I saw the biography they did of Jesus on A&E and he lived in Bethlehem and Nazareth, not Alberta."

"There's mountains out there, right? And there's always mountains in Bible stories." Tara was faltering. "Maybe it's about what it might have been like if Jesus came to Canada." She frowned, then went on with a new firmness. "My nana knew everything about Jesus. She always had a Bible in her purse. There's no way she'd forget where Jesus went and what he did."

Greg held up his palms in mock surrender. "I guess your grandma must have met Jesus when he did his cross-Canada tour. I'm sorry I tried to educate you. I didn't know your fucking grandma was personal secretary to Christ."

Tara plonked her plate of toast down on the counter and leaned toward Greg in a mean-looking hunch. "Don't freakin' talk like that about my nana. She was the nicest person in the world. She took me to church and the Dairy Queen every Sunday. She taught me it's wrong to swear and I never will. And when I have my baby, I'm calling her May, after my nana." As she finished, she stepped back from Greg and put her bad hand on her belly. It hit Russ for the first time that there was a baby inside her. A baby with bones and blood, arms and legs.

"So you're actually having it?" Greg asked. He crossed his arms and settled in his chair. "You actually think you can take care of a baby?" Tara just glared.

Russ felt clammy behind the knees, and he couldn't do any of the things he should have. He should have told Greg to get out of the house if he was going to be such a jerk, and he should have moved to Tara's side. He should have at least said, Take it easy, why don't we go for that drive before it rains? But he felt cold all over and couldn't move. He'd felt the same way before a BMX race that his stepdad made him enter. Russ had never raced, didn't have the flashy elbow pads and goggles that the other boys wore so easily. He had clutched his handlebars and stayed in place when the other racers exploded away from the starting line.

"What'll you call it if it's a boy?" Coop suddenly asked in the midst of the quiet.

"We'll call him Cal," said Russ, just as suddenly. "For Calgary."

The Art of Embalming

Diana Aspin

dreem on
denial can kill th magik lanterns

th smell uv wild roses hunee n love
whistuling harmonee with th meadow
larks in th pine treez being who we
relee ar all thos cells selvs living
yr eyez in th morning gold rays
serching thru th mist for food
briteness finding it finding
th watr
—bill bissett

Clive Pinner, named after his great-grandfather, Art, slipped the book of poems into his backpack and peered into his locker mirror. The broken mirror made a jigsaw of his long, pale face. It shattered his eyes and mouth. As he smoothed down the red curls at the nape of his neck he caught the reflection of Toby Dagleish leaning against the locker next to his.

"Hi," Toby said, his voice faintly mocking.

Shutting his locker door, Clive nodded. He took in Dag-the-Fag's long legs, his leather pants, the bronze silk shirt draped in the hollow beneath his ribs. The button above the silver stud of his pants was open, revealing a tear-shaped area of belly.

"Bissett's reading in Toronto tomorrow. The Bibliophile on Church Street. Seven sharp."

Toby's eyes were pools of ink. Clive felt a prickle of sweat on his upper lip. Heat swam to his cheeks. He became aware of his dull clothes: plaid shirt, jeans, Doc Martens.

"You seemed to dig bissett's stuff when he read to the class."

Clive struggled to keep his breathing even. Where were all the imaginary conversations he'd had with Toby? Conversations in which he was ultra cool, sexy even.

Worse than his tongue turning into a piece of cheap leather, though, was what he did next. Keenly aware of the heels that stopped hitting the dusty wood floor, of the turned heads, the stares—for Toby was the only in-your-face gay person at Muskoka High—he snapped back, "Not my kind of thing."

Not his kind of thing! As though Toby's yearbook photo wasn't tucked into the secret pocket of his backpack; as though he didn't read bissett's poem "dreem on" over and over. Each time imagining himself so close to Toby he felt his hot breath waft his cheek, felt Toby's hand, with its elegantly tapered fingers, on his thigh. Felt the blond wave that swept Toby's forehead brushing his own.

"Not *your* kind of thing?" Toby raised an eyebrow at Clive and smiled. A smile involving his full, pouting lips, but not his eyes. Under an arched brow Toby's eye, like that of a hurricane, seemed to gather scorn. Then it bore into Clive. You're a skinny little runt of a coward, the eye screamed; you're not even worth hating. With a grunt, Toby pulled himself from the locker and sashayed on down the corridor.

Clive's heart wobbled in his chest. Shit! For the past few months he'd taken to freaking out: he sweated, his lungs seized, his heart flip-flopped like a dry fish.

"Here, idiot." Jewel's voice sounded hollow and far away. Her plump black-nailed fingers grabbed his books and slipped them into his backpack. "What's with Toby?"

"Nothing," Clive said. "Let's split."

His best friend ran along beside him, tugging at his sleeve. "What do you mean, nothing?"

As they hopped on the bus, Mrs. Rochford, the driver, asked, "What's with you two?" Reena Rochford sat up front behind her mom, her pet rat, Executioner, tucked under her tangle of dark hair.

Jewel stopped to lift Reena's hair. "Hi, Ex," she said loudly. "At least rats don't lie." She scratched the rat's chin and he ground his tiny orange teeth in pleasure. Jewel offered Reena a chocolate crème egg from the cache in her pocket, and they quietly nibbled all the way back to Sky Falls.

In the gravel parking lot of Tackaberry's Auto, the school bus ground to a halt. Jewel leapt off, tripping over Tombstone, Clive's gray curly-haired mutt. Through the park, her open ski jacket flapping, she raced to the public dock.

"Wait up!" Clive yelled. Alarmed, his dog swayed right, tottered left, yelped, then farted. Tombstone Pinner was a yelping, farting radar for human emotions; he dealt with any overload by keeling over and playing dead.

Clive put a hand out to soften his dog's blow but Tombstone had spotted Jewel leaping onto the frozen lake, her long braid flying. She was heading for the fishing huts about a hundred yards from shore. He knew her pockets were crammed with chocolate eggs. For a medium-sized dog he could move pretty fast when tempted. Long shaggy legs going like steam pistons, he set off after her. *Woof*! Come back! *Woof*! Wait up!

By the time Clive, puffing and panting, reached the fishing huts, Jewel, warmed by the sun, had shrugged off her coat. She was sprawled in a lawn chair outside One-Eyed Charlie's hut, the one with the fancy drapes, while Tombstone sniffed around inside it. Digging an egg from her pants pocket, she peeled off the foil and sank her teeth into it. "I thought we were best friends." She spat foil in Clive's direction.

"We are."

"So what's going down with Toby?"

"With who?"

"Toby."

"Nothing."

"Liar. I thought best friends told each other everything." Jewel pinched foil from her tongue.

Best friends! Clive punched his fists into his pockets. That was one of his problems: He and Jewel were best friends, and that was all. The guys were always asking if he'd made it with her yet. He just smiled when they asked—wouldn't you like to know! What he'd like to know was why he loved a boy called Toby instead of a girl called Jewel.

It wasn't as though Clive hadn't tried a million times to summon up the feelings he was supposed to have. Jewel had freaky hair for starters; that dark rope of a braid snaking down the back of Charlie's ice fishing chair, the late-afternoon light pulling shades of blue, black and purple from it. And her full breasts were a turn-on for every guy on the planet but him. He wondered how she and Destiny Webber could be sisters, Destiny so much like a stick insect, Jewel rounded curves.

Clive sighed and stared miserably at Jewel's nipples, raised by the cold, beneath her pink sweatshirt. He thought about his dad, Gordy, Sky Falls' funeral director, about the way he was always trying to figure out if Jewel was more than a friend.

"What are you looking at?" Jewel snapped, jumping up. Shards of foil showered from her. "You some kind of pervert?"

Clive stormed off toward the rocky shoreline. No way was he a pervert! He leaned heavily against the ice-slicked rock and took a deep breath. If you're not a pervert, Clive Pinner, what are you? A freak of nature, hissed the nasty little voice inside him.

That's what some of the guys at school called Toby. Freak of nature. Dag-the-Fag. Sicko. And worse. Much worse. Clive's throat felt narrow as a straw as he sucked in air.

"I take that back." Jewel tramped through the rock's slushy runoff toward him. She touched his arm. "There's no way you're a . . . "

Clive shrugged her off and turned away; he didn't want Jewel to see him freaking out. Tombstone, peering at them from Charlie's distant fishing hut, barked in alarm.

"Look at me." Jewel jerked Clive back by his sleeve.

Clive lurched forward, dug the heels of his hands into his thighs and wheezed, "I can't . . . I can't . . . " His heart skipped rope. He tugged at the neck of his shirt. The collar ripped from its moorings. He slid to the ground. He was going to die!

Then Jewel was over him, her usual bossy self. "Breathe," she ordered, while Tombstone, over to see what all the commotion-emotion was about, danced at his feet like a circus bear. "Breathe."

Clive shot her a twisted smile. "Easy for you to say."

Jewel dropped to her knees and placed an arm around his shoulder. "You're having an anxiety attack, kiddo." With her mittened palm, she made tiny circles between his shoulder blades. She'd learned this from her mom, Dee-Dee. Dee-Dee Webber was Sky Falls' psychotherapist-cum-massage-therapist-cum-Tarot-card-reader-cum-past-life-expert.

It was rumored that Toby had been seen strolling down the dirt road that led to Dee-Dee Webber's Healing Haven; maybe that was why, lately, he seemed to spring back from each insult so quickly. But Clive wasn't Toby. He didn't want to be called Sicko. He didn't want to have his hand slammed in his locker door by Tim Pearson, Sky Falls' bully, or have his lunch bag heeled into the ground by Bull, or have the shit kicked out of him behind the bleachers by—yes—Bull.

"One, breathe, two, breathe, three . . . "

Clive was glad for the chocolaty smell of Jewel's breath; soon her circling hand calmed him. They leaned side by side, their backs against a cliff. "I feel so stupid," Clive said.

"You know what's wrong with you?" Jewel pushed herself from the rock and snapped off an icicle. "These anxiety attacks. All Mom's clients have them—until they've spat out what's bugging them." She jabbed him with her icicle. "Wanna hear this story she told me?"

Clive rolled his eyes. Tombstone rubbed his nose into the space between Clive's jeans and his boot and whimpered; Clive smoothed out the fan of grizzled hair above his dog's golden eyes. "Go on then."

"Well," Jewel began, "Alexander the Great, some sort of hero, was going into battle and his knees were knocking. 'Let's not go!' his knees begged. 'Pretty please!' Guess what he said to them."

Clive shook his head.

"He said in this booming voice, 'You think you're shaking now, knees! You'd be shaking more if you knew where I was taking you.' That rocks, eh?"

"Yeah, it rocks," Clive said glumly. And before he could stop himself, "So does being normal."

Jewel bobbed and feinted, slashing the air with her icicle. "Normal?" She drove the icicle between a cavernous crack in the ice.

Clive thought of that tear-shaped area of Toby's belly. He thought of the dyed blond wave that swept Toby's forehead. Of how he would like their minds and bodies and souls to be as tightly and securely wound as the strands of Jewel's braid.

"What do you mean, normal rocks?"

Clive couldn't explain. Not while she played at warriors with a stupid icicle. In the old days he'd have broken off his own icicle and fought her to the death. But now, even if he wanted to tell Jewel about himself—and he did—how could he? Jewel, I'm a faggot. Cool, eh?

Once the words hit air there'd be no going back.

"Cat got your tongue?"

"You wouldn't understand."

"Drop dead!" Jewel smashed her icicle against her thigh. Running back to the hut, she slipped into her coat and marched off, one side of it flapping, the other side heavy with chocolate eggs. Tombstone, alarmed, followed, zigzagging in her wake.

"Come back!" Clive yelled.

"Jerk!" Jewel shouted over her shoulder. "Loser!" She marched on, then spun around. "Moron!"

Tombstone whimpered as he ran, keeling over every few yards. Then he rolled onto his back and lay there on the ice like a dead thing.

The sight of him in the distance, looking like an abandoned upside-down table, stirred Clive's love for him, along with a sadness almost too much to bear.

Clive huddled under the light at the public dock until the clump of shimmering birches on the far shore, at the edge of the Skinner property, surrendered to silhouette and a clipping of moon began to rise behind them.

How long had he known he was different? He remembered feeling different even before kindergarten. Back then, though, it was a no-name feeling. Like someone handing you an orange. You know it's an orange because of its color, and its pitted skin, and the oil that flies off it when you twist the peel. But no matter how hard you try, you can't figure out the word for it. Then suddenly he was twelve and he had the word for why he felt different. And he hated it. Then he got the red-hot hots for Toby Dagleish and he stopped pretending, at least to himself.

Clive fished the laminated picture of Toby from his backpack and studied it as he'd done a hundred times before: the bright darkness of Toby's eyes, the even teeth, the blond wave sweeping his forehead. By the lockers, how could he have treated Tony like that? Like a piece of shit. But if he'd been enthusiastic about the bissett reading, everyone in that corridor would suspect that he too, was a freak of nature. A fag.

If Clive had been Toby—harassed, alienated, beaten up—he would have hung himself by now. Seriously.

Clive shivered and thought, with sickening dread, of his dad, Gordy. Bearded, macho Gordy Pinner, waiting for his only son to bring home a nice girl. It wasn't much for a father to ask, was it? Clive thought of his great-grandfather, Art Pinner, Sky Falls' first ever funeral director. At almost 102 years old, there wasn't much left of Art: wheelchair-bound, frail as a fall leaf and talking crazy most of the time. Perhaps the Pinner family was destined to have its screwballs and he was just carrying on the family tradition.

The previous week, Clive's dad had been lost in thought over a coffin, adjusting a corpse's head on its pink pillow, rearranging a freshly washed gray curl at its temple. Gordy was putting the final touches on what he called a "memory picture" of old Sadie Sinclair, a last view that wouldn't give her relatives endless nightmares. He'd drained her blood and replaced it with embalming fluid. He'd sucked out her organs, sluiced the cavity with preservative, fleshed out her cheeks and scrubbed her teeth with Bon Ami tooth powder. Then he'd stitched up and lipsticked her lips.

"I'm outta here, Dad," Clive whispered, glancing down at Sadie, mesmerized as always by his dad's transformations. Sadie looked granny-ish, like a woman who bakes and knits and chucks babies under the chin. Not like the cranky, beady-eyed person from the trailers down Biggar Lane. Not like the Sadie he knew who shot black squirrels with a .22. The Sadie who drank Scotch from the bottle and kept company with Sky Falls' Mad Margaret. Rising from a bouquet of satin and lace, Sadie's head looked more like a trophy than her real, true self. The last time Clive talked to Sadie she'd looked enormously like Sadie: baggy work pants, a red checkered shirt and a baseball cap with an orange Day-Glo fish attached to its brim.

"Quit walking across my lawn!" she'd yelled at him, the fish bobbing in agreement. Which was Sadie through and through. Clive suspected Sadie would put some shot in his dad's rear if she could get her hands on him. Drop that lipstick, Gordy, she'd bellow. And what's with those damn prissy curls, eh?!

"I'm going out, Dad," Clive repeated.

Gordy, busy arranging Sadie's manicured hands, left over right, hands slightly cupped for a natural effect, lifted his broad hands from hers. He rubbed his red beard and frowned. "A date?" Then a grin, a flash of gold filling.

Clive's mouth dried up. A sharp pain, the size of a pebble, lodged itself in his throat. "No, Dad."

"Somewhere special?"

Clive took a deep shaky breath. "Nowhere special," he said, turning, fleeing. He'd charged smack into the electrical hoist used to move the cadavers from the prep table to the casket, almost knocking over his dad's tricks of the trade on their steel cart: scissors, augers, basins, clamps, needles and thread. And the trocars, used to suck the guts right out of you.

The incandescent moon was above the birches now, a sequin glued to the midnight-blue bolt of sky. Under the dock light, Clive took out his book of bissett's poems: *What we have*. Reading the poems always cracked him open; some tight scared part inside of him unwound and he felt larger, bolder. Even his breathing deepened and settled into a rhythm of its own. Clive read:

denial can kill the magik lanterns
th smells uv wild roses hunee n love
whistuling harmonee with th meadow
larks in th pine treez being who we
relee ar all thos cells selvs living
yr eyez in th morning gold rays
serching thru th mist for food
briteness finding it finding
th watr

Being who we really are, all those cells, selves, living.

Clive thought about his own cells. He imagined himself living like he really should, his insides matching his outsides. Like Toby, he thought. Like Sadie before his dad got his hands on her. And what about the denial that could kill the magic lanterns? He imagined them as smaller versions of the lanterns on his patio at night, the ones that lit up all the dark and creepy corners of the yard. Would denial kill the magic lanterns inside him, the ones that lit up the real Clive? And: your eyes in the morning! Awesome. How could bill bissett have known how he felt about Toby's eyes?

It seemed to Clive that in some weird way time had folded like a pack of cards, and bill bissett was writing his words at the very moment Clive was reading them. It seemed that personal! He sensed the poet next to him, scribbling away, looking just like he did on the cover of his book: his white blazer, his enormous shades.

Yes, bissett was writing these sweet words, right here, right now, just for him, Clive Pinner. Old Gramps Pinner was right: life was miraculous; it did work in mysterious ways. Bissett was saying to him: Go for it, kid.

Clive had forgotten it was his dad's monthly poker night. The kitchen reeked of rubber boots, beer and pizza. Frank Miller was regaling his dad's buddies with stories about his son, Shoulders, who'd applied to go to Indiana State. Whenever Clive saw Shoulders on the field, or watched him strut his stuff down the school corridors, he felt a frisson of shame at his own puny unsporting self.

"He's always been tough, your Shoulders, eh?" Rod Tackaberry, Sky Falls' auto mechanic, said. His voice was flat, his face longer than ever since his wife died.

Clive's dad said, "That kid's going places."

"Going places good." One-Eyed Charlie fixed Gordy with his good eye.

Clive snatched a carton of milk from the fridge and slammed the door. I hope Shoulders leaves this town and never comes back!

"I remember that little guy," Rod Tackaberry said, smacking his cowboy hat firmly onto his head. "Knew he was headed for a football field even then."

Clive knew that if his sister Amy had been there she would have cheered them on. Amy loved Shoulders; she'd been saying she would marry him since she was six.

There was a ripple of agreement about Shoulders, followed by comments about his heritage. Shoulders had been adopted by Alice and Frank when he was a baby. Shoulders was pure Mohawk Indian. "You must be proud of him, Frank," Gordy said, dishing out cards.

Clive stared at his distorted reflection in the fridge door. His dad's words had been like a punch in the gut. Proud of him. If his dad thought Shoulders was a son to be proud of, what did he think of him?

Clive's milk overshot the glass. "Shit," he whispered, biting back tears.

His great-grandfather, slumped in his wheelchair between Gordy and Rod, lifted his hairless head and squinted in Clive's direction. "Everything okay there, Sonny?" he asked. "Lost something?"

Clive lay in bed feeling the vibrations of Moose Radio through Amy's wall. His sister was everyone's favorite. For starters she was the spitting image of Gramps' mom, after whom she was named. The small framed photo in the living room proved it: same oval eyes, same curly hair. Gramps said Amy had the same wicked temper. He was a disappointment to his dad, Clive knew that. A failure at sports, no girlfriend, and no plan to be a funeral director like the Pinner men before him. After the music stopped, he listened out for the sound of Amy sucking her thumb, which, at age fifteen, she still did. All night long, like a train shuffling along its track, bissett's words jogged through his mind. *Being who we really are, all those selves living. Being who we really are. Being who we really are.*

Until at dawn, exhausted, sitting by the window with Toby's photo in his lap, the words seemed to shake loose from his head. They entered his torso, his arms, his legs, the very core of his being, and he knew what he had to do.

On Church Street, at the back of the Bibliophile, a rickety old table leaned under a pile of books, bizarrely decorated T-shirts, Styrofoam cups and a wooden rattle. Folding metal chairs were set in a semicircle, and a paper-thin woman with a tragic sort of face sipped coffee and jiggled her foot. A plump woman in jeans and a denim cowboy shirt sat with a baby on her lap, its pudgy hands grabbing air.

Over in a corner, a group of kids huddled around bill bissett, a tall man with fine blond hair fanned out across the epaulets of his leather jacket. Clive looked away shyly when he saw two boys shoulder to shoulder, their hands linked in the space between them. He tried to imagine that happening in Sky Falls—and couldn't.

A woman with a long skirt, work boots and a shiver of bracelets appeared. "Okay! Let's begin!" *Let's begin.*

Clive looked around to see if Toby had come, but he hadn't; he wasn't sure whether he was glad or sad about that. It's only a reading, he told himself, his heart starting up.

Bill bissett lifted the rattle from the table and stood with it raised to his shoulder, eyes closed. He breathed deeply in and out, then raised the rattle above his head and smacked the air sharply with it three times.

Clive's jaw dropped as the man began to chant. Amazing sounds issued from his parted lips, like colors it seemed to Clive: deep midnight blues, high-pitched yellows, throaty reds. A silence fell about the room; even the baby stopped its fussing and regarded the poet solemnly.

Then, swaying to a rhythm only *he* could sense, bill bissett tipped his head, as though attending some sound deep down inside him. The silence in the room wasn't an awkward silence but one in which Clive's gut relaxed and his heart steadied.

As the poet read, the mother undid the tiny pearl buttons of her cowboy shirt. Cradling the baby's head in her open hand, she drew him in. The baby turned his plump face to her breast, twitched as his lips sought the nipple and latched hungrily onto it.

"... the human soul did not look afraid," the poet said, his voice so generously gentle, "... is this what happens when we are freed of other people's trips, our own."

Soon the poet had them laughing, a poem about snot on the bookcase above his bed, one about Mr. and Mrs. Rabid Raccoon, another about tiny anchovies with feet and lips. Clive smiled as the tragic face of the thin woman morphed into its less troubled, more open self and the two boys unlinked their hands, gave themselves high fives and kissed.

Kissed!

Changing tracks, the poet spoke so softly that a hush fell. The audience leaned forward as one to catch his words. "Gypsy dreams," he began, "we always get forgiven, we can count on it, if we even halfway keep faith with our dreams."

Clive stirred in his seat. *He* had dreams. But no way did he keep faith with them. Like Toby, or the dead Sadie Sinclair and her friend Mad Margaret, this man was not afraid to show his feelings; turned inside out *he* would look exactly the same. Clive felt himself opening. It wasn't just him either. The baby pursed its lips around its mother's nipple, its eyes rolled back ecstatically into its head. The tragic woman's leg stopped jiggling.

"Isn't there always someone looking in on us, isn't there," the poet asked, "when we think about it, isn't there always more going on than we thought… is it angels gazing so so lovingly at our losing again… "

Clive sighed.

The baby burped. Brrrr-up!

"Any requests?" Bisset held the rattle to his chest.

"Yes!"

Toby's voice races along Clive's skin like a jolt of electricity, lifts the hair from the back of his neck.

Turn around, Clive tells himself. *Now!*

And when he does, there's Toby Dagleish, *his* Toby, his beautiful in-your-face Toby, leaning against a wall.

"I wish I were the one!" Toby shouts, raking his fingers through the amazing blond wave at his forehead. His dark eyes rivet Clive to the chair.

Clive turns away, sweating. His hands tremble. His stomach cramps.

"I wish I would be the one you would be in love with," the poet begins.

Clive has never been this frightened. What has he set in motion by coming here? If he has the courage to turn back, will Toby still be there?

"I wish I would be the one you would fall in love with, talking strong and intimate with each other." Bissett sways, as though his whole body is an instrument from which his word-music flows. "The vessel plowing through the ice and frozen dolphins."

Turn!

Turn!

It is the bravest thing Clive Pinner has ever done. His eyes lock with Toby's. *Yr eyez in the morning gold rays / serching thru th mist for food / briteness finding it finding / th watr.*

Camping at Wal-Mart
Ania Szado

Eureka parked the Airstream too close to the garbage Dumpster and she's too stubborn to move it, even though at night half the neighborhood comes driving up with their headlights off to slip their trash bags in with Wal-Mart's.

"I can't believe it," I tell Eureka. "Can't these people wait for garbage day?"

"Oh, Evelyn, it's summer," she says, as if I can't *smell* that it's summer, "and they probably got their garbage pickup cut to once a week."

Eureka thinks nothing of changing towns once a week, taking her whole life with her, but she don't think it's strange that those people can't handle a change in their garbage pickup. Eureka's from the that's-just-the-way-God-made-them school. It's always "Settle down now, Evelyn! No reason to get in a flap! That's just the way God made that lady driver. She's going places, that little lady. Nothing we can do about it."

Mouth the words with me: *Nothing we can do about it. That's just the way God made her.*

I'm gonna tell you something that Eureka doesn't know I know. This is it right here: Eureka doesn't even *believe* in God!

I wish I could really ask Eureka, *If you don't believe in God, then who did make that little lady and all those fine people out there?* But I can't ask her, because Eureka is a recovering alcoholic, and to keep on being a recovering alcoholic, she's not allowed to not believe in God. That's why it's a secret.

Eureka lets things be what they are. She's really my granny, but she's been watching me for years. I'm gonna be fourteen soon—as old as my mom, Cathy, was when I was born. When I was almost thirteen, Cathy said she was gonna leave town and take me with her—"Little Evvy" she called me, even if I'm taller than her now, I bet—so Eureka just walked out and started up the truck with the Airstream hitched on, and I hopped in right beside her, because ever since Eureka got to be a recovering alcoholic I've had to keep a close eye on her.

Our first night at this Wal-Mart, someone knocked at the door, and I started staring at Eureka like we were in trouble for sure. But she just waddled over, wiping her hands on her dress, and crouched down at the door with a friendly smile, and I could just see below her jiggly arm that a nice-looking guy was there, and his girlfriend was waiting on his motorcycle. And he said, "Hi. I was admiring your trailer. You folks come all the way from the coast? I wouldn't mind making you an offer if you're thinking of putting down roots here. Always wanted an Airstream."

I know this trailer is a collector's item. When we stop in cities there's people that always stare. They look at us like we don't deserve it too, just because Eureka's so wide and I'm, whatever, scrawny, or maybe I don't wear makeup so I don't look like a model yet, which is what I'm gonna be when Eureka lets me. Eureka's careful, and that's why the Airstream still looks so nice, and still a bit shiny, and not hardly dented, and why I'm not a model yet. I know those people might look nicer than us with an Airstream trailer, but that don't bother me, because one day I'm gonna look nice too, sitting here, right here, all alone in the driver's seat, hauling this hunk of aluminum all over the country.

The other time my mom said she was gonna take me and go somewhere, just me and her, and Eureka said, "No way, Jose," in her calm voice like vanilla pudding, Cathy yelled real loud, "It's my goddamn God-given right," and Eureka said, "There ain't no such thing."

That was my first clue. After that, I watched Eureka pretty close.

We are not the only people in this parking lot. There's a family with a tent trailer across the lot. They shop all day and put the tent up at night. They never seem to buy anything, but I've seen them waiting for the doors to open in the morning.

I think our truck has broken down again. We've been camping here for six days now, and the only time Eureka stays somewhere so long is when there's no gas or the engine's busted. Mostly she'll find someone, maybe someone from the back warehouse or a hardware store, or one time it was a guy from a slaughterhouse, someone who knows about motors, and they'll just fix it for her. She says big men like big engines and they're happy to help. She sends me shopping or walking a while, but I know what's up. First they tinker with the engine, then they fiddle with Eureka.

Eureka says we might have to go meet those people with the tent trailer, because it would be the neighborly thing to do. I just look at Eureka like she's nuts.

Okay, I'm gonna tell you a sad story and it's totally true. There's two girls living in that tent trailer with their dad and his girlfriend, and they never, ever, if you can believe it, lived anywhere else. Jennifer told me. She's nine, which isn't as bad as it sounds.

Eureka made me go and talk to them after I got back from the store. She always sends me shopping when we need toilet paper or cheesy crackers or whatever. She always says I'm so skinny that if someone looks at me I should just turn sideways and I will disappear. That's not true, though, because my shopping jacket is pretty baggy.

When I got back from Wal-Mart, those girls' dad was by the Airstream. Jenn and Reba were hanging out, staring at me, and Eureka said all happy, "Evelyn, honey, these girls can't wait all day! Off you go back to the store with them and have yourselves a nice time." She looked like she was gonna give me some money, but she just squeezed my hand.

Jenn says her dad's girlfriend sleeps all day in the car and her dad always says not to wake her. How can someone sleep all day for nine years in a row?

There was another clue right as soon as we stopped in our first town. Eureka left the keys in the washroom at the truck stop and a lady came running out after her—actually a real lady with little heels and a little jacket that matched her dress—and after she gave the keys to Eureka and Eureka opened the truck door, the lady just stood there looking at her and at me. Then she reached into her purse and pulled out the Holy Bible, and she said in her pretty voice, "In the Scriptures, the good Lord tells us—" And Eureka didn't even let that lady finish. She just climbed in and closed the door.

Jenn is tiny. She's almost as short as Reba, who is only seven, but she's smarter. When I ask her "How come the shopping carts don't roll down the moov-a-tor?"—that's what she calls the flat escalator that goes to the basement level—she looks at me like I am so dumb. I say we should go down and up again so we can make sure Reba isn't following us. But really it's so I can get another look at the wheels on those carts.

Halfway down, I stretch my arms out along the moving handrail and say, "I'm going to be a model, you know."

"You're too short."

"Eureka thinks I'm tall as anything," I say.

"You just think you're tall because your dress is too small," Jenn says. "Your sleeves are too short. Your arms hang out like a monkey. And I can see your underwear."

I drop my arms and hold my dress lower. I'm mad at Jenn now. I forget about the shopping carts. I move my eyes around, looking for a mirror. At the bottom of the escalator, Jenn walks off first. It takes ages for us to pass a mirror, then all I see is my face, looking almost like a crybaby.

Jenn stops in the girls' department and smiles at me. "Let's pick out something nice for you." She smiles at me for a long time.

I want to hug her.

I hardly even look at the dresses Jenn points out. I'm thinking I could live in that trailer with her, and she could dress me up and go to model go-sees with me. She could even sign my pictures for me, the ones I send to boys who write, if they write nice things. I keep on thinking about it all the way up to the main floor. I don't even know which dress Jenn has under her sweatshirt when we burst out into the parking lot. She's giggling, so I do too.

In the Airstream, Eureka is sleeping. I strip down to my underpants and Jenn helps me wiggle into my new dress. It's navy blue, with pleats that start at a white ribbon below my chest and go all the way down. The hem zigzags just above my knees. Jenn closes the buttons in the back then stands behind me without saying anything. I don't know what to say either. I can feel Jenn's breath on my neck. I can smell the sweat from her. My arms are locked to my sides, pressing everything inside me into a tight hot bundle. It takes me a minute to realize that Jenn is holding them there. The insides of her elbows are damp where they cross over my arms. Her hands are flattening the pleats over my belly. Her little body is pressed against mine and the posts of the buttons are pushing into my back, up and down my spine. It takes me a minute to really know all that.

By then she's already out the door.

This morning the stink is gone from the Dumpster, just like that. It's a cool morning, a bit windy. Eureka says we're leaving. It's my birthday, but Eureka's tired. She woke up and said she feels old today, but she didn't say "How you feeling, Evelyn?"

She didn't notice that I'm older today.

Across the parking lot, Jenn is sitting on the hood of her car with her legs dangling down. Reba is sticking stones in Jenn's sandals, under her toes, and Jenn's feet are jumping.

Jenn slides off the car and Reba begins to run. Jenn runs after her. Their mouths are open. They are laughing. They look very far away.

Eureka turns the key and the engine starts up. I'm still standing at the Airstream window in my nightgown when we start to move.

I think I will stand here all day today, like a photograph going by. I'll take a marker and write on the window "MISSING". Let Eureka drive up front while my face and my word flash by all the people on all the sidewalks.

Years from now, those folks will still be looking for me. They'll see my real picture, my model picture, and say "I've seen her face before, before she started wearing that navy dress."

The dress is under my mattress. It's flat, still asleep.

GIANT STRAWBERRY FUNLAND

BY JOE OLLMANN

1

HITCH-HIKING TO TOWN

BUT THERE'S NOTHING, SO I JUST PLAY THE FUCK-UP, HITCHING IN-
-TO TOWN WHEN I SHOULD BE PICKING STRAWBERRIES.

SCREEEE.
CAT

GOIN' TA TOWN?
CAT

YEAH.

YOU'RE ABE AND SALLY MANN'S BOY?
CAT

YEAH.
HOW'S YOUR DADDY LIKE THAT BLUE HAIR OF YOURS?

OH, HE FUCKING LOVES IT.

SCREEEEE!
FORD

FL 62

I WAS BEING FACETIOUS, MY DAD DOESN'T REALLY LIKE MY HAIR!

MY FATHER IS LIKE, THE PERFECT RACIST CARICATURE OF A FARMER.
farmer 289
farmer n 1 a person who owns or manages a farm. 2 This chap below.

SILENT, SUNBURNED AND WISE.
UH-YUP.

MY MOTHER IS ALSO MOSTLY SILENT.

BUT STUTTERS WHEN SHE DOES SPEAK.
THAT'S N-N-NOT ----FUNNY.

SHE USED TO LAUGH MORE WHEN WE WERE LITTLE.

BUT SHE WEARS HER HAIR PULLED TIGHTLY NOW.

AND PRESERVES EVERYTHING IN PICKLE JARS.
chestnuts
wheat

2
BUSINESS

MY BROTHER KEN, THE SAVIOUR OF THE FARM...

...FELL IN LOVE WITH THE IDEA OF "BUSINESS" THE YEAR DAD BOUGHT US BABY CHICKS FOR EASTER.

I PETTED MINE AND KEPT IN MY ROOM. I GAVE THEM ALL NAMES AND TAUGHT THEM TRICKS...
snake
fang
hulk
SOUP
PORK BEANS

...AND I GUESS I FELL IN LOVE WITH THOSE LITTLE YELLOW FUCKERS.

KEN FED HIS AND WATCHED THEM GROW AND HIT ON ALL THE LOCAL POULTRY-FARMERS FOR ADVICE ON WHERE TO SELL THEM.
OZZY

KENNY! THE CHICKENS GOT OUT! THEY'RE ALL GONE!!

WE SOLD THEM TODAY. DAD SAID TO SELL THEM ALL.
DISCO SUCKS

WHAT?
HERE. YOU GET TEN BUCKS.

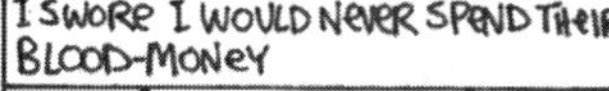
I SWORE I WOULD NEVER SPEND THEIR BLOOD-MONEY

SOB!

BUT TWO WEEKS LATER, I BOUGHT COMICS AND A SKATEBOARD MAGAZINE.
HEY KIDS COMICS
KAMANDI
FLASH!

AND DREAMED OF CONCRETE FOR ME TO SKATE AWAY ON.
SELL GRIT
KAMANDI
WIN PRIZES!

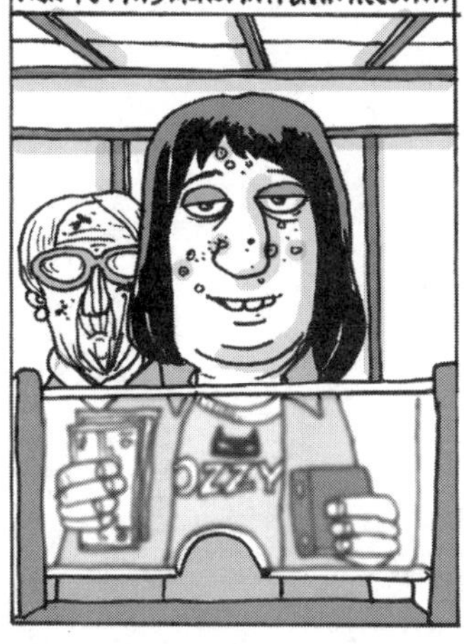
KEN PUT HIS MONEY IN A BANK ACCOUNT.
OZZY

AND DEVELOPED A HARD-ON FOR MONEY THAT HE NEVER LOST.

PRIAPRISM; THAT'S A CONDITION WHERE YOU HAVE A PERMANENT ERECTION.

MY BROTHER KEN HAS PRIAPRISM FOR MONEY.
$

AFTER HIGHSCHOOL, HE WENT TO BUSINESS SCHOOL FOR TWO YEARS.

HE CAME HOME WITH A CHARLIE SHEEN WALL-STREET HAIRCUT AND A PLAN TO SAVE THE FAMILY FARM.

3

MUSIC

THAT OL' TIME
CK 'N ROLL
ORDS - CD'S - VIDE

HEY MAN, ANY-THING NEW?

NEW U-2 CAME IN, HOOTIE AND THE BLOWFISH GREATEST HITS... CHRIST!
The Ramon

YEAH.

THAT SONIC YOUTH I ORDERED...

HASN'T COME IN YET.
The Ramones
DISCS

I HAD GIVEN MY COPY OF "GOO" TO SADIE BEFORE SHE MOVED AWAY.
ALL RIGHT, MAN. SEE YOU NEXT WEEK.

SHE DIDN'T HAVE THAT ONE. IT WAS THE ONE TIME I INTRODUCED HER TO SOMETHING COOL.
OCK 'N
ECORDS - CDS - VID

BEFORE SHE MOVED HERE, I THOUGHT I WAS SO "PUNK."

BECAUSE I OWNED THREE NIRVANA CD'S AND BECAUSE THAT MUSIC SCARED THE SHIT OUT OF THE OTHER FARM KIDS.

THEN CAME SADIE.
G.I. JOE

BIG-CITY GIRL WITH BLUE HAIR,

A TATOO ON HER STOMACH,
D.O.A.

AND A CD COLLECTION THAT BLEW MY FUCKING MIND AND CHANGED MY LIFE FOREVER.
YOU'VE NEVER HEARD OF THE MINUTE MEN?!
NO.

AFTER I KNEW SADIE AND ALL THE MUSIC SHE INTRODUCED ME TO...
WHAT DO YOU HICKS LISTEN TO, ANYWAY?
HERE.

I HAVE THREE NIRVANA CD'S.

...I KNEW I WOULD DO ANYTHING, EVEN GO TO BUSINESS SCHOOL, TO GET AWAY FROM THIS HICK FARM TOWN.
THIS IS COOL.
DUH.

4

SADIE

YOU DON'T COME TO SCHOOL WITH BLUE HAIR AND A T-SHIRT THAT SAYS "FAGGOT"...

faggot.

... IN A TOWN WHERE EVERYONE GOES TO THE SAME CHURCH...

...AND TEENAGE BOYS ACTUALLY RAISE CATTLE OF THEIR OWN TO ENTER IN FALL FAIRS, UNLESS YOU ARE LOOKING FOR TROUBLE.
YOU'RE THE BEST, GIRL...

SADIE WAS SENT TO THE OFFICE BECAUSE OF HER SHIRT. I WAS THERE FOR SKIPPING SCIENCE CLASS AGAIN.

WOW! WHAT A BUNCH OF FARM FASCISTS. THEY ACTUALLY WANTED TO SEND ME HOME TO CHANGE!
faggot.

UHHH, WHY DO YOU HAVE THAT ON YOUR SHIRT?
faggot.

WHY NOT? I MEAN, FUCK SHIT UP, FREAK OUT THE STRAIGHTS, RIGHT?
OH YEAH, RIGHT.
BUT I WOULD NEVER HAVE HAD THE GUTS TO WEAR THAT SHIRT.

IN DETENTION HALL THAT NIGHT, SHE SHOWED ME THE ZINE SHE PUBLISHED, "PUSSY-WALLOW." I WAS FREAKED-OUT. AND SHOCKED. AND SCARED OF HER. AND I FELL DESPERATELY IN LOVE.

5
KEN AND ABEL

I DON'T KNOW IF MY PARENTS NAMED US KEN AND ABEL FOR A JOKE OR NOT, BUT WE GOT ALONG AS BADLY AS THOSE TWO BIBLE DUDES DID.

EITHER ONE OF US COULD HAVE, AT ANY TIME, KILLED THE OTHER WITH A STONE.
CORN POPS

WE'RE TOTAL OPPOSITES. KEN IS BIG AND FAT AND HARD-WORKING AND CAN FIX CARS AND SHIT.
METALICA

I'M SKINNY AND USELESS EVEN AT HOLDING A FLASHLIGHT FOR MY DAD.
NOT IN MY EYES!!

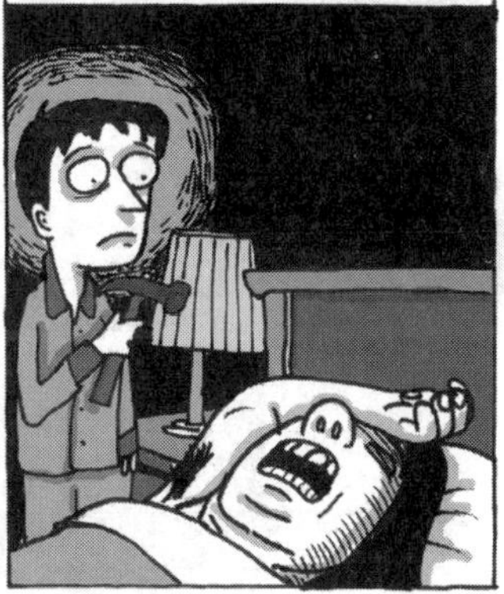
I USED TO FEEL BAD THAT I HATED KENNY SO MUCH. BECAUSE HE'S MY BROTHER, BECAUSE IT'S NOT NICE TO HATE YOUR FAMILY.

ONE TIME, MOM AND DAD TOOK US TO THAT MOVIE "POCAHONTAS."

I WAS REALLY INTO THE ENVIR-ONMENT THEN...

...AND WHEN SHE'S SINGING ABOUT THE WHITE MAN RAPING THE EARTH, I WAS LIKE, ALMOST CRYING.
white man, You Think that the earth was only made to hold Your girth! but it's NOT.

KENNY WHISPERED IN MY EAR, AROUND A MOUTHFUL OF CHEWED-UP POPCORN;
CALL ME CRAZY, MAN, BUT I'D REALLY LIKE TO FUCK THAT CARTOON CHICK, EH?

KEN IS LIKE POCAHONTAS SAYS IN HER SONG; "YOU KNOW THE PRICE OF EVERYTHING, AND THE VALUE OF NOTHING."
WHAT?

JUST FOR ONCE, I WISH MY PARENTS COULD SEE SOMETHING I DO AND THINK IT'S SO FUCKING GREAT.
BAKERY

LIKE THEY DO WITH EVERYTHING THAT KENNY-WONDER DOES.

I GOT A LETTER ALL THE WAY FROM TORONTO ONCE...
A.MANN

...FROM A GIRL WHO HAD READ MY ZINE, "FARM HAND JOB," AND THOUGHT IT WAS THE COOLEST SHIT EVER.
ICE CREAM TO BALLOONS MAKING HAPPY TIMES!
Dear Abe,
Oh fuck man, your zine is the coolest thing ever!
That part about your school year book was hilarious!
How old are you?
I'm fifteen. My friend Dana gave me your zine
If you are ever in Toronto we should hook up...
Here's my email:

THIS GIRL WROTE ALL THE WAY FROM TORONTO!
$10 CUT.

BUT I CAN'T EVEN SHOW THAT TO MOM AND DAD.

6

SADIE AND ABE NOT SITTING IN A TREE

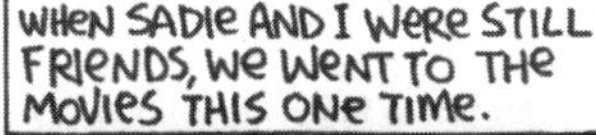

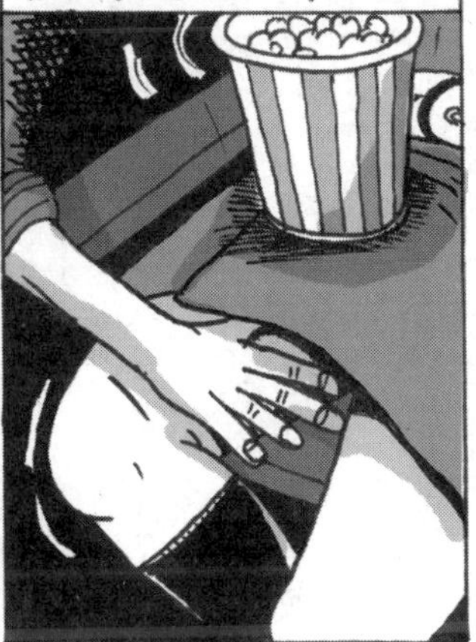

JESUS CHRIST, ABE! WHAT THE FUCK ARE YOU DOING?!

NOTHING! SORRY!

WE SAT IN SILENCE WHILE SCHWAR-ZENNEGER KILLED PEOPLE FOR THE EDIFICATION OF THE AUD--IENCE OF APPRECIATIVE HICKS.

EVVY-BODDY NOSE HOW TO DIE, SCUMBAG. HEE, I SHOW YOU HOW...

BLAM! BLAM!

I WANTED TO NEVER TALK ABOUT WHAT HAD HAPPENED. BUT SADIE WAS SO STRAIGHT-UP, AS SOON AS WE GOT OUTSIDE, SHE STARTED INTO IT.

WE STOPPED HANGING OUT.

HEY, ABE.

HEY.

SO, YOUR GIRLFRIEND DUMPED YOU FOR THE OLSEN TWINS, EH?

LEAVE ME ALONE.

7

GIANT STRAWBERRY F-LAND

SO, WHAT MY BROTHER KEN LEARNED IN TWO YEARS OF BUSINESS SCHOOL CAN BE RE- -DUCED TO A SINGLE IDEA. "YOU DON'T SELL A PRODUCT ANYMORE, YOU SELL AN "EXPERIENCE!"

WHY SELL LEMONS, WHEN YOU CAN SELL THE NOSTALGIC SCENT OF LEMONS IN A SPRAY FORM?

LEMON

STRAWBERRY-RELATED FROU-FROU,

THEY DRAGGED THE GIANT FIBRE-GLAS STRAWBERRY THAT KEN AND DAD BUILT OUT OF THE BARN LAST NIGHT.

TODAY IS THE GRAND OPENING.
GIANT
ERRY
LAND!
RIDES! PIES! MEET MR. BERRYMORE!

IT'S IMPORTANT TO MOM AND DAD.

IT'S KEN'S BIG DAY.
RIGHT GUARD
OLD SPICE
BRUT

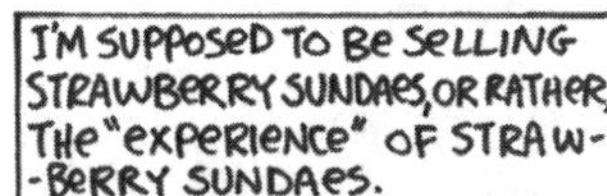
I'M SUPPOSED TO BE SELLING STRAWBERRY SUNDAES, OR RATHER, THE "EXPERIENCE" OF STRAW-BERRY SUNDAES.

GIANT
STRAW
FUNLA
RIDES
PIE

AND WEARING A STRAWBERRY SUIT.

AND THAT'S WHY I HITCH-HIKED INTO TOWN, I GUESS.

KEN IS MANNING THE INFLATED JUMPING CASTLE HE RENTED.

AND I GUESS HE CAN WEAR THE FUCKING STRAWBERRY SUIT TOO.

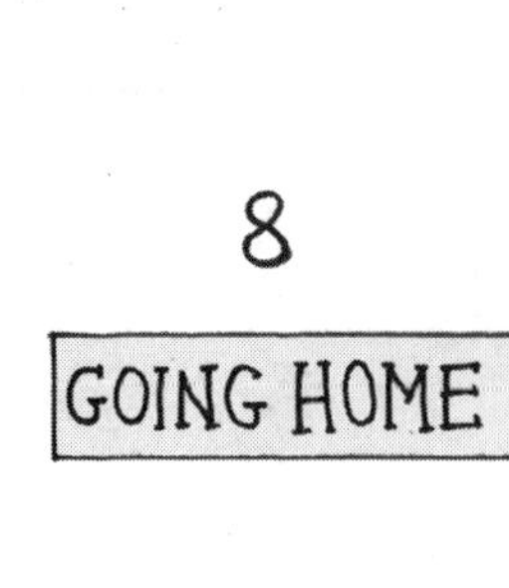
8
GOING HOME

I GOT SOME FRIES AT THE CHIP WAGON AND ATE THEM IN THE PARK.

ON A WHIM, I WALKED TO THE GAZEBO AND LOOKED FOR THE GRAFITTI ME AND SADIE LEFT THERE ONE NIGHT.

IT'S STILL THERE.
SADIE + ABEY
i LET'S FUCK SHIT UP!
Nike
Brock loves Gwen
Metalica!

I MISS YOU, SADIE.

I CAN'T PUT IT OFF ANY LONGER, SO I START WALKING HOME.

I WAS SUDDENLY NERVOUS. WHEN YOU DO SOMETHING WRONG, YOU NEVER REALLY FEEL BAD UNTIL YOU HAVE TO FACE THE PERSON YOU DID IT TO.

IT'S DARK WHEN I GET HOME.

THERE ARE NO STRANGE CARS IN THE DRIVEWAY.

I MEET MOM IN THE DOORWAY OF THE KITCHEN.

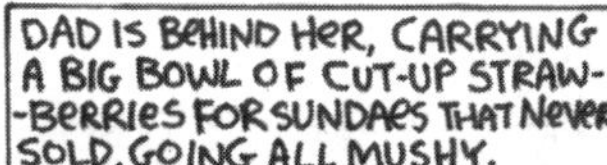
DAD IS BEHIND HER, CARRYING A BIG BOWL OF CUT-UP STRAW-BERRIES FOR SUNDAES THAT NEVER SOLD, GOING ALL MUSHY.

WELL?

N-N-NO ONE EVEN SHUH-SHOWED UP.

NO ONE?!

SUDDENLY, MY HABITUALLY SILENT FATHER IS ALL TALKATIVE. MENACING.
A FAT LOT YOU CARE NO ONE SHOWED UP.

HE PUTS DOWN THE BOWL AND COMES TOWARDS ME.

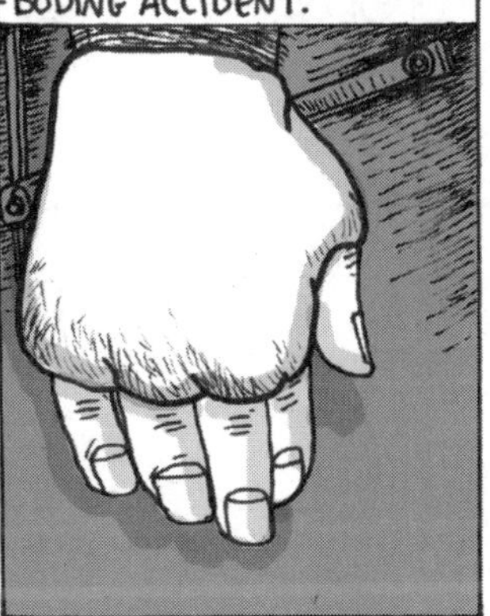
HIS HAND IS IN A CAST; CRUSHED WHILE MOVING THE GIANT STRAW-BERRY LAST WEEK. AN ILL-BODING ACCIDENT.

HE'S HOLDING THE CAST OUT IN FRONT OF HIM, LIKE A SCEPTER, OR A CLUB, AND COMING TOWARDS ME.

WHERE WERE YOU?

THIS FAMILY...

THIS FARM...

YOUR BROTHER... YOUR MOTHER AND I... WE... I WILL NOT...

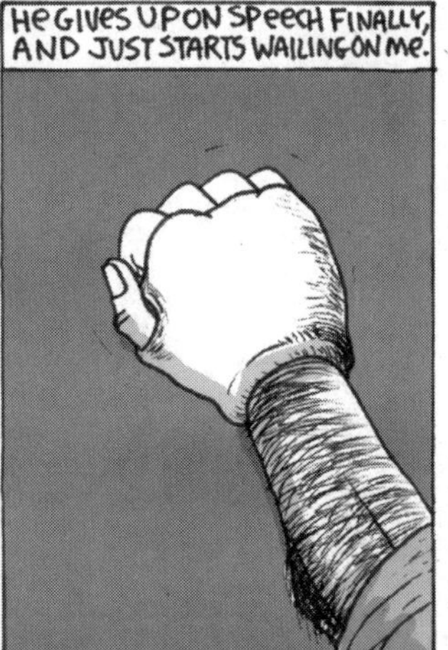
HE GIVES UP ON SPEECH FINALLY, AND JUST STARTS WAILING ON ME.

BEATING THE FUCK OUT OF ME WITH HIS CAST. MY DAD, WHO NEVER EVEN SPANKED ME, IS BEATING ME LIKE A ROGUÉ-GORILLA, HIGH ON RAILS.

AND I REALIZE HOW EMBARRASSING ALL THIS MUST BE FOR HIM. HE FINALLY STOPS WHEN HE SEES THAT MY NOSE IS BLEEDING.

MY MOM DOESN'T EVEN LOOK AT ME, JUST POURS SOUPY STRAW-BERRIES INTO FREEZER-BAGS, PRAGMATIC TO THE LAST.

IRRESPONSIBLE... ...PANT-...SELFISH. ...LITTLE...HUFF. ...PANSY!
AND THAT WAS ALL. AND, TRULY, IT WAS ENOUGH.

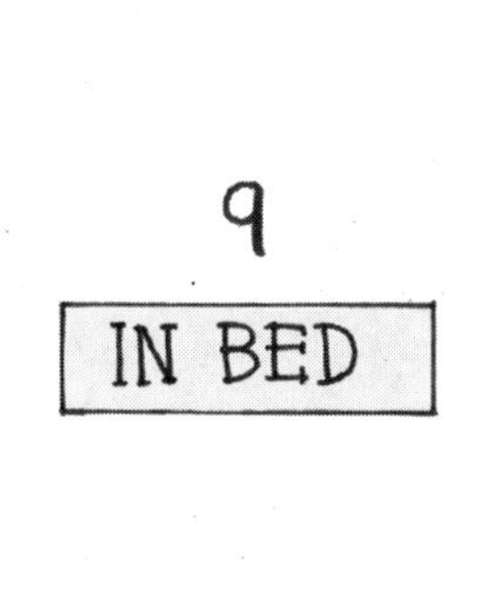
9
IN BED

I KNOW I SHOULD HAVE BEEN THERE TODAY. BUT, LIKE THAT WOULD HAVE MADE CUSTOMERS SHOW UP?

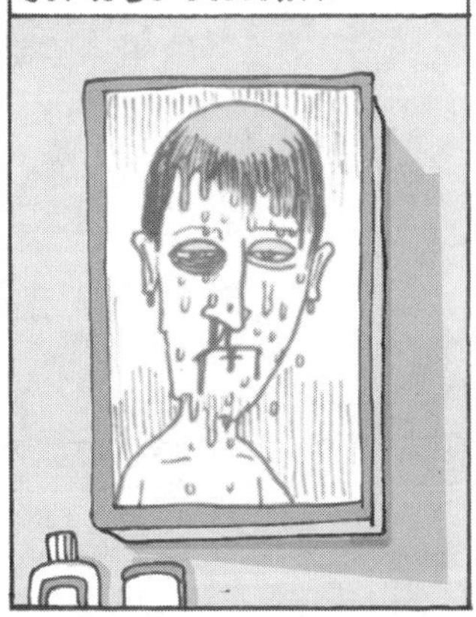
THEY'RE JUST PISSED THAT KENNY-WONDER'S IDEA TURNED OUT TO BE BULLSHIT.

I HAVE KLEENEX STUFFED UP MY NOSE, AND MY FACE IS SORE.

I HOPE I'M BRUISED TO SHIT, SO DAD CAN SEE WHAT HE DID.

I GET INTO BED AND LISTEN TO THE FIRST MIX-TAPE SADIE EVER GAVE ME.

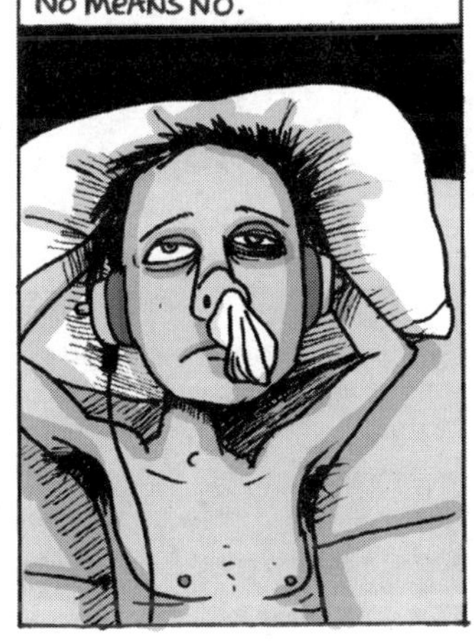
SONIC YOUTH, PIXIES, HÜSKER DU, NO MEANS NO.

I CRANK IT UP WITH THE HEAD-PHONES PRESSING AGAINST MY SORE EARS.

I CAN SEE THE GIANT STRAW-BERRY ON THE SIDE LAWN.

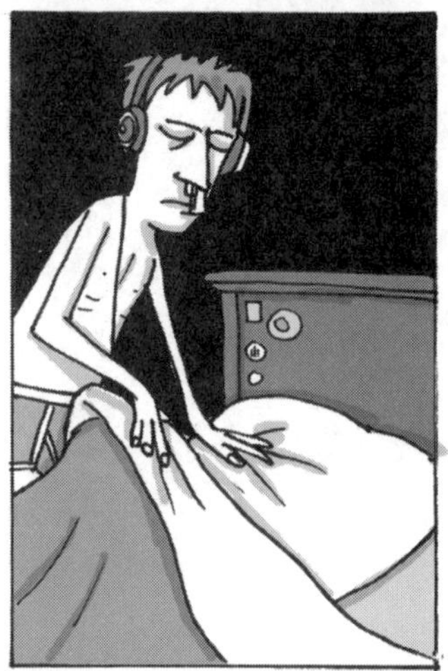

I'M CRYING INTO MY PILLOW.

THE END.

Piglet
Janet McNaughton

The bus passes a highway just before it swings into the mall. On this bright fall morning, as we make that turn, I see two kids standing on the shoulder of the road in costumes, holding a sign. One is dressed like a witch. One is dressed like a pumpkin. The sign says "Honk if you love our costumes." The costumes are terrific. Whoever made them can really sew.

I nudge Charlene. "Look at the kids."

And she says, "Oh look, Charlie, look at the pretty costumes." She holds Charlie up to the window so he can see, their heads together. Their hair blends in the sunlight, dark brown with red highlights, like some exotic wood, identical. Charlie, who is two, is suitably impressed. He flaps his arms and makes approving noises. Charlie can talk, but often prefers noises. When Charlene asked, the doctor said not to worry, this is okay.

"Those costumes are great, but why are the kids holding that sign?" Charlene says.

I shrug. "I don't know."

Charlene's forehead wrinkles. "You don't suppose someone forced them to stand there, do you?"

"Some kind of weird punishment?" I ask. She nods. The costumes were nicely made. The kids looked happy. "No," I say, "it must have been their idea."

Charlene hugs Charlie tighter. "Well, I'd never let Charlie do that, even if he wanted to. People might get the wrong idea."

I've noticed that people and their ideas occupy a large space in Charlene's mind. Sometimes I wonder how she got through her pregnancy as a single teenager in a small town, worrying that much about what other people think. But even though she's my cousin, that isn't something I can ask. Charlene moved to the city and into our basement apartment a year ago when she was ready to finish school. My high school provides day care for single mothers, something

Charlene couldn't get at home. Mom used to say, don't let it give you ideas, but she doesn't joke about it anymore. Charlene and I are friends now, even though she's almost twenty and I'm fifteen. Mom says, "You should spend more time with people your own age, Becky." But we both know Charlene needs the help, and I've noticed Mom's just as crazy about Charlie as I am.

The mall is decorated for Halloween. Charlie loves it. Halloween is why we're here. This is going to be Charlie's first trick-or-treat event. When Charlene asked him what he wanted to be, he said, "Piglet!"

That's because of me. I started reading my old Winnie-the-Pooh books to Charlie and he took to Piglet right away. Now I call him "very small animal." We make pig noises together and Charlie giggles as if we are the funniest people on the planet.

Charlene wasn't crazy about the idea. "Maybe you'd like to be Elmo," she offered.

"Not Elmo. Piglet," Charlie said. He crossed his arms over his chest, and the subject was closed. Charlie's a good kid, but stubborn.

I don't know if you've noticed, but you can't just go to a big box store and buy a pig costume, size two, off the rack. But, in the sewing section, Charlene found some soft pink plush. It felt like a cloud. It was even marked down. Charlene ran her hand over it like it was the finest velvet. She looked up and smiled. "It's really nice." She bought a pink zipper, some matching thread and a pattern that could be adapted to make any kind of animal costume for little kids.

In the toy store we found plastic animal noses, pigs included. "Fabulous," I said. "I'll get two. One for Charlie, one for me." I held one up to my nose. "Look, Charlie, oink, oink." Charlie laughed so hard he actually fell over. Lucky he's close to the ground. After, I bought us some burgers for lunch with money Mom slipped me in the morning, and then we took the bus home.

Charlene didn't have any trouble convincing the home ec teacher to let her make Charlie's costume as her project for the term. The school is set up to help single mothers, and that costume was a lot harder than anything she'd be expected to make otherwise. I guess the teacher knew it wouldn't end up unfinished at the bottom of Charlene's locker either. Unlike some people's sewing projects. Mine, for example. Soon Charlene was staying late after school to finish the costume while I took Charlie to the playground.

The Friday before Halloween, Mom and I left Charlene to put the finishing touches on the costume while we took Charlie to the farmers' market to find the Perfect Pumpkin. Charlie walked from pumpkin to pumpkin, circling each one. I knew he was looking for something, but I couldn't tell what. Finally, he said, "I want one with a face."

We laughed and explained we'd give the pumpkin a face ourselves. "And you can help," Mom added. The idea made Charlie's eyes big and round.

That night Charlene was almost as excited as her son. "Will you try on your costume for Becky and Aunt Kathy?" she asked Charlie.

"Pumpkin come too," Charlie said. He insisted. Charlene had to take Charlie, the costume and the pumpkin into Mom's bedroom so he could change.

He reappeared a few minutes later wearing a fuzzy pink suit and a hood with two floppy pink ears. He was wearing the plastic pig nose I'd bought him. "Piglet!" I said. "Where's Eeyore?"

Charlie giggled. Then he turned around so we could see the curly tail Charlene had sewn to the back of the costume. He looked like one of those marzipan pigs you sometimes see at Christmas. "Charlie," I said, "you look good enough to eat."

Charlie slept in his costume every night that weekend. By Monday, Halloween, it was a little grubby. When Charlene took him to school, still dressed in his costume, I heard her say, "Charlie, Halloween's over tonight. Tonight you sleep in your pajamas. Piglet needs a bath." There was a Halloween party at Charlie's day care, of course. When he came home, his costume was no longer a little grubby. It was really grubby.

"Time to carve the pumpkin," Mom said. Charlie got right into it, scooping out the seeds and pulp with his hands. When we were finished, his costume was smeared with pumpkin pulp.

"What can I do?" Charlene cried when she saw him. "There isn't time to wash it. It's almost dark. I'm taking him out now so he doesn't stay up too late."

"Oh, Charlene, don't worry. He'll be fine," Mom said, "Just wash his face and hands."

When they left, Mom said, "I think Charlene fusses too much. It does a child good to get dirty once in a while."

Charlie was home just as the first trick-or-treaters came to our door. He held up the plastic pumpkin we'd given him to hold his treats.

"Everybody give me candy!" he cried. It was only about half full.

"I didn't take him too many places," Charlene said. "Only to people we know."

I took him by the hand. "Come on, Piglet," I said, "let's get you changed."

"Oink, oink," Charlie said.

While Charlene gave Charlie his bath, I put the costume into the washer with a load of laundry. It came out looking like new. All the seams had held. "You're going to get an A in home ec this term for sure," I told Charlene.

A whole week went by before Charlene got the note. I guess it takes a while for things like that to filter through the system.

"I have to see the guidance counselor in study period tomorrow," Charlene said. "I wonder why?"

"Oh, it's probably just a standard what-do-you-plan-to-do-career-wise interview," I said. "Everybody has them."

"You think so?"

I nodded. But I was wrong.

When Charlene came home, her face was still blotchy from crying. She wasn't talking, but it didn't take a genius to see something awful had happened. When Mom invited Charlene and Charlie to stay for supper, Charlene still wouldn't tell us what had happened. "Maybe I could phone you after Charlie's gone to sleep," she said, her voice tight and small. "You could come down and I could talk to both of you."

I was glad she'd included me. I had to know what was going on.

When we went to Charlene's apartment, she handed us a photocopy of the letter. The address and sender's name had been blacked out. I read over Mom's shoulder. It was a letter to the school, from one of our neighbors, it seems, complaining that Charlene "had taken her child door to door on Halloween dressed in a filthy pig costume." It suggested Charlie should be investigated for possible child abuse.

"This is ridiculous!" I said.

"What did they say to you in school, Charlene?" Mom asked.

"They got the nurse to look at Charlie. They asked me a lot of questions—where he sleeps, how often I give him a bath, what he eats, question after question. I tried to explain, but they didn't seem to want to talk about Halloween. It was like they were following some procedure. They said they might call in a social worker."

Mom was quiet for a long time. Then she spoke. "I'll make an appointment to see them. Do you think your home ec teacher would talk to them too? You put a lot of time and effort into that costume."

Then I spoke. "I should come too, Mom. I'm the one who started Charlie on Piglet." Mom looked at me a moment, then nodded. "Okay, Becky. That's a good idea. You probably spend more time with Charlene than anyone."

We couldn't get an appointment until the end of the week. We did what we could to make things easy for Charlene in the meantime. We could see she wasn't sleeping, worrying they might take Charlie away from her.

On Friday, after school, we met Charlene at the counselor's office. The home ec teacher was there too.

In the hour that followed, Mom said things about Charlene she'd never said to me. "Charlene is my niece," she said, "but we didn't know her well before last year. I was worried when she first came to rent our basement apartment. I thought she might be a bad influence on Becky. Maybe someone who had already messed up her life so badly would have wild parties and do drugs. But Charlene is a fine young woman. Her whole life revolves around Charlie and making a good home for him. This is just a terrible misunderstanding."

Then we explained about Piglet, about Charlie insisting on a pig costume. We told them how Charlie had slept in his costume and how the mess from the day care party and the pumpkin made him look filthy before he went out trick-or-treating. The home ec teacher talked about the care Charlene put into the costume. Then we waited to hear what the counselor would say.

"Well, that's a very impressive show of support," she said. "The nurse assures me that Charlie is healthy and shows no signs of abuse. The day care workers think he's fine. I think we can all agree this was just a misunderstanding."

Charlene, who had said nothing until then, burst into tears. It was a long time before we could get her to stop. Then we went to the day care, where someone had stayed late to look after Charlie. When Charlie came running to her, Charlene scooped him into her arms and I saw her smile for the first time all week. She hugged him and kissed him all over until he started to giggle. "I love you, Charlie," she said.

That night I couldn't stop thinking about what had happened to Charlene, and what might have happened. I went to bed, but my mind would not stop. Why would anybody write a letter like that? It was such a mean thing to do. Then I remembered those kids on the side of the highway, the day we went to the mall. How Charlene wondered if it had been some kind of weird punishment. I'd thought then that she worried too much about what other people thought. And later, on Halloween, when Charlie got so dirty carving the pumpkin, Mom did too. After a long time, I drifted off to sleep with the image of those kids in my mind, dressed in their costumes by the side of the highway for reasons I will never know. And just before sleep took me, I remember thinking how little Mom and I had understood about Charlene and her life.

Alchemy
Madeleine Thien

In my memory, I followed Paula to the end of the aisle, past the hair products, shampoos, the colored lights, through an empty mall, a parking lot, Granville Street at night with kids and adults panhandling, to a bus all lit up, down a quiet street to her house, where she closed the door behind her, smiling. I stood on the lawn outside. From there I could see everything: the back shed, the porch with the rabbit hutch, her open window with the blue curtains billowing out. Before disappearing she had said, "The rabbits are gone," and I understood that as a sign. Move on, she was telling me. I'm on my own now. So I left her.

I remembered that last night. I had wanted a sign from Paula. Not everyone believes in signs. But the more you need them, the more you see and the more you believe. I found a white hair today and pulled it out. I call that a sign. After all, sixteen is young.

In school we've been learning about time. How human beings have hardly put a dent in it. If the history of the Earth were mapped against a single year, we would only show up on December 31, at 4:11 in the afternoon. I would have told Paula that, and we would have mulled it over late at night. We would have laughed and said that, in the history of the Earth, she and I, her father and mother and Jonah, were nothing. They would fall away from us without a bruise or a scratch. We could blow them off our bodies. We could say, with confidence, that in the grand scheme of things, in the long run, they meant as little as dust. "Less," Paula would say. And I would say, "Less."

Paula's mom worked downtown at the Hotel Vancouver. She was a housekeeper and smelled of fresh sheets and mild sweat. She always came home first, hung her coat neatly in the closet, unbuttoned the first three buttons of her blouse, and started cooking. Paula's father was a gruff yet caring man. He fixed cars for a living, came home with grease under his fingernails and the smell of oil on his skin.

I preferred Paula's home to mine and so I stayed over at her house most nights. At dinner Paula's dad once said to me, "Do you know how much it costs to keep an extra body, Miriam? Tell your parents to pay up."

Her mom made a noise like, "Ssss, shush." Paula stared at her plate, motionless. Her dad shook his head, apparently hurt, and picked up his knife and fork. "Eh, Jesus. I'm kidding, okay? Can't I do that in my own home? Any friend of Paula's is welcome here." The four of us ate quietly. Paula's mom brought out drinks, cola for me and Paula, Molson's for her dad, water for herself. She brought out dessert, a Boston cream pie, left over from the hotel kitchen that day.

Afterwards, in the bathroom, I stood back while Paula threw up dinner. Her hair, bleached blond, stuck to her face. She rinsed her mouth and said, "I only throw up dinners. You only have an eating disorder if you throw up everything." Paula told me that there were four kinds of bodies: the X, the A, the Y and the O. "You're an X," she said, "small waist and evenly proportioned chest and butt." She turned sideways. "What do you think I am?"

"An X."

"Wrong," she smirked. "Nice try. I'm more of an A. Heavy on the bottom." She picked up my wrist and measured it with her fingers. Her thumb and index finger touched. "You're lucky. Everyone wants to be an X."

We stayed up late, talking about Jonah and how the halls were empty because the senior boys had gone away to play basketball and about how our math teacher had hair growing on his back. If you stood behind him, you could see it push past his collar, a hairy finger. Paula and I pressed our faces into the pillows and laughed. A breeze came and blew her curtains back into the room, light from a passing car traveling down the wall, across our beds, and gone. She said, "Move in here. Why don't you just move into the spare bedroom? If you hate your family so much, you might as well, don't you think?"

"I don't hate them."

"Well, whatever. You hardly go home anyway."

"I'll ask," I said, though I knew I wouldn't. In my home we barely spoke. My parents had long since given up on their marriage. They were busy working, making ends meet, and hardly noticed whether I was home or not.

"We could be sisters then." Paula lay back on her pillow. "We'll share everything."

Paula wanted to be a veterinarian. That meant that, after dark, we'd slip out of her house and into the backyard, where her mom kept hutch rabbits.

Once a week, at supper time, her mom pulled one or two from the cage, broke their necks, skinned their bodies and drained the blood in the kitchen sink. She made rabbit stew, simmering the meat until it was tender, and you could smell the potatoes and carrots and meat all through the house and down the street.

The first time we snuck outside, Paula unlatched the door and poked her face up to the cage. "Be free," she whispered. "Be free or be stew." The rabbits came and stood in the long grass, their noses twitching. We lay down, and they crawled timidly on top of us, onto our heads. "They like our hair," Paula told me. "They feel safe there." She tried to coax them across the backyard, crouching on her hands and knees, leading the way to the fence. But they were nervous and would only take a few loping steps before something scared them, a bird overhead, a motorcycle on Knight Street. They scampered back to their hutch.

"What can we do?" Paula asked. "They're not wild, after all."

We stayed out on the back lawn listening to the traffic. At one point a light came on in the kitchen and we froze. Paula's dad stood at the window, a glass of water in his hand. He took forever to drink it, staring straight at us through the glass, but we trusted the dark and willed ourselves invisible. When the light in the kitchen went out, we breathed easy again, felt the chill in the wind, came back to life.

The nights I slept over, I would wake up with my face in Paula's hair. It leaped away from her, full of static. The smell would wake me up, apples and dish soap and sweat. I wondered what it would be like to wake up beside someone night after night, hair in your face, legs crossing heavily under the blankets. If the smell and feel would tire you out, like it had my mom and dad. They slept in separate rooms, Mom on the couch and Dad in the bedroom. Sometimes they sat in the same room, though neither of them would acknowledge the other. They had perfected it, made it an art to see something but believe it wasn't there.

Once, when Paula and I were lying in bed, she asked me, "Are you a virgin still?"

"Of course," I said, thinking of Jonah. I stared at her fingers on the top of the blanket, spread out and still.

"Aren't you?"

She lifted her hands, holding them over our head like planets, constellations, something we'd never seen up close. "I'm not sure," she said.

We lay together quietly under the blankets. For a long time lying there, I wondered if I should say something more, but then the moment passed. I could hear her breathing grow heavier. Before she fell asleep, she turned over and held on to me. Her grip was so plaintive that I felt sorry for her and held on too. I had the sense that some things were impossible for her to say.

In school we'd been learning about species. We had to imagine billions of years, different species rising like bubbles to the surface, all this time passing. But I could not imagine ten years, fifteen, twenty. My sixteen years felt like eternity, but I knew I wouldn't be like this forever. In all my life, the total sum of it, I was a species rising and falling. One day I would wake up and all of it would be gone.

At first when Paula and I talked about Jonah, we were conspirators. Together we laid out a course of action. She made sure I stood behind him at the line-up in the cafeteria, that I sat in front of him in French class, that we happened by his locker three times a day, every day. She planned out the life we might have and whispered it to me in the hallway, one hand excitedly grasping my elbow. He would take me into his confidence, slowly. He would unburden secrets he never shared with anyone. A long time in the future, he might kiss me.

One day Jonah appeared in front of my locker and said, "Let me drive you home, Miriam." Outside my parents' apartment, below their window, he put his car into neutral and reached over, running his hand from my chin to my stomach. I leaned into him. He kissed me, and I felt like I was being pushed to the bottom of a swimming pool, everything distorted, unfocused yet clear as glass. I felt myself moving through years and years, coming up different all of a sudden.

Once, in PE class, I watched Jonah running laps. He was falling behind, the other boys were far ahead of him, but he kept on, one hand grasping his chest then blurring down. He ran past me, breathing hard, but he blew me a kiss from the center of the palm of his hand. When I sat in front of him in French class, sometimes he whispered small requests, an eraser, an extra pen, and I passed them back without looking. But how I loved to look at him. He had dark hair and his eyes were round and dark and lovely. He had a soft body, not pounded immovable by sports, just regular and wide and comfortable.

Paula smirked when I told her this. She said, "That isn't any reason to love someone."

"It is for me."

She bent her head down. Now that Jonah had entered my life, she no longer approved of him. "Don't say I didn't warn you. You don't know what you're getting into."

She looked at me, her face blank, then turned and left. I didn't follow.

Later on, when Jonah and I slept together in his bedroom, I imagined looking down on us from the ceiling. I pictured how dark and naked our bodies must be, how small the two of us were. Right then I wanted to tell Paula that there are some things you have to go through on your own. Some relationships withstand life, some are there for a moment, a stepping stone, and then you push away from them.

But I never did because Paula said, "Don't talk to me about Jonah. I don't want to know."

"I won't tell you anything then."

"I thought you were going to move in here. I thought you were unhappy at home and you wanted to live with me." She lay down on her bed, yellow hair spreading in a circle. We had learned about Joan of Arc, and I imagined holding a match to Paula's hair; it was so dry it would catch in an instant, sprout into a ball of flame. "Don't lie to me anymore," she said. "Just say whether you will or not."

"I have my own family, Paula."

Some part of her seemed to give way. "But I need you here."

"Why?" I said, exasperated.

She turned away. "Go home then. I don't want to see you."

I wanted to tell Paula what was happening, how one thing leads to another. How a boy like Jonah feels like a necessary thing. He has a way about him, like a curved handle, so easy to hold, so easy to see. He can smile and something flares up in you, catches on your heart, opens you up to things you wanted but never asked for. He can change the way your mind forms words, shapes sentences, imagines their capacity. He has a heart you think you can drink from. I've heard that it's common, there are lots of boys, and girls too, who are like this. Their faces have promise in them, but how can you be promised something you will never stop wanting?

Once, after Jonah and I had sex, he said, "You really like it, don't you? It scares me how much you like it." He smiled at me knowingly, and I nodded. I never knew what to say.

I slept at Paula's house less and less. At school she would corner me in the bathroom and ask me to come over. I never gave firm answers. I was waiting for

Jonah to come by, sweep me into his car, forgive me. It seemed like I was always doing something wrong—I held him too tightly, told him I loved him. It never came out right. When I said it, the words sounded more like a plea.

"I'll see," I told Paula.

She nodded her head. Her hair was a different shade. Clairol "Stardust," she told me. She was losing weight too, and it made her face thin and freakish.

I did go over, and that night we lay outside on the back porch, the stars muted by the city lights. She said, "I've been thinking about running away." She had her eyes closed as if she were imagining it right then, some new place farther inland, a new city identical to this one, but different in all the right ways.

Sometime after midnight, she stood up and walked slowly down the back steps. When she returned, she was carrying the cage of hutch rabbits. We lay on the deck watching them, then Paula undid the latch. Reaching in, she lifted the rabbits out one by one until all five sat shivering on the deck. "Go," she said, waving toward the stairs. "This might be your last chance." They stayed where they were, frozen by the traffic sounds and the half moon. Paula leaned down and blew on each of them gently. They crept forward. "Go on." They froze.

She gathered the nearest one in her arms. Then she stood and walked across the verandah, the rabbit bundled against her chest. At the railing she stopped, stretched her arms out and held it straight in front of her. There was laundry on the line, shirts pinned up like paper cut-outs. A light came on in her parents' bedroom. Paula opened her arms. I saw the rabbit falling slowly.

The traffic on Knight Street kept going by and going by. She ran down the back stairs. I heard her say "Oh no" in a flat voice. I didn't look. I gathered the other four and put them back in the hutch. Paula laid a piece of newspaper on the concrete walkway, over top of the one she had dropped. She looked up at me and said, "My fingers slipped."

I said, "It's okay. There are lots of others."

That night, in the middle of sleep, I heard voices, a man and a woman. They were whispering, and he was impatient with her. I thought I felt Paula get up and leave me but when I woke up in the night I was confused because it was only the two of us in her bedroom. Paula had one arm across my waist; she had her face buried against my arm.

Jonah came over to my house twice a week and I helped him with his science homework. We memorized the periods of geologic time scale, traded them back and forth as if they were codes. "Triassic, Jurassic, Cretaceous, Tertiary, Quaternary," he giggled. I laughed at him.

We sat with our legs dangling out the window, and I said again, "I love you."

He looked at me, his face confused. "How do you know?" he asked.

"I just do."

He said, "You're crazy."

When he lay on top of me I looked up at him and willed myself to feel joyous, exuberant, but it was like something on the other side of the world. He caught my eye for a moment and I saw an expression pass across his face. Afterwards I tried to name what I saw. Pity, perhaps, more pity than love.

When Jonah left, I walked to Paula's house. At Knight Street, I stood on my curb. My mom said this was the most dangerous street in the city, all the semis, four-by-fours, speed demons. I thought of walking into the street. But I wasn't brave enough to do a thing like that. Standing on the sidewalk, the traffic whipping my hair from my face, I felt the sensation of flight.

Paula's house was just around the corner. I walked across her front lawn, then rapped on the window. When she opened the door and saw me, she didn't look at all surprised. She poured two glasses of brandy and we watched *Mask*, a movie with Cher and a boy who had the elephant-man disease. The sun went down through the window behind the television set; it filled the glass and steeped the room in sunlight. In the movie, Cher fights for her son because she loves him so deeply it cuts her open. Paula filled our glasses again and again. The bottle shone like a coin in the room.

Paula turned to face me. She said, "I've got the other bedroom all set up."

I could feel the brandy slipping down my throat, holding in my chest and pumping warmth like a spare heart. "I told you, Paula, I have my own home."

She looked taken aback, then she nodded. "We're best friends. Even best friends don't tell each other everything."

Paula took another drink and looked at me thoughtfully. Then she pointed through the window at the back shed. "See that? I used to fix cars in there with my dad. I'd lie on my back on one of those trolleys, and he'd roll me under. It's lonely under there, and dark. And then one day I just stopped going. My mom said to me, 'What's the matter with you? Don't be so lazy.

Your father needs your help.' I told her that I didn't want to go to the shed, I didn't want to be with him. I was too old to go there."

I looked down at the carpet, shaking my head. The alcohol faded through me in a slow wash. "Paula," I said. "Stop talking."

"My mom told me, 'This is how families fall apart.' I didn't want to believe her, but I did. So I kept going back. I can't stop it. I think maybe I'm the one who's sick. Sometimes I go into the shed and roll myself underneath the car and I pretend I've been hit and I'm lying in the road, almost dead. Just in case, just so I know beforehand what it might feel like."

I knew what was coming next and I didn't want to hear it. I shook my head to block it out.

"Listen to me. It doesn't matter who you fuck or how do you do it. It's all the same, it always hurts. Why won't you just stay here? If you were here, this wouldn't happen."

I hit her across the mouth to stop her. A loose hit, palm flat, the smack high-pitched. Her mouth fell open.

She shook her head, hysterical. "I'm not lying."

"You shouldn't let him."I couldn't look at her when I said it. "Why do you let him do it?" Then I stood up and walked stiffly across the living room, down the hallway, to the front door. Paula's mother came awkwardly to the top of the stairs, her weight pulling her side to side. "What's wrong?" she asked. "Who's crying?"

I shook my head and pulled on my shoes. Paula's voice rose higher and higher. Her mom said, "Paula?" and ran down the stairs, one hand pressed to the opening in her nightgown. When I opened the front door to leave I could hear Paula sobbing, "Leave me alone. Please, just leave me alone."

I started walking, past Kingsway and onto Slocan, where the traffic lights disappeared and the street was soft in darkness. I slowed down, paid attention to each car sliding by, the lights settling on me for half a second.

A man in a car drove up beside me. He pushed his head out the window, whistling. "Beautiful," he said. I turned and stared at him. He smiled, motioning me toward him.

I went toward his car, all the feeling in me lost. I opened the passenger door and thought, This is what it all comes to. I'd seen pictures of girls like me, here one moment then gone the next. When I climbed into the car, I thought of Paula sitting on the floor in her living room, face in her hands, her mom's arms wrapped around her. Paula's expression when I turned away from her. We eased away from the curb and he said, "Where are you going?"

I told him I was going home.

"Do you want to go there?"

I nodded.

He smiled knowingly. "Are you sure?"

"Yes."

He turned the radio on and let one hand drift over to rest on my thigh. I thought, Everything has led to this. This is what it comes to.

But he drove me home. He let his car idle behind my parents' apartment building. When I put my hand on the door handle, he said, "Let me kiss you."

I looked him full in the face and saw he was older, so much older than me. He leaned toward me, and I remembered what Paula had said. It doesn't matter who or how. I turned my face to him, the street empty and the car warm. He kissed me, and I felt his moustache on my skin, a passing touch. Then I got out of the car and walked home.

The next morning, Paula ran away. She left her house as usual, carrying only her schoolbag, and didn't come home. I learned later, from Paula's mother, that she had left a note in the kitchen, telling her mother that she would take care of herself and not to worry.

In the spring, once or twice, I walked by Paula's house. From the outside it looked the same, the windows in her bedroom open and the blue curtains moving gently in the breeze. We had picked the material for the curtains at Fanny's Fabrics, and Paula's mom had sewn them exactly as Paula had wanted. I stood on the sidewalk out front hoping that wherever Paula was, they would never find her and make her go home again.

Once, Jonah lay his hand against my neck, and I was startled. He said, "Sometimes I look at you and you are very beautiful." I wondered if he meant to be terrible or if there were some truth in this, a tiny piece, but too little to buy happiness, security, love. I held on to him and felt my mind, my heart and my body separating. Wherever Paula was, I wondered if she had come across a formula that would keep these parts intact, if the act of leaving had taught her some truth I still could not grasp. After Jonah left, I sorted through the mail but nothing came.

In the weeks after Paula ran away, a counselor and a youth officer at our school called us to their office one by one. They pulled me out of geography class, and my stomach filled up with dread. In their tiny room, I sat as still as possible, staring at the floor. The police officer was at the back. Paula's mom was there too, foreign-looking in her work clothes, blouse and pleated blue skirt, nylons and black moccasins. She touched me gently, one hand against my back, then she went and sat in the corner.

The counselor smiled at me. She said, "We want to help Paula just as much as you do, Miriam."

"I haven't heard from her."

"Do you know where she might have gone?"

"No."

"Do you have any idea why she left?"

I shook my head.

The counselor poured coffee into a Styrofoam cup, then stood and circled the room, offering the pot to the officer and then to Paula's mom. They both covered their cups with their hands and shook their heads and everyone sat in silence. Paula's mom whispered, "Surely you know something. Can't you guess where she is?"

The school counselor caught my eye. "Her parents are very worried. We're all very worried about her safety."

I said, "I don't know."

Paula's mom said, "But she told you everything."

This startled me. I looked down at my hands, thinking of Paula, the two of us stretched out on her living-room floor, the brandy flooding us with warmth. How when I left her house that night, that warmth evaporated. I thought we had both known the truth, but Paula was the only one brave enough to say it then, and not me. "A few months ago," I said, "I slept over at Paula's house. I woke up in the night and her father was standing beside our bed. He was touching her hair. He had his hand over her face. She turned away from him and held me and later on I woke up and she was crying, but I pretended I was asleep."

I folded my hands in my lap and looked up. "What do you think it meant?" No one answered me. I said, "I know that in her own house, Paula was always afraid to sleep alone."

I looked up at the woman because I was afraid she wouldn't believe me. I held her gaze and felt a humming in my chest like a burst note.

When I left the office Paula's mom followed me into the hallway. Her face was coming apart and she said, "What are you trying to do?" I stared at her hair, curly brown and wisping to gray. She said, "How can you do this? How dare you lie like that?" and I felt blank, an opening inside where the humming was, dead air.

I turned and walked down the hallway, leaving her standing there alone. I didn't know what difference it made—if the truth would be of any use to Paula now or if it was too late. But I believed her. I had believed her from the start, and this was the only thing I knew how to do.

I remembered Paula buying hair color in the drugstore. She couldn't decide between one and the other, Clairol "Brash" or Nice 'n Easy "Natural Light." I was impatient and said, "Let's go, Paula. They're all the same." She balanced them, one in each hand, as if she could tell by the weight. She glared at me. I thought, If you could change your life with a shade of color, if it had ever been that easy, we would not be standing here in the first place.

I waited for Paula to write me. I kept in my head a list of things I would tell her. How her house was the same as ever but they left her bedroom window open, as if hoping one morning she would climb back in again. That grade eleven was the same as grade ten. That things got a lot worse before they got any better. We had learned the history of gold. How people had rushed up the coast, panning for it, because they believed that the nuggets might be as abundant as the fish. And long ago, how people had tried to make something out of nothing, filling beakers with coins and the seven metals made from seven planets, how they hung their hopes on this, like a coatrack.

Then I only hoped. Because Paula did not write and I did not know where she was, I tried to dream it. I imagined a place of great abundance. Fish in the seas and terrible beauty.

Slice
Gary Barwin

My mother buried me with a handful of flour. He will rise, she said, and threw the shovel over the fence. Then she went inside and began to sing like a lizard.

No. Though her mouth was empty of soil, she didn't sing. But how would I know, buried in the backyard with a handful of flour?

Underground, everything was different. The worms bickering in the dirt, the millipedes cracking droll and ironic jokes under damp rocks, the yapping and slobbering of dogs burying their bones. My mother, silent, went to bed and pulled the covers over her head.

Was she feeling guilty? Do guilty-feeling people climb into bed in high-heeled shoes? Do they ignore the hammering of truant officers, of Boy Scout leaders, of can-he-come-out-to-play friends? Even Grandma, with her armful of cake ingredients, gave up knocking, went to the next daughter down the list.

The morning splintered as night threw a champagne glass full of dew into dawn's empty fireplace. A millipede cracked a good one about an ant, and my mother got out the shovel. She had forgotten the eggs, the milk and a few other things.

There was brightness for a few seconds until Mother filled the hole.

It rained all that day. I could hear the raindrops thrumming, the earthworms irritated and cranky, heading for the surface. My mother shouting on the telephone, railing against world history, built-in shelving, politics, the ocean. She'd lost her eyes in the ocean.

Not her actual eyes. Here I'm speaking metaphorically. Or I would be speaking metaphorically, if my mouth weren't filled with soil. It's like when I said her body was lithe and spiteful as a lizard's. The ocean had pulled her bones out and washed them like driftwood on the waves.

There was a boat.

Small, wooden, propelled by oars. Don't ask what was in it. If I was so clever, would I be a living bone buried in the corner of the yard?

A recipe, maybe. A child. An extensive Julia Child video collection. All of history rolled up small, then baked in a bread to escape detection at the checkpoints.

Why is it dark underground? Why are there no birds? These are the mysteries. I'm just buried.

The next day there was sun. The world was warm and I began to rise. I pushed away worms, squirrels, broken teacups, swing sets, patio stones and barbecues. I was a vast loaf and the rec room became dark in my shadow.

Maybe I have exaggerated a little. In truth, I was no garage-sized loaf, but a bread slice, large as a bedroom wall, and I made the birds cower. The sky was light and tawny through my translucent body, and my mother, peering from beneath the covers, noticed the change.

About the Authors

Gil Adamson was born in North York in the sixties on New Year's Day, so her mother got a box of groceries from the city. She has lived in Australia and Canada, and has a brother named Andrew. When Gil was a teenager, she was much better at reading people.

Diana Aspin wrote her first book at age six. Fifty years later, in 2003, her first book of short stories, *Ordinary Miracles*, was shortlisted for the CLA YA Book Award. When Diana was a teenager, her parents fought like cat and dog; though sad, she became the class clown, had good friends and laughed a lot. Her sense of humor and the absurd has steered her through many awful situations. Writing helps too!

Writer and musician **Gary Barwin** writes poetry and fiction for adults, children and young adults. His latest books include *Frogments from the Frag Pool* (with Derek Beaulieu) and *Doctor Weep and Other Strange Teeth*. His YA novel *Seeing Stars* was a finalist for the CLA YA Book Award and the Arthur Ellis Award. Gary teaches music at Hillfield Strathallan College and lives in Hamilton, Ontario, with his wife, three children and way too many chores. When Gary was a teenager, he used to pretend to read really complicated books. Now he just pretends to understand them.

The excerpt in this collection is from **Martha Brooks's** 2002 Governor General's Award–winning novel, *True Confessions of a Heartless Girl*, a book that has been translated into French, German, Spanish, Italian and Japanese. As a teen Martha broke a few hearts until, at the ripe old age of nineteen, she met her future husband and lifetime boyfriend, Brian.

Ivan E. Coyote is the author of three collections of short stories, *Close to Spider Man, One Man's Trash* and *Loose End.* She is a freelance writer, CBC Radio love child, a columnist for *Xtra! West* and a creative writing instructor at Capilano College, in North Vancouver. Her first novel will hit the shelves in 2006. When Ivan was a teenager, Air Supply was cool and e-mail hadn't been invented yet.

When Brian Doyle was a teenager, growing and learning in the Ottawa Valley, he picked up his love of stories and anecdotes. His keen memories of youth and the dozens of jobs he had to work at to put himself through school figure prominently in the settings, the people and the atmosphere of his work. Brian has received many honors and awards for his writing. He has switched from the recorder to the ukulele.

Anne Fleming's first book, *Pool-Hopping and Other Stories,* was nominated for many nice awards. Just published, her second book, *Anomaly,* is a novel about two sisters growing up in Toronto in the seventies and eighties. As a teenager, Anne ate grilled peanut butter sandwiches and played ringette.

Lisa Heggum is an award-winning teen services librarian who began her career in New York City. She currently lives and works in Toronto. When Lisa was a teenager, she always said "No way!" when her mother told her she should get a job at the library.

Lee Henderson is the author of *The Broken Record Technique,* a collection of short stories. His first novel will be published in 2006. Henderson is an associate editor at *Border Crossings* magazine and writes regularly about visual art. He lives in Vancouver but was born in Saskatoon, where as a teenager he knew the kid (now dead) who stole all the bikes off the U of S campus, chopped them up, and resold them to street punks to make his rent money.

James Heneghan, born in Liverpool, England, now makes his home in North Vancouver, B.C. He worked as a fingerprint technician with the Vancouver Police for twelve years and taught high school for twenty years. Many of his books for young people are award winners (e.g., *Torn Away, Wish Me Luck, The Grave, Flood* and *Waiting for Sarah*). When James was a teenager, during World War II, he was in the Scouts and helped build air-raid shelters in people's homes.

Sheila Heti was born on Christmas Day 1976 in Toronto. She has published two books, the story collection *The Middle Stories* and the novel *Ticknor*. She is the creator of the popular lecture series *Trampoline Hall*, at which people speak on subjects outside their areas of expertise. Her work has been translated into five languages. When Sheila was a teenager, she hated women.

Susan Kernohan writes short stories and works in a library in Toronto. Her poetry and stories have been published in various literary journals, and she's working on a story collection called *Dead Man's Pajamas*. When she was a teenager she hung out at Global Donuts and always ordered black coffee and a Global Dip.

Carrie Mac is a tattooed maverick who was raised in small-town British Columbia, where there is no shortage of eccentric people and shady goings-on to spy on should a small four-eyed child with a colossal imagination and insatiable curiosity have the notion to do so. When she was a teenager she thought the hellish doom of adolescence would never end.

Derek McCormack is the author of three books of fiction—*Dark Rides*, *Wish Book* and *The Haunted Hillbilly*—and a non-fiction book, *Christmas Days*. When he was a teenager, he read Baudelaire and dreamed of living in Paris. He still likes Baudelaire. He lives in Toronto.

When **Janet McNaughton** was a teenager, she read constantly and was terrorized by cheerleaders. Today, Janet is a full-time writer of books, mostly for and about teenagers who don't fit in. And, since writers tend to be awkward, introverted people, Janet now has many like-minded friends and is perfectly happy.

Joe Ollmann is a cartoonist who lives in Montreal, where he bumbles about, speaking French poorly. While his first two books, *Chewing on Tinfoil* and *The Big Book of Wag!*, gather dust on finer bookstore shelves everywhere, he diligently works at completing a third. He is the art director at *ascent magazine*, a yoga magazine of all things. When he was a teenager, he was married and the father of two girls and working in a box factory. He remains the father of the two girls and recently added a small boy-child, but is no longer in a box factory.

Michel Rabagliati was born in 1961 in Rosemont, a working-class neighborhood of Montreal. He later studied graphic design and illustration and worked in this field for more than twenty years. When he was a teenager, his dream was to make comic books, but it was only at the age of thirty-eight that he really took it seriously. This proves that the dreams of youth are strong. His books include *Paul in the Country*, *Paul Has a Summer Job* and *Paul Moves Out*.

Stuart Ross, a Toronto writer, editor and writing teacher, was first published at age sixteen. His recent books are *Confessions of a Small Press Racketeer* and *Hey, Crumbling Balcony! Poems New and Selected*. His online home is hunkamooga.com. As a teenager, Stuart wore tikis and read B.S. Johnson.

When **Arthur Slade** was a teenager he played guitar for hours at a time, wrote short stories and one novel, and also tried to write poetry, but it was awful. Thankfully he stuck with fiction and now he writes full time from his home in Saskatoon. His novel *Dust* won the 2001 Governor General's Award. He is working on his tenth published book right now.

Susannah M. Smith is the author of *How the Blessed Live*, a dark fairy tale of a brother and sister. Her second novel, about a taxidermied love affair and a ventriloquist's dummy, is forthcoming. When Susannah was a teenager she had huge glasses, a perm, and posters of Einstein and a unicorn on her bedroom wall. She currently lives in Ottawa where she wears contact lenses most of the time.

Ania Szado's novel, *Beginning of Was*, was a regional finalist for the 2004 Commonwealth Writers' Prize, Best First Book. Ania has two kids and lives in Toronto, where she runs, writes and procrastinates. When she was a teenager, she never imagined she'd one day be so happy.

Madeleine Thien was born in Vancouver and now lives in Quebec City. She is the author of *Simple Recipes*, a collection of stories, and a novel, *Certainty*. When she was 19, she went up in an airplane for the first time, and down (slowly) in a parachute.

Tim Wynne-Jones has written over two dozen books, including *Some of the Kinder Planets* and *The Maestro*, both of which won the Governor General's Award. His fourth YA novel, *A Thief in the House of Memory*, was published in the fall of 2004. When Tim was a teenager, he failed English.

Story Sources

"Fish-Sitting" by Gil Adamson, from *Help me, Jacques Cousteau* (The Porcupine's Quill, 1995), reprinted by permission of The Porcupine's Quill.

"The Art of Embalming" by Diana Aspin, from *Ordinary Miracles* (Red Deer Press, 2003), reprinted by permission of Red Deer Press.

"Slice" by Gary Barwin, from Doctor *Weep and Other Strange Teeth* (Mercury Press, 2004), reprinted by permission of the author.

"True Confessions" by Martha Brooks, from *True Confessions of a Heartless Girl* (Groundwood Books, 2002), reprinted by permission of Groundwood Books and Farrar, Straus and Giroux.

"The Cat Came Back" by Ivan E. Coyote, from *Close to Spider Man* (Arsenal Pulp Press, 2000), reprinted by permission of Arsenal Pulp Press.

"Recorder Lesson" by Brian Doyle, from *The First Time: True Stories Volume 2* (Orca Book Publishers, 1995), reprinted by permission of the author.

"The Defining Moments of My Life" by Anne Fleming, from *Pool-Hopping and Other Stories* (Polestar Book Publishers, 1998), reprinted by permission of Polestar Book Publishers.

"The Unfortunate" by Lee Henderson, from *The Broken Record Technique* (Penguin, 2002), reprinted by permission of Penguin.

"Mermaid in a Jar" by Sheila Heti, from *The Middle Stories* (House of Anansi Press, 2001), reprinted by permission of House of Anansi Press.

"Rock Paper Scissors" by Susan Kernohan, from *The New Quarterly*, No. 84 (Fall 2002), reprinted by permission of the author.

"Real Life Slow Motion Show" by Carrie Mac, from *Prism International*, Vol. 43, No. 2 (Winter 2005), reprinted by permission of the author.

"The Jeweler" by Derek McCormack, from *The Wish Book: A Catalogue of stories* (Gutter Press, 1999), reprinted by permission of the author.

"Giant Strawberry Funland" by Joe Ollmann, from *Chewing on Tinfoil* (Insomniac Press, 2002), reprinted by permission of the author.

"Paul in the Metro" by Michel Rabagliati, from *The Adventures of Paul* (Drawn and Quarterly, 2005), reprinted by permission of the author. Hand-lettering by Dirk Rehm. First Published in French by *Les Editions de la Pastéque*, Montréal, Canada. Published in English by *Drawn & Quarterly*, Vol. 5, Montréal, Canada.

"This Is the Story of My Family" by Stuart Ross, from *Henry Kafka and Other Stories* (Mercury Press, 1997), reprinted by permission of the author.

"The Deluge" by Arthur Slade, from *Tribes* (HarperCollins, 2002), reprinted by permission of HarperCollins.

"Making the Dragon" by Susannah M. Smith, from *Secrets from the Orange Couch*, Vol. 1, No. 3 (December 1988), reprinted by permission of the author.

"Camping at Wal-Mart" by Ania Szado, from *Taddle Creek*, Vol. V, No. 1 (Christmas Number 2001), reprinted by permission of the author.

"Alchemy" by Madeleine Thien, from *Simple Recipes* (McClelland & Stewart, 2001), reprinted by permission of McClelland & Stewart and Little, Brown and Company.

"Dawn" by Tim Wynne-Jones, from *The Book of Changes* (Groundwood Books, 1994), reprinted by permission of Groundwood Books.